HAVE MY BABY

DIRTY DILFS #1

TARYN QUINN

Have My Baby
© 2017 Taryn Quinn
Rainbow Rage Publishing

Cover by: LateNite Designs
Photograph by: Sara Eirew Photography
Model: Mike Chabot

ISBN: 978-1-940346-49-6

First print edition: September 2017

PROLOGUE

Almost five years ago

The guy in the suit in the mirror wasn't me. He couldn't be. I wasn't ready to pack it all in yet.

I'd only graduated college a couple of years ago. Marriage? A baby on the way? Fuck, middle-aged guys did that stuff. Me? I was still young and fancy free.

But I wasn't. Not anymore. Not since the morning Marjorie Maplewood had walked into my office at Hamilton Realty, waving around a white stick that didn't belong to a popsicle.

This kid is yours, Hamilton. Don't try to pretend it isn't. What are you going to do about it?

It had never occurred to me that the child wasn't mine, but I'd probably stared at her for two full minutes before finding my voice. Marj hadn't appreciated that, and she'd burst into such loud sobs that my loyal assistant, Shelly, ran in from the reception area with a handkerchief, a mint, and plenty of judgment.

An hour later, we'd been engaged and planning a wedding. Okay, maybe two hours.

Now I was facing my reflection in a spotted mirror in a back room at Our Lady of Peace Church, and the ticking minutes might as well have been a time bomb that wouldn't be kind enough to kill me.

Jesus, you're an asshole. She's the mother of your child.

And I was marrying her. I knew my duty. It wasn't our child's fault. Truth was, I already wanted that baby. I had as soon as I'd stopped panicking.

Hell, I was still panicking, but I was moving forward anyway.

A soft knock came at the door and I turned, expecting my father. He was one of the few pleased as could be about this union. Marjorie's family wasn't as well-to-do as ours, but they had good social positioning. My father sold property for a living—as did I now—and was always negotiating deals and searching for angles. My mom leaving the family when I was a kid, certainly hadn't softened him. If anything, he'd become harder and more inflexible.

Everything has a price, Seth. Even people. Especially people.

But it wasn't my father. The woman standing in the doorway, her dark hair wreathed in a crown of tiny wildflowers, would never worry about social standings or brokering deals. She called me on my shit and made me laugh while doing it.

"Hey, you," Ally said, and I smiled for the first time since I'd walked into this narrow, stuffy room.

What that said, I didn't want to analyze.

She took a step forward and for a moment, light surrounded her, making her pale blue dress seem even paler. Almost…white. And if I tilted my head, that crown of flowers on her head could be attached to a veil.

Almost immediately, the tightness in my chest eased and I could breathe again. I wasn't going to run out of oxygen before I even walked down the goddamn aisle.

"Ally Cat," I said, my voice sounding scratchy even to my own ears. I moved forward and gripped her shoulders, drawing her back enough that I could search her eyes. Then she slugged me in the gut and the spell was broken.

I wasn't marrying Ally. That wasn't what we were about. We were buddies.

We'd met in Mrs. Danforth's third period English class in tenth grade on the second day of school. Ally had been absent the first day, and I was a transfer from the godawful prep school my father had sent me to in Connecticut. I'd lasted a year there, which was three years fewer than my twin, Oliver. Then I'd landed in public school in our small town, still unsure if I was making a colossal mistake—sure, prep school had sucked, but school was never fun—and I'd been half as interested in starting *Of Mice and Men* as I was at looking down Marcie Culpepper's V-neck top.

Then Ally had hurried into the classroom, her hair done up with crazy sticks, her arms full of books, and dropped into the empty seat beside me. She'd taken one glance at the way I was hunched over my desk to ogle Marcie's boobs and smirked.

Between that and the fact that I'd assumed she'd ditched the first day of class, I'd figured she was totally badass. I found out later her mom was sick and she'd stayed home with her to keep her company. But my badass opinion of Ally had remained all these years.

This badass chick was my best male friend…who just happened to have a pair of tits.

Sure, occasionally, I noticed more about her than a friend should. Like how her hair always smelled like fucking sunshine, or that her legs seemed six miles long. I always shut that crap down immediately. She'd been dealing with her mother's illness all along, and with every passing year, her mom grew frailer. I was Ally's support system. The only certainty she had in her life.

Just as she was mine.

"Seth? Hey, wise ass, you okay?"

I flexed my hands on her shoulders, not quite ready to let go. Normally, I didn't grab hold of her as if she was my only lifeline, but it sure as hell felt as if I was facing an abyss.

One of my own making.

"What's going on?" She reached up to lay her hands over mine, and the softness of her skin made me swallow hard.

I had to haul myself back. To remember who I was marrying.

"Nothing. Last minute jitters, I guess." I smiled and let her go, tucking my itchy hands into my pockets.

Ally smiled, relaxing finally. "Understandable. It's not every day that Scorer Seth gets put on lockdown."

See, she was glad I wasn't going there too. She'd even mentioned my old stupid high school nickname. Scorer Seth, the guy who never missed when he set his mind on a woman. Now I was engaged, and of course, Ally wouldn't want me going there. But she never had.

Our entire friendship, we'd kept each other firmly in the friend zone. It was safer. Didn't make sense to risk screwing up a good thing, not when we had so few others we could count on.

We were it for each other. And we always would be.

"Scorer Seth never learned." Giving in to the urge to touch her one more time, I reached up to adjust her flower crown, and she immediately followed my hand to adjust it herself. That was my girl, always double-checking my work.

I grinned and moved back to the mirror to work some more on my tie. My eternal downfall. Knowing that, she let out a sigh and walked over to fix it for me, accomplishing the task in two seconds flat. When she started to move back, I grasped her wrist and her gaze flew up to mine.

"Promise me this won't change," I said urgently.

"What?" She let out a nervous little laugh, the kind I rarely heard from her. No matter what, Ally had her shit together. "You want me to promise to always fix your ties? Okay, I can do that—"

"No. I want you to promise we'll still be this way together. That just because I have a wife now, we'll still be like…this." I gestured between us with my free hand. "That you won't pull away."

She laughed again, averting her gaze. Telling me without words she'd intended to do exactly that.

"We'll always be friends. But your wife will be your best friend now. As she should be. If you're worrying about me, don't. I'm good." She tried to shake off my hold, but when that didn't happen, she shook back her hair instead. "I've got it all handled."

"What if I don't? I don't want this to change. Fuck, Al, you're my best friend."

Gently, she pulled away. "We'll always be friends," she repeated. "I better get to my seat. It's almost time. Break a leg, Hamilton." She flashed a weak smile. "Or whatever you say in times like this." She leaned up on tiptoe and kissed my cheek. "I'm so happy for you."

She was gone before I could reply.

I reached up to cup my cheek. My skin was still tingling from her lips.

She hadn't promised me. The only promises I could count on now were my own. The ones I'd already made to my unborn child, and soon, to my wife.

I would do what was right.

1

ALLY

I HOPPED BACK A GOOD THREE FEET, BUT IT WAS WAY TOO LATE. "Aww, come on."

I stared down at the puddle of coffee dripping from the worn Formica tabletop to the red vinyl booth. The cracked pot in my hand held a jagged edge that could be a prop in a Quentin Tarantino movie. Right down to the coffee-stained orange lip.

If I had to sacrifice my last pair of white Converse sneakers to the coffee gods, at least it should've been goddamn full octane coffee, not decaf.

"I'm sorry, Mrs. Diggs. Don't move, okay?"

Mrs. Diggs, one of the diner's regulars, shuffled to the end of her booth and cupped her mug in her manicured hands. She picked up her feet—clad in bright orange and white sneakers—as the coffee raced toward the wall of windows.

I winced. Dammit, the baseboards needed a scrub again. Maybe I could convince Mitch to let me stay late or come in early one day. I'd been picking up as many shifts as he'd allow me to, but at least if I did this it wouldn't require talking to people.

I was pretty much talked out.

"Are you all right, dear?"

"Fine. I just don't want you to get cut, okay? Give me a quick second and I'll brew you a fresh pot." Disgusted, I dropped my threadbare towel over the glass and scraped the shards into a pile as I shimmied my way out from under the table. "Sage, can you grab me another towel?" I hollered over my shoulder.

My best friend's head popped out from around the corner. I gave her a rueful smile as I lost the battle against the river of coffee.

Sage rushed over with a pile of towels and crouched beside me. She blew a honey blond curl out of her face. No matter how many pins Sage Evans jammed into her twisting pile of curls, one invariably escaped. Luckily it only enhanced her heart-shaped face and huge green eyes.

"What happened?" She started mopping up the escaping coffee.

"Careful." I grabbed her hand just before a hook-shaped shard of glass took a chunk out of her palm.

"Jeez, what did you do?"

I set what was left of the pot on the table. "One too many times left on the burner while empty is my guess. I barely tapped the side of the table and pop-crash."

"Coffee." She wrinkled her nose.

"Full pot no less." I managed not to let the growl or the string of swear words free as I reached back under the booth and mopped up the coffee under Mrs. Diggs' feet. "Okay, you're set."

The woman put her feet down as I crawled back out from under the booth. A pair of dark jeans and black boots stopped two inches from my coffee-splattered khakis.

I knew those boots.

My gaze skipped up to the way his jeans molded to strong thighs and a bulge behind his zipper that had caused me way too many sleepless nights.

My best friend since high school tucked his thumb into his pocket and drummed his fingers lightly against his leg. "Is this a new customer service thing?"

My mouth tipped up at one corner. If he only knew what kind of service I wanted to offer. "Jerk."

Even with the slightly burnt decaf wafting up from the floor—and covering me from knee to toes, couldn't forget that part—there was no denying Seth Hamilton's delicious toasted sugar and sex scent.

It was some ungodly expensive cologne. I wasn't exactly proud of the fact that I'd gone to a department store's counter to take an extra whiff of it. I'd hunted it down so I didn't seem like some perv by burying my face in his chest to get a better inhale.

However, the bottled version wasn't nearly as divine as it was on Seth. Probably had something to do with his stupid pheromones.

Or the fact that his alarmingly perfect body chemistry made everything smell good—even during that one night we spent together with his daughter up all night with a fever.

I've relived that night more than I care to admit. Not the awful part. I'm not a freak. But I can't help remembering the aftermath when we melted into a heap on the couch in half-hysterical laughter from exhaustion and relief. Yeah, so I shouldn't have noticed, but I'm human.

It wasn't like I jumped him.

I thought about it for a hot second. To be honest, I think about it all the damn time. When you didn't get any attention of a sexual nature, it tended to take over the whole frontal lobe. The fact that he was so delectable didn't help. However, the idea of tilting our perfect friendship into naked time was too much to deal with. Much of my life was the same refrain.

Me lusting after my best friend. Him completely clueless. Me more than willing to let him stay in the dark. It was a pathetic song that I couldn't stop playing.

I scrubbed my tingling palms on my thighs and noticed his untucked white dress shirt. He was still wearing a navy sport jacket so he wasn't completely off the clock, but definitely not in sales-mode. His dark hair was tousled from the breeze off the water, a pair of mirrored aviators hid his equally dark eyes, and his perpetual scruff made my insides buzzy. Who the hell needed caffeine when Seth came into The Rusty Spoon?

Or the thoughts of me on my knees in front of said man.

Good God, pull it together, girl. I slapped my thighs to kill the last of the buzzing. "Hi."

"Hi yourself." He bent at the waist and I got a blast of that sugar sex. He took off his sunglasses and his eyes crinkled at the sides as he smiled. His gaze slid from me to Sage. "Two-woman job? Must be serious."

"Hey, Pita." Sage rolled her eyes before bunching all the towels together. "I'll put on that pot for you." She stood up and dropped the pile on the lunch counter so it wouldn't drip all over the floor.

"Thanks," I murmured.

"Wow, ten points for the full-on shatter, Ally Cat." He helped me to a standing position, then hustled around the counter for the garbage and dragged it over to me. He must have heard the crunch and click of glass because he cupped his hands around mine and pulled them over the bin. I didn't bother trying to save the towel, just shot the whole thing in the trash. "No cuts?"

"I'm fine, Dad." Or I would be if he'd let me go. Because seriously, I couldn't deal with tingles on top of mortifying coffee splatters. Not that I wasn't used to the eternal stains that were part of being a waitress at the diner. It just seemed extra embarrassing in front of Seth.

He flipped my hands palms up then coasted the pads of his fingers over the tops. "All good."

I curled my fingers into my palms. "Told you. The only casualty is my Chucks."

He glanced around the garbage to my shoes. "Yeah, they're toast."

"No, I'll just use them as my new mopping shoes."

He frowned.

"What?"

"Nothing." The little wrinkle between his brows cleared as he noticed Mrs. Diggs in the booth. "Aren't you looking lovely, Mrs. Diggs? New workout gear?"

"Charmer." But she preened and smoothed her bejeweled hand over the expensive designer Adidas jacket in the same orange and white of her shoes. "Nice to see someone watching after our Alison though."

"Always."

"Oh, brother." I turned to the counter lined with red vinyl stools and collapsed onto one to take stock of my situation.

Most of the coffee had hit the floor and my shoes, so I guess that was something at least. I stalked down the aisle and inwardly groaned at the squeak of my rubber soles. I hustled to the carpet in front of the door and scuffed my feet. I could actually feel the coffee squishing inside my shoes.

Ugh.

My life—up to my ankles in crap coffee. Of course.

I went around behind the counter to take care of the pile of towels Sage had left. "What's up, Seth? You don't usually come in this late."

"I actually have some papers for you."

My gaze swung back to him. He nodded to the back of the diner where he always sat. "Can you take a few minutes?"

It was only then that I noticed the folder in his hand. The white Hamilton Realty logo scrawled across the dense green glossy folder. My stomach twisted for a whole different reason this time.

Mom's house.

My house.

What could have been my house if it wasn't full of shitty memories and the stench of too much antiseptic. I closed my eyes as a wave of exhaustion chased the sad. It had been three months since my mom had finally passed away after a soul-crushing bout with cancer. She'd always been fragile, but the last five years had about killed me too.

By the end, all I wanted was peace for her.

And maybe a little for myself. I only let that part out in the deepest, darkest parts of the night where sleep and waking overlapped. When the quiet was finally comforting and the hiss of the oxygen compressor wasn't my constant companion for the first time in too many years to remember.

But then the alarm pushed me out of the quiet and into my current reality. Bills, life, the diner, plans…all jumbled together in my little planner. And the little secret pocket where I'd stashed the page of classes I wanted to take. I had sent off for a few brochures from schools in New York City, and I looked at them now and then.

It had been so long since I could think about what I wanted that I honestly wasn't quite sure what to do. But it didn't stop me from poring over my brochures and the college catalog online.

Too bad dreams didn't pay the bills.

I pressed a shaking hand over my belly. "Yeah. Let me make sure I can take my fifteen."

I hurried over to the sink. My rings clicked together as I soaped up my hands to get the coffee smell off them. "Mitch, I'm going to take my break."

He only grunted. Typical.

"Sage, you okay?"

She waved me off. "Sure. Take it now before the biddies come in for the early bird special."

"Truth." I smoothed my hand over my apron and stuck my order pad in the front pocket. I double checked that I had three pens like I always did. Patrons were notorious thieves. Not sure why they wanted my cheapie Bic pens, but they were forever walking off with them.

Stop stalling.

I was tempted to roll my eyes at myself, but that took too much energy and I didn't have much to spare. I grabbed a fruit plate and a scoop of cottage cheese to get me through the rest of the evening. Sage and I might have time for a bite after the dinner rush, but more often than not, it just rolled into dessert business and the endless coffee mug crowd.

I snagged a menu on my way down the aisle to him. Seth was sprawled in his favorite booth, his long legs encroaching on my side. I kicked his boot as I sat down and dropped the menu in front of him. "How you don't have that memorized is beyond me."

He straightened and placed his phone face down on the table, then propped the menu against the wall. "Just coffee this time."

"Oh. Have an appointment?" I ate a forkful of my cottage cheese.

He sneered at my plate. "So gross."

I forked up some more and held it in front of him. "So good."

"Disgusting."

I snagged a piece of pineapple to go with my forkful and chewed with a smile. "How would you know? You still won't try the wonders of my fruit plate."

"It's a texture thing."

"And yet you'll eat grits."

"Only Angelo's grits. Which reminds me." He flipped over his menu. "I have been dreaming about his kitchen sink omelet."

"Kinda lame dreams."

He glanced over the menu. "I can't have dreams about you naked all the time."

"Har-har."

He winked at me and I tamped down the hormones prepared to leap across the table.

Sage came over with a grilled cheese sandwich and slid it in front of me. In her other hand was a pot of coffee. "What are you having, Seth?"

I frowned. "I didn't order this."

Sage put her hand on her hip. "That fruit thing isn't going to hold you over for the rest of the day."

"Thanks. My ass won't thank you, but I do."

"Your ass is just fine."

"Sure is," Seth agreed.

What the hell was up with the comments? He didn't notice my ass. Did he?

I shook my head and peeled the triangles apart as the lava-like mixture of cheddar and muenster that spilled onto the plate made me moan. Cheese was my downfall. I could pretty much give up anything except that.

Noticing Seth's smirk, I dragged my fingertip through the cheese and brought it to my mouth. "What?"

"Should we leave you alone?"

"Fine by me. We'll live happily ever after, won't we, you gooey piece of perfection?"

Seth shook his head. He flipped his mug right side up on the saucer. "I'll just have coffee."

"You sure?" Sage asked as she poured.

"Yeah. I really want that omelet, but it'll have to wait until next time."

Sage nodded. "You got it." She glanced at me. "I got Mrs. Diggs."

"Oh, crap. I forgot." I swiveled to give the older woman a smile.

"No worries."

"She wasn't mad?"

Sage shook her head. "Too busy staring at this one's ass." She nodded at Seth.

He waggled his eyebrows.

Sage rolled her eyes. "I'll leave you guys to it."

As soon as she walked away, Seth folded his hands on the folder. "So about the house."

I looked down at my sandwich and picked up half. "Want?"

He smiled. "I wouldn't want to come between you two."

I shrugged. Fine by me. I sucked at sharing anyway. If he wanted to keep it about business, I could do that. "How'd we do?"

He blew out a breath. "I'd prefer to leave it on the market so we—"

"Nope. Can't. John Chandler gave me three months to sell and here we are a week past that."

His eyebrows snapped down and his jaw muscle flexed. I'd bet twenty bucks he was grinding his molars. But it was my decision, not his.

"I told you I could—"

"Nope." I yanked a napkin out of the dispenser to degrease my fingertips before I covered his clenched hands. "You know I can't." He'd been trying to throw money at all my problems for years, but my answer was always the same. Even if he had more money than most of the Crescent Cove population combined, I couldn't take money from a friend.

Especially not Seth.

God, not him.

"Let me talk to John. We throw him a hell of a lot of business. I can pull a favor."

"No."

I had a feeling the three months I'd been granted was already one of those favors. No matter how much history I had in this town, a banker wasn't going to let me slide when it came to prime land, even if it was on the fringes of lakefront property. Add in the mortgage I could barely scrape together now that my mother's social security was gone and the only math that made sense was selling the house.

John Chandler over at Crescent Cove Credit Union might be a sweet man who coached Little League on the weekends, but he was still a businessman. And there were rules.

Rules I was intimately aware of. My mother's modest life insurance policy did little more than cover her burial and a small memorial service.

"I've got a guy who's buying up some of the older…" He trailed off.

I squeezed him one last time before sliding my hands back across the table and picking up my sandwich again. "Shacks? You can say it. I know my house wasn't much."

He swiped his hand along the back of his neck. "Dammit, Al."

"It is what it is. She wanted a house on the lake, and it was all I could afford on my meager salary and what she had in the bank. It was enough for us." My bedroom had been little more than a closet, but my mom had been happy her last few years and that had been all that mattered.

"A new company is looking to build family houses on the lake to beef up the rentals for the season."

"The Kennedys kind or…?"

He nodded. "The middle-income kind of families. I'm not completely against what they're doing."

I broke off a corner of my toasted cheese and popped it in my mouth. "That's great. You know this town relies on seasonal visitors. Though I'm glad they're not just making mansions."

His eyes glittered. "No."

I knew Seth and his brother had been working hard to keep Crescent Cove from turning into the Hamptons part two. They were probably the only reason half the coast hadn't been razed and turned into huge houses and overpriced hotels.

But the Cove was a mix of wealthy and working class. Just the way I loved it. Though I wouldn't mind being one of the wealthy someday.

And maybe if I could get the house sold and get back to even, I'd have at least a chance at some kind of future besides drowning in debt.

"What's the offer?"

I listened to him drone on about the sale and the banks. I swallowed when he opened the folder and slid a printed page my way. The sale price wasn't as good as I'd hoped, but it would cover what I needed it to.

It would leave me with a big fat zero in my bank, but at least it wasn't a minus sign.

Right now, that was glorious and I was calling it a win. I folded the paper in half. "Thank you, Seth."

"Don't thank me. I'd rather you walked away or haggled for more."

I lifted my chin and pushed my plate away. "Do you think I'd actually get it?" He opened his mouth. "Without doing upgrades and all the things you wanted me to do to the house?" He shut it. "I thought so."

"Fuck." He slumped in seat a little. "I don't like any of this."

"You don't have to like it. Just make sure I don't get too screwed and be my friend. Simple things. It's all I really need." I put my leg out and twisted my ankle to show off my splattered shoes. "And a new pair of sneakers. Which I need to work to pay for. Just let me know when and where to be to sign the papers." I started to slide out of the booth.

"Your fifteen isn't over yet."

I paused.

"Almost. Fifteen minutes goes quick. You know that."

He pressed his lips together and his eyes flared with something. I didn't even want to think about what they flared with. It didn't happen often, but there were moments when I wondered if he thought about other, less platonic things when it came to me.

But it was much easier to file those moments away as aberrations and fantasies.

"Just one more thing."

"It's never just one more thing with you."

"You're killing me, Al."

"Right back atcha, buddy." Exasperation was the word of the day. When he leaned forward, his dark eyes were a little too serious. I straightened and pulled my hands away from my plate to land in my lap. I twirled my thumb ring as a sudden chill climbed up my hairline.

He leaned forward, suddenly earnest. Too earnest. When Seth Hamilton acted solemn, he was up to something, and chances were high I wouldn't like it.

"Will you have my baby?"

2

SETH

Silence was not the response I expected.

I wasn't sure what I did expect. The request wasn't a usual one, not even between longtime friends. Tenth grade was more than a decade in the rearview mirror, and here we were.

Still friends. Best friends, even. Our friendship had survived my marriage and divorce, among other things. If this crazy request of mine didn't kill her affection for me.

Anyone's bet at this point.

"Have your baby…what? What does that mean, exactly?" When I didn't immediately reply, she fanned herself with the laminated menu she'd given me. "Okay, wait, baby means Laurie. Of course it does. She's your only baby. Right? Right. So you must want me to babysit her or something? I can do that. Sure. Let me consult my planner for dates."

I stopped her from flying out of the booth. "Laurie isn't a baby. She's almost four. As she likes to tell me, that's almost halfway to ten, and ten is more than halfway to a big person."

As always, when talk of my daughter entered the conversation, Ally softened. I might have known that and used it to my advantage, if I hadn't been so addicted to how her cheeks turned pink and her smile warmed at my little girl's name. God knows Laurie's own mother hadn't been similarly affected.

Ally's love of children, and my child in particular, had weighed in heavily to my choice to ask her this very important question. And if I'd watched her with my daughter a bit too much lately, studying the exact curl of Ally's hair against her neck, or the way her dangling earrings made shadows, or how her mouth curved and teased out a dimple—well, I was a red-blooded man.

One who could only ignore the beauty in front of him so long without it slamming him in the forehead, apparently.

"She is a big girl. Growing bigger every day." The wistfulness in Ally's voice made me lean forward.

"So now that we've ascertained I wasn't talking about you babysitting my child, something you do on occasion anyway, let's go back to the point of this conversation. You. Having my baby."

Golden brown eyes settled on mine as a smile toyed with her mouth. "You missed April Fool's day by a mile, dude."

"This isn't a joke. There's no hidden camera. This is just me, your best friend coming to you with a simple request."

Her dark brows knitted. "A simple request to borrow my eggs? And what would you need with another baby anyway? You already have one. You work all the time, and if you had two kids, you'd have twice the work."

"I'd have another child to love and my little girl would have a sibling, something she wants more than anything else in this world." I toyed with the handle of my coffee cup. "Even more than she wants a mother, and that's the one thing I can never give her. Fucked that one up royally."

Ally sighed and tweaked my pinky, curled around the cooling mug. I'd barely touched my coffee. My throat was too tight.

"That wasn't your fault. You didn't know Marj was only it for the dough. How could you?"

"Oh, I don't know, that she was always more concerned about fur coats and jewels than baby formula and lullabies? If I'd been paying attention, that is. But as you said, I'm always working." I heard the bitterness in my tone and couldn't do a damn thing to stop it, though I knew I was screwing this up more with every passing moment.

I didn't want Ally feeling sorry for me or guilted into this situation. I wanted her to make the choice because it would be good for her and good for me and Laurie. A positive thing all around.

"She didn't breastfeed?"

"Is that relevant?"

"No, not really, just that it's such a healthy, nurturing experience. It's not an imperative, of course. A baby can be perfectly happy and cared for without it."

"I'd be fine with you breastfeeding our child." Just saying those words had my stomach tightening in weird and unexpected ways.

"Stop it." She hissed out a breath. "We don't have a child. Nor will we. I don't know why you're pursuing this, really, but it's not very funny. Now I should get back to—"

I reached out and snagged her wrist. "Let me spell this out for you before you run from me and concoct all kinds of crazy scenarios in your head. I want another child. I do not want another relationship, potentially with a woman who would harm our baby and not be viable long-term. I just want a healthy child. To that end, I am prepared to compensate you for your significant time investment. Four years at the college of your choosing, tuition free. If you desire to go to grad school, that will be covered as well."

She yanked back her hand and let it drop limply into her lap. "You've gone stark raving mad."

"Actually, I feel saner than I ever have. Instead of lamenting I can't have what I want, what my daughter wants, I can make it happen with a woman I trust. The *only* woman I trust." Swallowing hard, I gripped the handle of my mug and fought not to reach for Ally again. "I'm not exaggerating. It's you or no one. I can't risk it with anyone else."

Her lower lip wobbled and I clutched the handle until my damn knuckles went white. If she cried, I'd be done for.

"Not fair," she whispered. "So not fair."

"No, what's not fair is that you work your fingers to the bone in this place and you have dreams you can't see your way to because of all the bills."

She clenched her jaw. "As soon as I sell Mama's house—"

"What, you'll barely be out of the hole? I have more money than I know what to do with. I can make a good life for my kids. Both of them, including the one I'd have with you. And you'd be free, Ally. You could go to school like you want. I know you probably wouldn't want to quit here, and that's fine. But school would be taken care of, and then your dreams could be yours. Anything you want."

She turned her head away and stared hard out the window at some place I couldn't see. But she damn well wasn't seeing the tidy, well-kept Main Street of our small town, I was certain. Her gaze was farther off, on a future I couldn't imagine.

For all I knew, she'd leave Crescent Cove. With the money she'd receive, she could go somewhere else and start over for real. I knew she loved the diner, but more than anything, she spoke of fresh starts. Hard to have one in a town synonymous with so many bad memories for her. So much loss.

Sure, Laurie was here. I was here, plus Sage and her other friends at the diner. But there was a huge world out there, just waiting for Ally to make her mark. This way, she could. Without being tied down by anyone or anything.

As much as I might hate the idea of going even one day without seeing her smile or having her roll her eyes at me or hearing her laughter, it wasn't about me now. She deserved a chance to live the way she wanted to.

So did I.

"You're paying me for my eggs," she said quietly. "Like I'm a freaking chicken. Except my eggs are like fucking gold lined in platinum, if they're worth a college education."

A laugh tickled the back of my throat, but it was too constricted for me to let it free. "Anywhere you want," I gritted out instead. "A free ride all the way. Ivy League if that's what floats your boat."

Her chest quickly rose and fell, drawing my attention to her full breasts heaving under the starched cotton of her uniform. I tried not to notice. I respected the fuck out of her, but I also wanted to fuck her senseless.

Something I don't think I'd fully realized until that exact moment.

Even knowing what I was asking of her, what it would entail…I'd been focused on the end result, not the process.

Now that process was playing out in my head in lurid Technicolor, and my stiff dick was lurching against the zipper of my jeans. And she was still breathing hard and worrying the silver rings she wore on each finger, her mind whirling faster than she could give voice to her thoughts. Or else she didn't want to share.

I wanted to fuck her until every one of those thoughts tumbled out of her pretty mouth. To strip her bare until she could hide nothing from me. Her innermost secrets, her hot tits, her sweet pussy.

All of her, mine for the taking.

But I didn't say any of that. Not yet. There was one point I needed to clarify, however.

"You keep talking about your eggs. You think that's what I mean?"

"I don't know what you're getting at, because this is all crazy talk. You never gave me one inkling you were thinking like this before and now you're all in on baby central."

"Okay, yes, I know my technique could use some work. But I figured you'd say no, so if we can get to that part, then we can get to the part where I considerately give you time to think about it while I do my level best to convince you. Without acting as if I'm convincing you, of course."

"I can't decide if you're the dumbest dude on the planet for admitting that or the smartest."

"I'm an excellent closer. You know that yourself." I shrugged, hoping the gesture didn't look as jerky as it felt. Truth be told, acting overly confident about this situation was the only way I'd been able to gear myself up to ask her in the first place.

I was okay with her thinking I was nuts. I was even okay with her saying no. What I wasn't okay with?

Her pulling away from me because I'd officially moved out of the stress-free friend zone into the realm of one more man who wanted something from her. I did, but I wanted to give as much back.

As much as she would let me.

"Closing is one thing. Your openers, however, suck." Ally leaned across the table and gripped my wrist, twisting my arm toward her so she could see the time as she'd done a million and one times before.

Normally, I barely paid attention. But apparently asking her to have my baby had subtly changed the ions and molecules in the air between us, because the brush of her fingers on the back of my hand made my balls clench. My spine locked as I fought not to draw back my hand.

But she noticed that I tensed. Of course she did. She was as perceptive as the damn cat I'd nicknamed her for years ago. "So what, you want to knock me up but I can't touch you now? You're all about that petri dish action, aren't you? You don't want to come right out and admit it, but that's what your goal is." She let out a whooshing breath as if I'd just handed her the winning lotto numbers. "You just want to inseminate me. Okay. Better. I'm not saying yes, of course. Still, even considering that you actually thought that we…that we could…is ridiculous."

Leaning forward, I snagged her fingers where they lay on the tabletop, holding firm when she tried to snatch them back. "That we could what?"

Her gaze darted everywhere but never landed on me. "You know quite well. Can you let go of me now, please? I need to get back to work."

I only tightened my hold as I leaned across the table. She didn't shrink back. Far from it. Her maple syrup eyes—all those rich hues of gold and brown—flashed and locked onto mine. "That we could what, Ally?" I asked again, voice low.

Suddenly it was vitally important she answer me. That I hear her say the words, to solidify the reality of it happening in my head. Because it was sure as fuck real according to what was going on in my jeans.

"So we could have, you know, sex." She spoke so fast that I lessened my grip a fraction and she yanked free, popped to her feet, and grabbed hold of the folder containing the contract.

Both of them.

Though she didn't know about the second one yet. I hadn't gotten that far.

I started to lean toward her to snatch it back, then paused. *Hmm.*

Maybe it was better she read the contract on her own. Seeing it all in print might work to allay her fears. It wasn't as if I was asking her to let me breed her and marry her and lock her away forever in my tower. It was just a simple exchange between friends. No romantic relationship, but a pleasant, mutually satisfying one. She would give me something I wanted, and I would give her something she would never ask for but deserved.

Hell, I'd be happy to offer her the money right now on the spot, no strings attached, but she would never take it. So instead I'd made it a condition of our bargain. All neat and tidy and written down.

A wise businessman pivoted with changing conditions. And I was nothing if not my father's son.

"Too slow," Ally said, her confidence returning as she clutched the folder to her chest. "Better work on those reflexes of yours, Hamilton. Think you're getting old."

"Thanks for bringing that point up. Sit again for another moment." I inclined my chin toward the opposite side of the booth.

She sighed and sat sideways on the seat, balancing the folder on her knees far from my reach. "Finally reconsidering this insanity? I knew if you took a moment to just think, you'd realize this is insane. Just because Laurie wants a sibling it isn't a reason to be rash."

"Rash. Right." I stirred my now ice-cold coffee and dropped the spoon into the saucer. "She's told you too?"

"She's told everyone. When I picked her up at school last week, Mrs. O'Connor mentioned it to me. She had this idea that I was your girlfriend." Shaking her head, Ally smoothed a hand over that green Hamilton Realty folder that held the power to change both of our lives. "Ridiculous."

"So you keep saying. Ridiculous you'd be my girlfriend, ridiculous I'd want to fuck you to make a baby."

Her eyes flared wide before she slapped the folder on the table. "Keep your damn voice down. You know how this place is with gossip. If the wrong person hears that, they'll think you actually want to…do that."

My frustration level spiked, and laughing was the only thing I could do to alleviate it. Along with grabbing hold of the back of my neck to rub out a particularly pesky set of knots.

Not the only thing I wanted to rub out, but that wasn't going to be occurring at the diner. Probably. Unless she pushed me to untold lengths.

"Newsflash. I do want to do that. I want to spread you out on my bed and fuck you until you're so full of me it's spilling out of you. And then, just for good measure, I want to roll you over and do it again." Her lips trembled apart and I placed a finger over them. "But no, I don't want a girlfriend. I want you to have my baby, and I want it to be a good, positive thing for both of us. Unconventional, yes, but then we've always been that, haven't we?" I rose, unable to deny that I enjoyed looming over her while her big brown eyes tracked my movements.

"Seth," she whispered.

Her usage of my actual name instead of some insult said volumes.

"The second contract," I said lightly, pulling out my wallet to leave a wad of bills on the table. Far more than my coffee and tip should cost, but I always tipped excessively, especially at the diner. "Call me when you've had a chance to read it."

Slipping on my sunglasses, I headed toward the door. I could feel her heavy stare on my back. And knew she would probably flip open the folder to scan the contents before the door shut behind me with a cheerful tinkle of bells.

I'd made it up the street to my Mustang and was just about to open the driver's door when my cell vibrated in the pocket of my jeans. I pulled it out and answered her call without reading her name.

It could only be one person. The one who held a good chunk of my dreams and my future in her strong, capable, ringed hands.

"Hi there," I said, keeping my voice pleasant. Even with my aviator sunglasses, I still had to shield my eyes from the angle of the sun glinting off the lake directly in front of me. "That didn't take you long."

I heard a hiss that I guessed might be running water then the sound disappeared. "You told another human being about this crazy plan?"

"I told my lawyer. Whether or not he's actually human is up for debate, but most people seem to think he qualifies."

"The last hope I had was that this was another one of Seth's wild schemes. You know, like when we put the top down on your convertible and drove up to the Canadian side of Niagara Falls on senior skip day without any ID. All because you woke up that day and wanted to do something fun."

"And you thought I'd ask you to make a baby the same way." I nodded, inhaling a deep breath of water-tinged air. "Sure. I can see now why you're hesitating. If you think I'd view those two events the same way, no wonder you aren't inclined to say yes."

"But you laid all of it out in these papers." She lowered her voice until I had to strain to hear her over the gentle lap of the water against the sea wall. "You want me to get pregnant, and you want to pay me for my baby. Like I was some broodmare."

"A chicken and a broodmare. Nice to know how you see yourself."

"How I see myself? Um, no. That's all you, bucko."

I nearly smiled. I would have if this wasn't so important. "I want to pay you for your time. The gestation period is lengthy, and the change in your lifestyle for that period is worth compensation."

"So you keep saying," she said, sounding shriller by the minute.

"Which brings me back to the reason I asked you to sit down again in the diner. I was knocked off-course, but you've reminded me once again. Age. You're twenty-eight. Egg validity is an important concern."

"Egg what?"

"Validity. Once a woman nears thirty, her eggs start becoming—"

"Dude, you did not just call my eggs old. You're fucking lucky you walked out when you did because if you were still here, I'd slap you until you came to your senses."

"You'd be slapping me for a while then, because I've thought a lot about this. It's a sensible idea, and once you take some time to calm down and think, I have a feeling you'll agree. College is expensive, and this way you'll be covered. Any school you like," I reminded her. "And Laurie will have that sibling we both know she desperately wants."

"Cheap shot," she said in an undertone. "Using that little girl to get your way is the lowest of lows. But I should expect nothing else from a fabled Hamilton, now should I?"

Wincing, I gripped the phone tighter. "Wait. That didn't come out right. I meant—"

She'd already ended the call.

Immediately, I called her back, but it went straight to voicemail. I braced my elbow on the roof of my car and shut my eyes, hearing her pained voice on repeat in my head.

Hating every second.

"Fuck," I muttered, stepping back and yanking open my door.

Maybe I wouldn't have to worry about her saying no. God knows I'd bungled this situation in every possible way. And I might have screwed up more than just my slim chances of her agreeing to my plan.

I might have just lost my best friend too.

3

ALLY

I STARED AT THE CEILING AND FROWNED AT THE WATERMARK IN the corner. Had that been there before? I covered my face with my arms and pulled my knees up to my chest as I stretched out my back.

I'd been on the floor for the last ten minutes. Mostly because my furniture was either packed or sold off. If the ten-dollar college student special counted as sold anyway.

My day had started at five in the morning to open the diner, then I'd gone right to my—no, not mine anymore. *The* house. Now the only thing familiar were the ghostly shapes from my mother's old medical equipment on the battered hardwood.

Hospice had come to collect them last month and I hadn't had the heart to come back into her space since then.

I held my hand up to catch the speckled bits of sunlight that peeked from the trees surrounding this corner of the house. Dust motes danced through the fading rays as I dropped my arms over my knees to pull them closer.

My body ached almost as much as my head. Between the long hours at the Rusty Spoon and packing up the house, I hadn't had time to do anything more than fall on my face in sheer exhaustion. Lather-rinse-and-repeat.

Okay, so maybe some of it was to avoid thinking about Seth's question.

Because if I was so tired I was blind, I didn't have to re-read the two-page contract that he had tucked behind my tentative house sale contract.

I released my knees and sprawled out on the floor spread eagle. What the hell had he been thinking?

I was obviously going to say no. There was no way I could contemplate having his baby for a college education. First of all, paying me to be his broodmare was archaic. Second, I couldn't survive it.

Simple as that.

My nipples hardened and I crossed my arms over my chest. See? I couldn't even think the words sex and Seth and not react. The fact that my body wasn't cooperating with my firm *no* was getting really annoying.

I shut my eyes as the word firm teased out a memory of Seth shifting in the booth as he explained his plans for me. When he'd stood over me, there had been little doubt he meant what he said. Oh, the dark denim masked most of his…situation, but there was a bulge behind his zipper that I had to stop thinking about.

"Where are you?" Sage's voice rang out from the front of the tiny house. She really just had to walk in a small circle and she'd find me.

"Here," I called out.

"Should I worry that you're on the floor?"

I peered at the doorway, but instead of Sage's face, there was a huge arrangement of lilacs and daisies tucked into a copper watering can.

I didn't need to look at the card to know it was from Seth. My head thunked back onto the hardwood. "Dammit." I slung my arm back over my face. Why the hell did he have to remember both me and my mama's favorite flowers?

Couldn't he be like the guys I heard my friends complain about? The clueless boyfriends or husbands who bought them a vacuum instead of a bracelet for an anniversary?

That guy was easy to ignore.

This one?

Not so much.

Add in thirteen years of being my best friend and I was friggin' toast.

"Where do you want me to put this? And why don't you have any furniture?"

I hauled myself off the floor. "By the door is fine. In fact, put it in your car and take it home."

Sage put down the jumbo watering can. "I will take it home, but only because it's your home now too. Or did you forget that little fact?"

"Of course not." I tucked a stray curl out of my face and back into my fraying French braid. Like a damn homing beacon, I couldn't stop myself from crossing to the flowers. I brushed the back of my knuckles along the delicate lilac petals before curling my fingers back into my dirty palms. A fine layer of dust caked my hands, arms, and knees from packing and hauling boxes. "And that's why I didn't need all this stuff."

"We could have put it in storage," Sage said with a flutter of hands.

I dabbed at the sweat on my forehead. I needed a shower something fierce. "None of it was worthy of storage."

Her huge green eyes were about a blink away from tears. "There has to be something you want to keep."

"Would that be the cracked Walmart lamp, or the sagging wicker round chair circa 1994?"

"Stop. You can't throw everything away, dammit."

Sage actually stomped her foot. It was sort of cute in a fluffy half unicorn, half pixie kind of way. The unicorn half was the one that had a little mettle behind her words. She wasn't a pushover, even if she was the sweetest, most fanciful woman I knew.

"Some kids from the university came and took me up on my bargain basement deals."

"You didn't use Craigslist."

When I didn't disabuse her of that little statement, her eyebrows shot up.

"Are you insane? And why didn't you wait until I got here?"

I shrugged. "Not like I couldn't handle myself."

"You are on a semi-secluded road a quarter mile away from the main road and the lake. Anything could have happened."

"Okay, Ann Rule."

"Don't joke. We watch those shows together, woman. Anything could have happened. They could have kidnapped you and put you in the back of their van—"

"Before you get all bent, there was no van, Scooby Doo Magical Mystery van or otherwise. They had an old rusted truck with a flatbed that wouldn't even close properly. The most exciting part of the whole endeavor was us wrestling with bungee cords to get them safely back onto the highway."

Sage tipped back her head. "You're incredible."

"Thank you."

She shoved me. "Not funny."

"A little funny."

Her lips twitched, but she managed to keep a straight face.

"Aww, come on, Sage." I hooked an arm around her hips before wrinkling my nose and pulling away. "Sorry, I'm too dirty to be touching you."

She hauled me in for a hug. "Dusty is part of moving. At least you smell like sunshine. How you doin', girl?"

"God, I doubt it." But I hooked an arm around her and hugged her back. When the lump I'd been jamming down my throat and belly started to rise up, I eased away from her. "I'm okay." At least I would be as long as she didn't look at me with those big leafy green eyes puddled with tears.

"My mom sent over some food for us."

"Not diner food?"

She laughed. "Not diner food."

"God bless her. Though it's Mother's Day, she shouldn't be cooking. And God, I'm sorry. You shouldn't be here helping me on her day."

Sage waved me off. "We all made her a big French Toast breakfast."

As Sage spoke, I wandered over to the box half-full of the crocheted blankets my mom used to wear when she sat out here. No matter how warm or cold it was, she was forever bundled under the rainbow patchwork blanket.

That I would keep.

And a few others.

Okay, all of them. I could get rid of most of the junk we'd collected over the last six years, but not those.

Sage pulled the blanket out and buried her nose in the ancient yarn. I had to turn away again and suck in a long, slow breath.

I was not going to cry.

I'd already done that when I'd folded them up the first time. The lavender essential oils she'd been using at the very end had become her scent. As soothing and soft as her tissue paper skin.

My phone buzzed again, distracting me from thoughts better left in the past.

I'd been in denial mode for days. Three of his messages were still on my notifications. Every time I caught a glimpse of them, I flipped my phone over and ignored.

Even swiping them away, I'd have to read something.

Nope and nope.

"Still ignoring him?"

"Hmm?"

"Well, if you don't want to talk about the house or your mom, then jackass is the next best thing."

I rolled my eyes as I lifted onto my toes to reach the clock on the wall. Though Sage was all about finding Mr. Right, she thought Seth was an entitled pain in the ass with a cocky attitude. Some of that probably had to do with her even worse opinion of Seth's brother.

And, yes, Seth was most of those things, but even when he was being a complete jackass, he was still better than most men I knew. There were some rose-colored glasses involved. I could admit that much, but then he went and did things like the flowers.

I fought the urge to touch them again. *No.* I wasn't going to dwell.

Instead I brought the clock with me as I crossed the room. Carefully, I tucked the old starburst cabinet between two of the blankets. It might be hideous, but she'd loved the rose-gold clock. We'd moved a few times over the years and it always went with us.

In fact, she'd stolen it from a tacky hotel when I was seven. Back when my dad had still been around. We'd stayed in places like that most of my life until he finally disappeared for good. She'd taken that clock and the fifty bucks he'd left us and we'd driven east until we landed in the middle of New York.

And that was where we stayed.

Our life had been penny pinching and extra shifts and crappy little apartments until I'd scraped together enough to get us this house. When the doctor had told me—told us—that she didn't have much time.

She'd survived for five more years just because of Crescent Lake. Looking out of the sagging screen windows of the four seasons room had been her little piece of perfection.

I crossed to the La-Z-Boy chair she'd lived in for the last six months. Getting in and out of a bed had been too difficult for her, but she'd always wanted to be by her window. So I had made sure she had all her blankets and her window and her lake view.

It had been worth all her savings and mine too.

Every damn penny.

I jumped when Sage tipped her head against my shoulder. I rested mine against the crown of her head. "Today sucks."

"Yeah, I know," she said softly.

We stayed like that for I don't even know how long. Until my belly started howling its distress. Food didn't sound good at all these days, but man, the idea of something that wasn't on the Rusty Spoon's menu sounded glorious.

"What did your mom pack for us?"

Sage grinned. "Chicken and dumplings."

"Oh, man."

"Comfort food at its best. Still have plates?"

"I can scrounge some up if you go get the food."

Sage waggled her eyebrows. "Deal." She crossed the room and paused at the threshold to the living room. "I didn't forget my question, even if you're ignoring it."

"Hmm?"

"Don't give me that innocent face, Alison Marie Lawrence. I'm not done."

"Plates!" I said in a singsong voice.

She blew raspberries before she banged out the front door.

I sagged against the ledge of the half wall beneath the screen window. The problem with having a friend like Sage was that she liked to talk about feelings. Especially of a romantic nature.

The girl was in love with love.

So much so that she'd had a parade of boys, then eventually men, in her life. They never stuck around long because they invariably couldn't live up to Sage's high standards of romance. You just weren't going to find a Prince Charming in Crescent Cove.

I certainly hadn't. Though my issues might have had something to do with my caretaker status since high school. And meeting Seth.

He didn't even know he'd ruined me for other men. Without a touch other than a platonic hug or a game of touch football, I'd been his.

Pathetic.

So yeah, his current mission to steer me into Babytopia by way of his very impressive master bedroom had me ready for first place in track and field at the other end of the county.

Which was impressive since my idea of running generally consisted of dodging Sage, Amber, and Jean on National Pancake Day at the diner. Pretty much the only day every waitress was working.

"Okay, where are those plates? I'm starving."

I blinked out of my rambling musings. Honestly, there had to be something in the air.

I met Sage in the kitchen and pulled down two large bowls from the cabinet I hadn't quite emptied out. I had to dig through two boxes to find something to eat with.

A serving fork and slotted spoon for vegetables would have to do.

Sage laughed when I handed her the spoon. "Remember when I moved into my place and couldn't find the silverware?"

I flipped over a bucket and pulled over a box to serve as a makeshift table. "God, yes. We scoured your apartment. We even left the house to go to Target and buy another set."

35

"Mom called to let me know the box was still sitting under the kitchen table."

"Heaviest freaking box too." I stopped at the kitchen sink and washed my hands and arms with soap.

"Of course, it had to have all my silverware and pots."

I turned around and leaned against the counter as I dried my hands. "It took two of us to get it up those stairs."

"And then it busted twenty feet from the door." Sage transferred a healthy portion of the gravy-slathered chicken into my bowl. My stomach roared in reaction. She laughed and put on another spoonful. "Might need to zap it."

I took the bowl and shoveled a dumpling into my mouth.

"Guess not."

I grinned around a bite. "So good."

"So are you going to tell me what's up with Seth?"

I choked on a bite and stood to grab my Coke Zero out of the fridge. "Nothing's going on."

"Yeah, I believe that as much as Mitch's promise of a Friday night off."

"You get one?"

"Yeah, first Friday of never followed by when hell freezes over."

I laughed and took a longer sip of my soda before sitting back behind the cardboard palace. I forked in a regular-sized bite and chewed slowly.

"While I appreciate you not talking with your mouth full, I'm not reframing the question."

"He's my best friend, Sage. It ain't happening."

"What isn't?"

"Us. We aren't happening." That wasn't what I'd meant to say at all, but Sage took the ball and ran with it as if I wasn't talking crazy talk.

"Yeah, but you're simply biding your time on the sidelines. From what I've seen lately, he's finally gotten his hormones engaged."

That was the problem. He was only acting on an unexpected case of hormones and some misplaced sense of duty. Laurie wanted a sibling and Seth never knew how to tell his daughter no. At least not about this kind of thing.

And he knew I loved that little girl as much as he did. Dirty pool with a side of emotional blackmail.

Oh, and couldn't forget the left turn into naked time.

Nope.

But then he'd ruined it with a contract attached to my damn uterus.

My soda frothed over the top of the lip. I hadn't realized I was squeezing the bottle so hard.

Sage instantly crossed the room for a paper towel. "Oh, yeah. Nothing going on." She handed me a wad of them.

I crouched with a disgusted sound and mopped up the sticky mess before washing up and returning to our table.

Sage spooned up a dainty portion as I hacked at mine with the three oversized tines of my fork. I'd sold off my silverware since I wasn't going to need it at Sage's place.

"Things are weird, okay?"

She widened her green eyes comically. "Obviously, they're weird. I want to know *why* they're weird."

"It's stupid."

"Did you trip over his big feet and fall on his dick?"

"Oh, my God."

Sage dabbed at the corner of her mouth with her napkin. "It's the only thing that makes sense. Did you guys finally do the deed? You've been holding onto that V-card forever."

"You should talk. Yours is as intact as mine, pal."

Sage scooped up a roasted carrot. "Yes, but I've been trying to give mine away. You've been holding yours hostage."

"I have not."

Sage gave me a bland look.

"Not on purpose."

"Hey, it makes sense. You've had your focus split in a few different directions."

"Why are we talking about this?" I asked and stabbed a potato.

"Because that's my only guess for this weird behavior."

"Oh, honey. You don't even know how weird shit has gotten."

"Then enlighten me. Because I need to know why you aren't over with Seth and Laurie like you usually are on Mother's Day."

I bowed my head. If I thought about things too closely, then the guilt was going to choke me. I might be having trouble with Laurie's father, but that didn't mean it was fair to stay away from his daughter in retribution.

I yanked the tie out of my braid and sifted my fingers through the tangle of waves before I knotted my hair on top of my head. "It's complicated."

"Complicated came and went about ten years ago, hon."

I didn't know if I should tell her. The fact that I was going to say no made the point fairly moot.

I was saying no. I had to.

Didn't I?

Grumbling, I pushed my dish away and banged my forehead on the box.

"Okay, you have to tell me."

"Seth wants a kid."

"He has a kid. A cute one, if a little bit of a handful."

"She's bright and funny and really wants a little sister or brother."

Sage's eyebrows shot up. "Oh."

"He wants me to have it."

"I'm sorry? Come again?"

"He wants me to give him a kid."

"What? Like a piece of chocolate?"

I laughed. It was either that or cry. "So you see my dilemma."

"Not really. You already want to play Boom-Boom Room with him. This sounds perfect. You guys would make a cute couple. I mean, he can be annoying, and the idea is a bit weird, but—"

"He doesn't want us to be a couple. He just wants me to carry a baby for him and then hand it off to him like a fruitcake at Christmas."

"Huh."

"Yep."

"I think we might need wine." She rose and went to the fridge where a box of wine was stuffed down on the bottom shelf. She hauled it onto the counter and pulled out jelly glasses from the skinny cabinet.

When she set a glass in front of me, I took a swig of the sweet white wine. The shock on her face helped with my own insanity. It wasn't just me who had a problem with the whole scenario. It was straight-up crazy.

So why couldn't I just say no?

4

SETH

"No mo peas."

Staring at my daughter's stubborn chin as she shook her head in refusal of the healthy vegetable I'd added to our meals, I briefly reconsidered what I'd asked of Ally.

Did I really want another child?

Hell, could I *handle* another child? Basically on my own—along with the nanny I employed on workdays—since I didn't expect Ally to be tied down. She could be as involved as she wanted in whatever capacity she chose, but I'd proceeded as if she would choose minimal involvement. Thinking otherwise made things sticky.

Made me itchy in ways I couldn't define.

Now I had an almost four-year-old staring me down and a bowl of peas I didn't even want myself. But good example and all that. And if I wanted another kid, good examples were the rule of the day.

God, was I crazy?

Dutifully, I spooned up my vegetable. "Okay, if you don't want the rest of your dinner, as soon as I finish, we'll get you upstairs for your bath. School tomorrow. Mrs. O'Connor said you're drawing mermaids this week. That will be fun."

"No bath." Laurie pushed at her plate and inched back in her chair, step one in lurching to the floor.

She still wasn't the best at climbing, but she liked sitting at the big table without a highchair. As small as she was, she'd used one longer than some kids, but now she was done with it.

Done with everything judging from how many times she'd said no tonight.

"You need a bath. You were playing outside with Fritz for an hour this afternoon. Digging up Mrs. Polenti's flowerbeds no less."

It wasn't much of an admonition. Laurie and the neighbor's cocker spaniel were so cute together. Mrs. Polenti was soft on them too, so I knew she wouldn't mind a few trampled leaves.

Though as soon as I mentioned the neighbor's pup, I knew what I'd be in for.

"Daddy, I want a dog. Like Fritz." Laurie's big blue eyes zeroed in on mine. "I'd take care of it. Feed and walk it."

"What about clean up after it goes on the sidewalk? You have to scoop the poop into a bag and take it home to throw it out."

Her little nose wrinkled. "Eww."

"Part of being a pet owner, kiddo."

"Okay. Then I'd do that too." She sounded decidedly less enthusiastic.

"Maybe next year," I said as I always did.

Someday I intended to get her a puppy, but not until she was older and more responsible. And I'd figured out juggling the whole two little kids deal.

Yeah, I'd been plotting this scenario for a few months. Shifting things around in my head until I could figure out how to make it all work.

Ally was at the center of the plan. Without her, the rest fell apart. Considering she hadn't contacted me since our conversation at the diner, that wasn't a good sign.

She'd made it clear by not answering any of my calls that she needed space to think. But today was her first Mother's Day without her mom, and I couldn't just let the day pass without her knowing I was thinking about her. So I'd sent a simple bouquet of flowers with a brief card and hoped that sufficed. Even if she hated me, at least she knew I cared.

As far as the reverse, she hadn't come by to see Laurie today, and she always did on this day for obvious reasons. I couldn't blame her. Much. My offer had upset the balance, but it bugged me that Laurie was paying the price.

Not that my baby girl had mentioned Ally. Not once. She barely seemed aware of the day, though it was always a big deal in her preschool class. She'd brought me home a card she'd drawn, as was standard on a parent celebration day when the parent in question wasn't a part of the child's life. So she knew what today was. Knew what it meant.

Maybe that had something to do with her cranky mood since waking up from her nap. She had to miss her mom, right? Even if they'd only spent a few months together while Laurie was too little to remember much, Marj had carried Laurie for nine months. That created a special bond. It had to. Not that Marj had seemed overly affected.

Yet you're asking your best friend to bear your child then to walk away?

"Daddy, ice cream?" Laurie picked up a couple peas between her fingers, squashing them together before popping them in her mouth. Her idea of a concession in the hopes of getting dessert.

"A scoop of ice cream after your bath, then you brush your teeth." I wasn't above bribery.

Laurie tilted her head, her blond pigtails falling over her shoulders. Every day she looked older. The chubbiness in her cheeks was fading, and her eyes were taking on a more knowing quality I was both proud of and worried about. I didn't want her to have to face the world. She'd never be alone—not while I had breath in my body—but there were far too many things out there that I couldn't shield her from.

And I would be taking on a whole new set of worries with a new one. Voluntarily.

Maybe Ally was right. I had gone mad.

"Okay," Laurie said after a moment's thought. "Strawberry?"

"It's Neapolitan," I told her. "Vanilla, strawberry and chocolate."

Again with the stubborn chin. "Just strawberry and brush my teeth for three seconds."

"Thirty," I corrected, grinning in spite of myself. My daughter was a negotiator to the core. Just like her daddy and Uncle Oliver and our father before us. Always wheeling and dealing.

"Thirty what?"

"Seconds." I reached over to ruffle her cornsilk hair. She was also a con artist. "You can have a scoop of mostly strawberry and then brush your teeth for thirty seconds." I looked at her plate. "If you eat a few more peas."

With a loud sigh, she grabbed a couple and smashed them into her mouth, chewing and swallowing so fast I feared she would choke. Then she made a face. "I hate peas."

"You liked them last week."

"Elizabeth doesn't like peas."

"Oh, so if your best friend doesn't like them, you can't like them?"

She nodded as if that made total sense. "Ally doesn't like them either."

Halfway to my feet to clear the dishes from the table, I paused. And sank back down as heavily as a stone in a lake.

Just her name slayed me.

"Is she coming over today?"

Like an idiot, I stared wordlessly at my daughter. I honestly didn't know, and that was my fault. On another Mother's Day, she would. It was almost guaranteed. But because of my crazy scheme, I'd put distance between us. And distance between her and my little girl.

"I'll find out," I replied, unsure exactly how.

I was trying to give Ally space. Trying to not push or cause her any more discomfort on a day that already had to be tough. Not being there for her on this first holiday without her mom was like a physical ache in my gut. She wasn't just the woman I'd asked to have my child. She was my best friend, in many ways my other half. The person I wanted with me when I was going out for a good time or just kicking back with a beer and a movie.

And Jesus Christ, I'd told her I wanted to fuck her. In lurid detail.

The kind of detail that had kept me up late every night since, fisting my cock and imagining the shock on her face. The way her pale pink lips had trembled open, as if she was stunned I would ever say such a thing.

But I had. Now there was no coming back from it. We could only go forward. The one thing I wasn't going to do was apologize, because I wasn't sorry for being honest. I was just mad at myself for not realizing sooner that the occasional flickers of interest I'd dismissed as being due to a lengthy dry spell were so much more.

It wasn't like I wanted a relationship. Experience had taught me I sucked at those. Enjoying the process of getting Ally pregnant, however, was a completely different ballgame.

If she ever talked to me again. Which I wouldn't know unless I tried.

"I'll call her," I decided, standing up and grabbing Laurie's plate as she reached for another couple of peas. I waited while she grabbed them and pushed them into her mouth, shaking my head with a smile. "Fork next time, young lady."

She gave me a toothy green-smeared smile. "Call Ally now?"

I could do that. Sure, why not? It wasn't a big deal, calling my best friend on an important holiday.

That I'd told her I wanted to fuck her until my cum spilled out of her was incidental. Besides, I didn't want it to spill out. I wanted it to stay inside until her belly grew rounded with my baby.

Our baby.

Swallowing hard, I carried our dishes to the sink and rinsed them off before loading them in the dishwasher. "Why don't you go up to your room and pick out what you want to wear tomorrow then start getting ready for your bath?"

Sending Laurie off to dig through her drawers was always a dangerous proposition, but she preferred to dress herself these days, even if that meant she ended up more often than not in mismatched—and sometimes strange—outfits. Not like I was the fashion police. She was reaching for her independence, and so far, we hadn't yet hit an impasse. It was coming, I was sure, but it wouldn't be over rainbow leggings and light-up sneakers.

"Okay." She heaved herself off the chair, her feet landing on the tiled floor with a thud. She circled the table and grabbed me around the legs, hugging me hard. "Love you, Daddy." Then she ran down the hall, ponytails streaming, and I grinned.

Moments like that were why I wanted another one. Also possibly a healthy streak of masochism.

After I heard Laurie's footsteps climbing the stairs, I dried off my hands and tugged out my cell from my pocket. No missed calls or texts, which meant Ally hadn't responded to the texts I'd sent. I'd only checked twenty times today, so not sure when I thought they might've come in.

Nada.

Nyet.

Eh, fuck it. I was calling her anyway. She couldn't hide from me forever. If her answer was no, well, I'd just have to change her mind.

Steeling my shoulders, I hit the number one saved number. She didn't answer for so long that I figured I'd get voicemail.

"Hi." She sounded tired.

My hackles rose. Everything rose, truthfully, including my dick. Since when did her silky voice have the power to wake up my cock?

For that matter, since when did I hear her voice as *silky*? I was on the verge of turning in my man card and signing up for eternal blue balls all in one week.

"Hi. How are you?"

"I'm okay. How are you?"

So she thought we were going to keep it cordial as if we were strangers. No dice.

"Why do you sound exhausted?" I asked.

"I stayed up late fucking my neighbors. Is that all right with you?"

That I actually gripped the edge of the sink instead of realizing right away that she was screwing with me, proved how messed up I was. She'd said things like that a million times, and I'd tossed back my share of those kinds of replies as well. We didn't get overly personal when it came to sex, but we'd never shied away from most topics either. I didn't know much about her sex life, and I was okay with that.

Or I had been, until I had decided I should become part of it. For babymaking purposes only, of course.

Mutual orgasms would just be a bonus.

"I know today is a rough day for you." I relaxed my grip on the edge of the sink. "I wanted to make sure you were okay."

"Yeah, it's been rough. A lot of days have been lately." She let out a breath and I wished like hell that there wasn't a phone between us so I could hold her.

Not to make a baby. Not to soften her up for my wild plan. Simply because she was my closest friend, and her pain was palpable.

"Wanna come over?" I asked softly.

Any other time, I wouldn't have had to voice the question. She would've just shown up, and we wouldn't have talked about the meaning of the day other than to maybe hipcheck each other or sling an arm around each other's shoulders before she left for the night.

We weren't touchy-feely. She was basically like my best guy friend, except she was even better—and she also had one hell of a body, which thankfully was only a recent obsession of mine. *Very* recent.

If I'd allowed myself to notice her curves before, we couldn't have remained platonic friends for so long. I'd have banged her and probably driven her out of my life years ago.

There was a reason I didn't try to have relationships anymore, and it wasn't just because I didn't trust easily. I wasn't built to be a married guy.

Or maybe that was just what I told myself.

"Do you think that's a good idea?" she replied, just as softly.

"Why the hell not? You've spent part of every Mother's Day here since Laurie's birth. Hell, even when Marj was pregnant, you were the one here on Mother's Day making a fuss over her. More of a fuss than I made."

By then, things had been so strained between Marj and me that I'd had trouble tamping down on my feelings long enough to do my husbandly and fatherly duty. But I'd made breakfast and gotten her flowers and tried to pretend we were a real family.

And I'd ignored my bitchy wife when she crabbed about Ally "always hanging around" instead of appreciating her kindness.

"Being a mom is special," Ally said, and I felt like an asshole all over again. "So is being a dad."

"Yeah, it is." I grabbed a sponge and wiped halfheartedly at the sink. "Look, I'm not asking you to come over here so we can discuss things. I mean, unless you want to."

"Why would I want to? I've spent the last few days hoping you had developed amnesia and had forgotten the whole asinine idea."

I tried to rein in my temper. I'd told her we didn't have to discuss this right now, and today was a difficult day for her. Of course she wouldn't be in the best frame of mind.

"Judging from your silence, you haven't. So I'm not really sure what else we have to say to each other, since you've lost your goddamn mind. Telling me you wanted to—" She broke off and hissed out a breath. "Lunatic."

"Is telling you I want to have sex with you that startling that you think I must've developed a mental condition?"

"When you say it like that… Yeah, maybe. It certainly came out of left field. Though I get that it's just the means to an end to you."

"No, it isn't."

"Yes, it is."

"No, it fucking isn't. Okay, maybe it started that way, and maybe I never noticed you had tits before, but—"

She huffed out a laugh. "See? And they've been here all along."

"I just never saw you that way. Intentionally. Not because you aren't hot. You're just—"

"Not your type. Yeah, yeah, Hamilton, I know it and I'm cool with it. We stay in our lanes. You're the one who's suddenly swerving all over the place. Maybe this is just the male version of a ticking hormonal clock. I didn't know it happened to dudes, but possibly something went off inside you and you panicked. It's no big deal. We can just move on from here and forget we ever brought up the subject."

"Wrong answer. It is big, and if you ever stopped freaking out at the mere idea I could want to fuck you, you'd find that out for yourself."

"You want to fuck me to make a baby with me. A baby you can then raise as a storied Hamilton child without my involvement to taint him or her."

Her words stole the breath from my chest. "You honestly believe I'd view your involvement that way?"

"I don't know. You're the one who told me I could run off and be a free bird as soon as I gave birth. Didn't really seem like you wanted my input. And for that matter, I wouldn't do it anyway, so why are we still talking about it?"

"Because you can't seem to talk about anything else. Which is pretty damn funny considering you supposedly find the idea so off-putting. Me thinks the lady doth protest too much."

"Oh, fuck right off."

"I'd love to. When can I expect you?"

She growled at me and the tight band around my chest loosened for the first time since I'd walked into the diner during her shift on Thursday. That sound was pure Ally. She might be annoyed and questioning my mental balance, but she didn't hate me. And I wasn't entirely convinced she hated the idea of us making a baby either.

I could work with both of those things.

"Look, we'll just hang out. Laurie's been asking for you."

"She has?" Ally cleared her throat. "Again, using your child is a dick move, Hamilton."

"I'm not using her. Just saying I'm not the only one who misses you." All right, so I hadn't intended to phrase things quite like that.

I didn't miss her. Did I? That would be nuts. It had only been a few days since we'd seen each other. You couldn't miss someone in that time.

Even if the tightness was back in my chest at the possibility she wouldn't come.

"Now you're sweet talking. Pulling out the big guns, huh?"

"Nah. I haven't pulled out the biggest gun yet. But if you'd like me to…"

"Hear that sound? It's me not being amused by your sexual innuendoes."

"Who mentioned sex?" I used my most innocent voice as she audibly swallowed a laugh. "You filthy-minded pervert."

"Yeah, it's all—"

"Daddy!" Laurie screamed from upstairs.

I didn't think. I barely held on to the phone as I rushed down the hall and up the stairs, my only thought my little girl.

"Seth? Seth, what was that? Did I hear a scream? Oh my God, was that Laurie? Is she okay?"

Turning the phone against my shoulder, I hit the top of the stairs and booked toward Laurie's room. She wasn't in there, but the door to her en suite bathroom was open. And water was running.

"Oh fuck," I muttered, my heart slamming in my ears.

"Seth? Goddammit, Seth." Even Ally shouting into the phone couldn't distract me from crossing the room to the bathroom.

I stepped over the threshold, my eyes bugging out at the sheer number of bubbles flowing everywhere. The tub was full and the bubbling water was still rising, and in the middle of it sat my little girl, her hair wet, and her eyes wild.

"I can't turn it off, Daddy," she shrieked as I moved forward and did the honors, barely managing not to curse a blue streak. I pulled the stopper up, rather amazed that Laurie had thought to put it in, and waited while several inches of water flowed down the drain. Her assorted Care Bears and other toys floated in what was left.

Laurie squealed in dismay. "My bubbles!"

"Yeah, well, my bathroom floor. Why are you in here? You were supposed to pick out clothes and get ready for a bath, not start it yourself."

"Seth! You better answer me, you jackass! Is she okay?"

Somehow, I smiled in the middle of chaos. That was the gift Ally had given me since the first day we'd met.

Once the water was at a much more reasonable level, I put the stopper back in and brought my phone to my ear. "Your god-daughter chose to nearly flood the bathroom instead of waiting for me to start her bath."

Laurie popped halfway out of the water, her little face screwed up in annoyance. "I do it myself."

"Oh really? And you did a fine job." I braced my fist on my hip. "I'm going to let out some more of this water and—"

"No. Bubbles. I like it." Laurie crossed her arms and glared. "Is Ally coming over?"

"See?" I said into the phone. "Did you hear that? The princess herself just requested you."

"Don't be mean to her. She just likes her bubble baths."

"Fine. She couldn't have waited five minutes for me to get up here and start her bath for her?" Spying the almost empty bottle of Cookie Monster bubble bath on the side of the tub, I sighed. "And maybe not finish off the bottle of bubbles in one go?"

"There's some left. It needed more," Laurie said stubbornly, plopping back down in the water and sloshing a small tidal wave over the side.

"Women," I muttered.

"Sorry we're such a trial to you manly sorts," Ally said, but the dry humor in her tone made the year Laurie had just chopped off my life worth it.

"Daddy, out." Laurie stuck out her chin. "Private now."

"Say what?"

"Daddy, private now!" She flung a handful of soapy water at me and I backed into the other room, casting a glance at the ceiling.

"She won't let me stay in the room for her bath."

"Since when?"

"Ask her. So you gonna come over or what? My bathroom tiles will thank you later."

"Daddy," Laurie called. "Shut the door, pweese."

"Did she just ask you to close the door?"

"She sure did." And I was doing it—partially, though it was damn sure staying cracked so I could keep an eye and both ears on the situation—because hell if I knew what was protocol at Laurie's age.

I'd been unsure about continuing to help with her bath as she grew older, but sometimes Ruth, the nanny, wasn't there to help. I was her father, for fuck's sake. It was my job. But if Laurie felt ready to do it on her own, I supposed I could give her that space.

Especially if Ally could help make sure my daughter—and my bathroom—survived intact.

"Fine, I'm coming over. But to see Laurie, not you."

"Whatever. I'm grateful regardless. Bring alcohol."

"Moscato?" Ally asked, mentioning what we'd turned to more often than not lately.

"Nah. A six-pack of whatever you find at the corner store will do." A thud came from within the bathroom and I tipped back my head. "Make it a twelve-pack. And hurry."

5

ALLY

I HUNG UP THE PHONE AND FROWNED AT SAGE WHEN SHE TOOK my glass and poured it into hers. "Hey."

"You're going off to play Mommy to jackass." She snorted. "Now that I know he really wants you to play Mommy, it makes it a little more amusing instead of just annoying."

"You think it's annoying?"

She shrugged as she swirled the wine. "I think it's very suspect that he calls you with a SOS a lot."

"He's just a little overwhelmed."

"Uh-huh. And he wants another one?"

I crossed my arms. I could feel the sweat and grit on me, but I didn't have time to get changed and I definitely didn't have time to take a shower. Maybe if he saw the real me he'd get that ridiculous idea out of his head.

I wasn't mommy material. I knew a few tricks when it came to Laurie, but it was because we were buddies. Not due to a maternal instinct—mostly.

It still didn't make sense that he wanted me to be a gestational host to his spawn. A spawn he planted himself.

Thank God for padded bras. Otherwise my damn nipples would

be on display. Just thinking about him planting anything inside me stirred me up in ways I didn't want to examine. And if my hand strayed a little farther down my body to cup my middle, then I was entitled. It was still a shock to think Seth might want me that way in any capacity.

At least if we did a fertility clinic then it wouldn't be so…messy. Getting skin to skin would only screw things up. I wasn't exactly the type of girl who could remove myself from the sexual component.

And it was only partially because I hadn't gotten truly naked with anyone in my life. I'd had a few opportunities, but it never seemed to work out.

I wasn't as picky as Sage, but I was definitely a special head case thanks to my home situation. Since my mom had only been gone for a handful of months, it didn't make sense that I'd jump right into the dating scene. Especially when I didn't have time to sleep let alone try to form coherent sentences during a date.

Did I mention that this situation was fucked up? Because it so was.

I grabbed my purse off one of the two chairs left in the kitchen. "You good to get home?"

"No problem." She gulped down the remaining butter-colored liquid and set the glasses in the sink.

I frowned at her.

Sage rolled her eyes. "That wine was like drinking a diet, watered down beer."

"Better safe than sorry."

"Okay, big sis, relax yourself. Just because Scorer Seth wants to get jiggy with it doesn't mean you have to analyze every move I'm making."

"I know." I blew out a breath and wondered why I'd ever told her about Seth's old high school nickname. "I know."

"Good. Now do I need to give you the talk?"

Horrified, I unrolled the sleeves of my T-shirt. "What talk?"

"I think you know about the birds and the bees. At least I hope you've at least watched those romantic cable movies after midnight that are almost porn."

"Um, that's a little TMI, don't you think?" It wasn't, but I was great at stalling.

"Is there anything off the table with us at this point? I now know you have been propositioned to be a gestational incubator."

"I suppose not. And no, I'm good, thanks. Think I know how Tab A fits into Slot B."

Big Tab A, from all the talk Seth was throwing around. Probably trying to sweeten the pot.

Sage glanced at my shirt. "At least that part's fitting."

I glanced down at my "I Can't Adult Today" shirt and my cutoff shorts. I really wished I had time to change. Then again, the quicker I got Laurie settled, the quicker I could go home and soak in a tub before work in the morning.

Or maybe I would just climb in with the kid.

I shook my head. No, that wasn't happening. Extra time at Seth's was a no-go tonight and for the foreseeable future.

I grabbed my iPad and my iPencil and dumped them into my purse. My Christmas present from Seth last year kept his daughter endlessly entertained. Could've been the eight coloring apps I had on it too.

Hurrying outside, I waved to Sage as I climbed into my trusty Subaru Outback. Then I headed to Seth's place on the opposite side of the lake. My old house was on the fringes of town, but I'd made this trip plenty of times. And most of them actually didn't involve a cry for help from Seth.

He was a really good dad, but Laurie was asserting her independence. She was very much like her father, and I'd known they would butt heads eventually.

I toyed with my arrow necklace as the lakeside road curved around the bend. The gazebo and the pier came into view. It was late enough that most of the pedestrian traffic was light as people finished up dinners and the shops started closing up for the night.

It was late for Laurie to be up. If she was already down for the night by the time I got there, I was going to string Seth up by his short and curlies.

My car made the steep climb up to the mansions on the far side of the lake. They were surrounded by gates of all kinds to keep the riffraff out, and the moneyed in. The house Seth had chosen for his home with Laurie after his divorce definitely wasn't at the top of the scale, but they definitely weren't slumming it.

Hamilton's never did.

According to my mother, a Hamilton had been in residence since the town had been established. In fact, the town had nearly been named Hamilton Cove, but some of the residents had fought for the name to be a bit more welcoming. Hamilton sounded so stern.

Much like the men, and the women, of the line. Seth even had his moments of stoic behavior, but Laurie had definitely changed him for the better.

I parked in the long, winding driveway and sat with my fingers wrapped around the steering wheel. There were wear marks from a hundred thousand miles of me gripping them. From the various levels of news about my mom's sickness, to money issues, to frustration—all of the handprints were carved into this wheel.

Tonight, it was nerves and frustration adding another layer to the already worn gray leather. I wasn't ready to face Seth, but his little girl trumped all. In fact, she was the reason for much of the drama in my life right now.

Seth wouldn't have looked twice at me if Laurie hadn't vocalized her very passionate view on having a sister. A brother wasn't really in her purview, though Seth tried to indicate she was open to either. We both knew it was female or bust in this princess's life.

I leaned over and dug my sandals out of my canvas bag, swapping my dusty ancient sneakers for more comfortable shoes. Especially if bath time troubles were in my future.

I was pretty sure my poor feet swelled to double their size the minute I took my sneakers off. I needed to be horizontal for a week.

My heart raced at the thought. No.

No.

No.

Not that kind of horizontal.

I peered into my bag for any other goodies. I was good at packing extras of most things, including clothing, but nope. Dusty T-shirt and cutoffs it was. My backup shirt had been used when a toddler sprayed me with ketchup yesterday.

I slammed the door and tromped through the river rock edging the wide driveway, then up the grand staircase. Solar lights flared from large lamps flanking the double entry door. The aged walnut wood screamed of money and affluence.

I didn't even get the pretense of knocking. A blood-curdling scream had me pulling the large door open.

"Laurie Elizabeth Hamilton, that is enough." A rare bellow from Seth kicked my heart rate into high gear as I hit the stairs at two at a time.

"No boys allowed!"

"I washed your hair two days ago and you didn't say a thing then, young lady."

Uh-oh. He'd dragged out *young lady*. This wasn't going to be good.

I came around the corner to find a frazzled Seth crouched next to the door with his fingers fisted in his hair. The dark wavy strands were sticking up in damp tufts. Wet splotches arced across his chest and his arms were beaded with water.

"Didn't even let you get a towel, huh?"

He spun on the balls of his feet and stood. "Thank God."

He was wearing his oldest jeans—you know, the kind that were worn at all the good stress points—with bare feet and a waterlogged blue Oxford dress shirt open a few extra buttons to show off way too much of his chest. There was obviously no justice in this world.

"I just tried to go in again. I'm her father, for God's sake. We just had a bath the other day without incident."

"That was the other day." I swallowed down my nerves. If he could act normal, I could act normal. I strode down the hall and knocked on the door briskly. "Hey, can I come in, munchkin?"

"Ally! Do you have my Care Bear bubbles?"

"Honey, you dumped your tubby bubbles, remember?" Seth called through the door.

"No! My bubbles. I want bubbles."

I looked over my shoulder. "Does she mean like blowing bubbles?"

Seth tipped his head back. So much throat and chest on display.

57

His chest was mostly smooth save for a sprinkle of dark hair between his pecs. I'd seen him without a shirt a million times, but now just seemed so much worse. *God, stop looking.*

"Honey, we play with those outside."

"No!" Laurie screeched.

My eyebrows shot up. "Tell me you have bubbles."

His dark brows knitted, then cleared. "Yes. I have to go get them." He started to stride down the hall then stopped. "Are you okay?"

I rolled my eyes. "You're asking this now?"

His gaze dropped to my chest and his eyes heated briefly. "Your shirt says maybe not."

I glanced down at the words on my chest and cursed my headlights coming out to play. Timing was wrong as always, but this time there was a weight to it I didn't want to examine. At all. "Yeah, well, adulting comes around whether you want it to or not." I opened the door and slid inside before he could say another word.

The little girl in the tub obliterated any other issue I had with daddy dearest. I put my hands on my hips. "I hear you're giving your dad some trouble."

Laurie grinned up at me, her freakishly long eyelashes starred from the water. She was sitting in about six inches of water that was mostly foam. She also had an array of plastic ducks, fish, whales, dolphins, and yes, Care Bears in the tub with her. She held a bright pink netted puff in her hand as she painstakingly washed her blue Care Bear.

Fittingly, it was a plastic version of Grumpy Bear.

Just like me.

Well, until this little girl was in my space. I couldn't be grumpy around her, even if I wanted to strangle her sometimes. Cuteness always won out.

She smiled up at me with a dimple winking. "This is a girls' party."

I kneeled beside her and brushed her damp bangs out of her face. "Is that so?"

She nodded and bit her lower lip in concentration as she washed under Grumpy's armpit.

"Grumpy is a boy."

She looked up at me with a knitted brow so much like her father's.

A blond version, but all the rest was the same. "Grumpy is a bear," she said as if that made all the difference.

I supposed for an almost four-year-old, it really did. I shrugged. "All righty then."

I turned on the taps to add to the water to bubbles ratio. From the looks of the bottle on the side of the tub, Laurie had been using a heavy hand.

When she lifted the bottle and started to pour more on the puff, I made a grab for it.

She stuck out her lower lip. "I need that."

I swooped up a froth of bubbles and settled it on top of her puff. "There you go." When she still frowned, I took another dollop and settled it on her nose.

She giggled.

Now we were in business. By the time Seth came back, I had her hair washed and was chaperoning her hygiene rituals. I'd already made the mistake of trying to help there.

I'd been an independent kid too, but I didn't remember a lot about my childhood. Just moving a lot. And I'd learned to shower far earlier than a lot of my friends. Sitting in bathtubs in some of the places we'd lived wasn't the best idea.

Seth knocked on the door.

"No! No boys."

A clunking sound made me frown and then Seth's lacrosse stick came through the door with a bottle of bubbles in the netting. I laughed and stood.

Laurie giggled. "Thank you, Daddy!"

I took the bubbles. "You're a dork."

"Daddy's a dork."

"Great. Thanks. She'll be saying that for days."

"Fitting."

"Har-har. Everything okay in there, girls? It's way past bedtime."

"Almost done." Laurie slapped her hand on the water. "Go away."

"I'm going."

I snaked a finger through the crack in the door and flicked a nail over the back of his hand. "We're fine."

He let out a slow breath. "Thanks."

"Of course." I rubbed my hand over my breastbone and went back to his daughter with the bubbles. I unscrewed the cap. "Okay, you get one blast of bubbles for each friend you finish washing."

"Deal." She dunked her dolphin into the water and it came out gleaming. She set it on the shelf along the back of the tub. "Go."

I pulled the double wand out and blew out a stream of rainbow bubbles.

"Me. I want to do it."

"Two more of your buddies and you got it."

The big whale and baby whale got dunked and deposited on the shelf. I dunked the wand and handed it to her.

"No, I want to do it."

"You are wet and soapy, kiddo. We don't want these to fall in, do we?"

She scrunched up her nose and lips. "No. I guess not." She shrugged and took the wand. She blew too hard and only got three bubbles. "Hey."

I took it back and dunked. "Easy. Soft. Yes, just like that."

When the stream of bubbles floated up, she clapped. Five minutes later, there were many squeaky clean fish guarding her tub and a pruny almost four-year-old standing with a purple towel on her head and fluffy pink Care Bears towel wrapped around her.

Before she could find another reason to extend her bath time, I swooped her out and deposited her on the bath mat. I wrapped another towel around her and started a rubdown. By the time she was mostly dry, she was still giggling and I was laughing with her.

I hadn't even known this was exactly what I needed to even me out.

"Okay, Daddy, we're ready."

He opened the door so fast, I knew he'd stood out there the entire time. I wasn't sure how I felt about that. Didn't he trust me?

Then I looked down at the crazy monkey in my arms and her adoring eyes only for him. There was no way I could get upset about that. Laurie reached for him and suddenly I was forty pounds lighter.

He looked down at me, his eyes flashing for a moment as he

dropped his gaze over my wet shirt. Yeah, good thing I had that padded bra on. I turned away from him to pick up the bubbles and empty bottle of soap.

He cleared his throat before burying his face in Laurie's neck. She giggled and squirmed, causing the towel on her hair to fall to the floor. "I'm just going to get her dressed."

"Yeah, good idea. I'll just clean up."

"Don't worry about that. You've done more than enough."

"It's fine."

"No, really. The nanny will take care of it."

"Right." Of course he had a nanny for her. I'd talked to her a million times. I didn't know her duties included cleaning a bathroom, but he was right this wasn't my house or my life.

He just wanted me to create a human, not take care of one. Even if he did call on me to help.

Would he do the same with my—our—his... God. How would I even classify him or her? Mine?

Ours.

I fisted my hands into my hair and tugged out my messy bun. "Fuck."

In the hallway, I could hear giggling and Seth's baritone voice. The love obvious between them. His heart was so huge for that little girl. It might be a little more reserved for others. He used charm to deflect emotions for other people in his life.

I'd seen it firsthand. The way my customers reacted to him. That half-grin and easy way with conversation left everyone at ease. And half the town's female population would jump at the chance to do what he'd asked me to do.

But they would want more.

Every woman wanted more in his eyes. Mostly because of the lenses that Marjorie had left behind when she'd walked away from Laurie. He just assumed most women wanted something from him. And part of me understood that.

He could grant me opportunities that I'd have to work my ass to achieve. But then again, they would be my achievements. No one else's.

Part of me wanted to just up and leave this town and start over. Even if that meant I would be in debt up to my eyeballs for the next thirty years. It would be my debt, and my life, and a fresh start.

I lifted the towel that had fallen off Laurie's head and hung it on the pink unicorn hook on the wall. And because I couldn't stand to leave the mess in the bathroom, I listened to Seth tell his daughter a bedtime story as I tidied up.

When the rumble of his voice faded and I heard his footfalls, I shut off the light and met him in the hall.

He frowned at me. "I told you—"

I held up my hand. "Already done." I crossed to him and ducked under his arm to enter Laurie's room. His burnt sugar cologne mixed with the baby shampoo scent of his kid and my hormones decided that was the perfect aphrodisiac. Did I mention my life was unfair?

I focused on the little lump on the middle of the full-sized mattress. The bed was way too big for her, but she was surrounded by Care Bears and stuffed animals from various Disney movies. Dory, Hank, and the guppy from *Little Mermaid* guarded her. A nightlight spun from her bedside table, shooting starlight around her room.

Pink and perfect in every way. This little girl had everything I didn't have growing up. No wonder he wanted to give her the world.

I just wasn't sure I was the one to help him.

"She's out."

I lifted my shoulder in reaction to his deep voice against my ear. He slid his arm around my waist and pulled me away from the doorway. He shut the door most of the way, then pulled me down the hall.

"I don't want to wake her."

I nodded. Understandable, of course. He needed to back up though. I couldn't handle him in my space for extended periods of time. Even if I'd initiated it this time. What the hell had I been thinking?

Oh, right. I wasn't really thinking. Actually, it had been a luxury I couldn't afford for years. I was really good at ignoring my feelings for him. Why did he have to go and ruin it? Now all I could imagine was what he tasted like.

Fuck.

I tried to pull away, but he pulled me back against him. "Don't go."

I closed my eyes. "Please don't."

"Don't what?" His nose coasted around the shell of my ear. "Touch you?"

"I'm filthy."

He buried his nose in my hair. "You smell like lilacs and sunshine."

"Liar."

"Baby shampoo and lilacs?"

I tried not to smile, but I had no defenses for this man. The worst part was I was sure he knew that. And Seth Hamilton was always on the lookout for weaknesses to exploit to get what he wanted.

How the hell was I supposed to move out of his crosshairs?

Did I want to?

His hand slid along my midriff, his thumb grazing the underside of my breast. I groaned. "Honestly, you have to pick now to do this?"

"I've been thinking about this for days."

I turned in his arms. "So this was all a ruse?"

"No. This was the last act of a desperate man. She's been a handful all night. She misses you."

"Low blow."

"You've spent Mother's Day with us since Marj left."

I shut my eyes. "I know." Didn't he realize how hard this day was for me? Not only because it was Mother's Day for Laurie, but the first without my mom?

He knew on some level. He'd sent me flowers, hadn't he? But all my emotions were raw today. It just wasn't fair that he was right here and finally noticing me.

Except he wasn't seeing me as a partner. No, he was only seeing me as a woman because I had a functioning uterus.

He wanted something from me. It was just handy that he was attracted to me. It was how the world had propagated all these years. Just a biological response.

He swiped his thumb along my jawline. "I know today was rough.

And it was completely unfair of me to push you to come over here and save me."

I ground my teeth together and growled. I looked up at him. "Don't be sweet, dammit."

His fingers slid up into my hair and he gathered it tight at the nape of my neck. "You got it."

I didn't have time to dodge or pull away from him. I didn't have the heart to do it either. I'd had a truly shitty day and I wanted to see what all the fuss was about.

Finally.

For years I'd seen women come and go from his life. A knowledge always seemed to live in their eyes when they touched him. I wanted that too. I wanted to feel something other than sad and frustrated.

I met his gaze. The dark, turbulent anger swirled with something else. Something I couldn't define. I had a limited scope with men, but I had some.

Nothing came close to this man though.

I shifted against him and my damp T-shirt met with his wrinkled Oxford blue. Working class and old money between us in every way. And then none of that mattered.

He lowered his mouth and covered mine. My eyes fluttered shut and I fell into the kiss.

Nothing soft and hesitant here. He was no fumbling boy. I was pretty sure he hadn't been one of those in a very long time.

His other arm wrapped around me from the back, gripping the hem of my shirt until his fingers curled into the belt loops of my shorts. His grip drew me up until I rose on my tiptoes, desperate for more.

He dragged me closer and opened me for his invading tongue. No easy transition into a carnal kiss. Instead it was a tempest of flavors and heat.

I curled my arms around his neck and hung on, giving back as much as I could manage.

I was out of my league. Hell, out of the galaxy, but I was determined to show him I belonged here in his arms.

Before I could allow myself to analyze that little thought, I was swept up into Hurricane Seth. He turned me around and pinned me to the wall, my toes dangling off the floor as he ground his hard cock against my shorts.

God, yes.

My fingers dug into his shoulders and I groaned into his mouth. We were a tangle of tongues and limbs. His hand coasted down my waist to my hip before a groan buzzed through my tongue and along my mouth. Mine? His? Who knew?

Then he swept lower to hook my knee and drag my leg up around his hips. I hopped up with the other and finally his hard length was right where I needed it.

The seam of my cutoffs dug into my panties and the little bit of friction was better than anything I'd done alone. Sweet merciful heaven, there was a God.

Not that I'd tell Seth he was on par with God. He didn't need that kind of help ego-wise, but yes. So much yes.

My sandal thumped to the floor and my eyes flew wide. We both froze, praying that the noise didn't wake the little girl across the hall from us.

Right across from us.

What the hell was wrong with me? I struggled and pulled my mouth away from his. "Put me down," I whispered.

"It's fine," he said against my cheek. "She didn't wake up. She's a heavy sleeper, except for the nightmares." He grazed his mouth along my cheek to my jaw and headed for my ear.

Nightmares? I shook my head to clear it. "We can't do this."

He jerked his head back. "What? Why?"

"Because we're right down the hall from her. God, what the hell was I thinking?"

"You weren't. That was the good part."

I wiggled until I slid down the wall and my foot hit the floor.

"We can go downstairs."

"What and make out on the couch like teenagers?"

"We can go to my room if it makes you feel better."

"No, it doesn't make me feel better." I pushed him away from me and jammed my foot into my shoe. "None of this makes me feel better."

"I promise you I can." His eyes were hot and his shirt was wrinkled. Oh, and another button had come free thanks to our little mauling make out session against the frigging wall. The little bit of hair at the center of his chest arrowed down his hard abs that were now showing.

Yeah, I was so not looking. I pulled down my shirt and cursed my overstimulated body. Everything was hot and tingling and it was all so wrong.

I spun on my heel and silently sprinted down the hallway to the stairs. I heard him curse under his breath behind me, but I kept going.

Yeah, I was running. Sue me.

There was no way I could handle any of this today. Not emotionally and definitely not intellectually. I'd found out why Seth made all the girls come around.

Five more minutes and I would have come.

And that was five minutes I could never get back, nor live through over and over again.

He caught me at the door and jerked me to a stop before I could make it to the safety of the night. To the normalcy of my piece of shit car.

"Dammit, Al." He turned me around and gripped both my upper arms. "Why are you running?"

"We can't do this. Not now."

His dark eyes fired. "Why not?"

My chest was heaving. My fight or flight instincts were in full-on escape route mode. "Please, let me go."

I don't know if it was the *please* or something he saw in my eyes. Whatever it was, he dropped his hands and I stumbled back and out the door.

I didn't look back to see if he followed. I could only pray he wouldn't.

My breath returned to normal when I was inside my car. I finally dared a look and quickly returned my eyes to front and center. To the moonlit water off the bank of his property.

To the lake that had been the only home I'd ever truly known.

I had to.

I couldn't watch him stand on that huge staircase and drive away from him. So I stared out the back window until I was on the road again, and I didn't look into my rearview mirror.

Not even once.

6

SETH

Shaking off the rain on my hair, I stepped into the darkened, intimate atmosphere of the Sherman Inn. My stomach was roaring and my mind was in knots.

As for my dick, I wasn't going there.

It had taken me days of wearing her down, but Ally had finally agreed to meet me for dinner and "some time" in town on Friday night.

"Some time" probably being an hour or less, considering her skittish tone as we'd talked that afternoon. But hell, after Sunday's kiss, I considered it huge progress that she was talking to me at all. She'd run awful damn fast the other day.

I couldn't even really blame her. I'd pushed for the kiss to happen and it had still almost blown my fucking head off.

"Table for two, please," I told the maître d'. I was running late, but Ally tended to run even later so I felt safe in assuming I'd be snagging our table.

Normally, I would've placed a reservation, but this wasn't supposed to be a date. Reservations screamed dates, according to Ally, so she'd wanted us to try our luck for a table. At one of the busiest restaurants in Crescent Cove on a Friday night at the start of summer.

Right.

"This way, sir," the maître d' said, proving me wrong. Even as I followed the tall, severe-looking man in black, Ally's voice echoed in my head.

Hamilton money buys tables. You don't need a reservation. Watch.

"Did someone just leave?" I asked.

The maître d' shot me a cool smile. "On weekend nights, we're booked solid all day and night. Your table, sir." He gestured toward a secluded corner table with a lake view and candles flickering under glass domes.

"You know who I am then." Why I needed the confirmation, I didn't know. Maybe some part of me hoped Ally was wrong. She had to be wrong now and then.

It wasn't as if I didn't know my family's influence in Crescent Cove. Of course, I did. Hamilton Realty had been a fixture in the community since my grandfather was a young man. I was also a regular at the Sherman Inn. But I'd never seen this guy before in my life.

"Yes, sir." He pulled out a chair and gestured. "Your server will be here in a moment with the wine list. Your companion's name so I can direct her to your table?"

"Alison Lawrence. She should be here soon—"

"Right behind you," she said cheerfully. "Got a table, huh?" she commented as I turned and tried not to swallow my tongue.

She wasn't wearing anything special. Correction—she wasn't wearing anything I hadn't seen her in a hundred times before. She had on a pale-yellow sundress with tiny purple flowers, cowboy boots, and a tight jean jacket, with her long hair flowing in every which direction and matted a little from the misty rain. It didn't matter. She was simply stunning.

How hadn't I noticed before?

"Miss," the maître d' said, pulling out the chair opposite me while I stood and stared. Mutely.

Smooth, dude. Real smooth.

Ally shot me a sidelong glance as she skirted around me to slip into her seat. "Thank you."

"Enjoy your meal." The maître d' melted away and almost immediately, our server appeared.

I dropped into my chair and accepted the wine list, ordering a bottle of rosé for the table before my brain clicked back into gear.

Ally kicked me as soon as the server went to fulfill my request. "Hi there, remember me? I wanted a martini."

"Since when?" Oh look, my lips could come unglued long enough to stick my foot between them.

"Since I felt like a damn martini. What is wrong with you?" She leaned forward and laid a hand on my forehead. "You're flushed. Do you have a fever?"

"Some virus is running through Laurie's class, so maybe." I eased away from her hand and she picked up her napkin. Her touching me right now was not the best idea.

My cock thought it was awesome, but that part of me wasn't known for its good judgment.

"And you left her with a babysitter just to come out with me?"

"She's not sick," I snapped irritably. "And I left her with her uncle. Oliver took her to the Faraday party so he doesn't have to stay long."

Ally paused midway through spreading her napkin on her lap. "He brought your little girl to a fancy work party? Why didn't you go?"

"Because I'm having dinner with you."

"Oh, right, because this is such an important event that you can't miss it."

"I haven't seen you since the weekend. Every time I stop in the diner, you're not there."

"Darn. Must've missed you." She glanced out the window. "Damn rain. Can barely see the lake."

"Yeah, you're wet." I brushed a damp curl away from her cheek and she bristled, backing away from my touch just as I'd done.

My words hung in the air between us. Heavy, rich with meaning well beyond what I'd intended.

"In your dreams, Hamilton," she said, her taunt falling short of the target.

She didn't know my dreams. I was only beginning to fathom their scope myself.

Our server returned with our bottle of wine. After pouring it into two glasses, I ordered Ally a martini even though her stare nearly burrowed a hole into the side of my head.

If she wanted a martini, a martini she would have. With an extra olive I could steal.

"He probably thinks I'm a wino," she muttered as she opened her menu.

"Can't please you, woman."

"Sure, you can. Stop ordering for me like this is a date. We never order for each other."

"I beg to differ. Did you or did you not order the tiramisu for me the last time we went out?"

"That's because it was a sacrilege you'd never had it. And you licked the plate clean." She disappeared behind her menu and I grinned down at mine, barely resisting the urge to make a sly remark.

Thankfully, we were back on an even keel. If she stayed hidden behind that menu, I might not be starstruck by just the sight of her again.

Maybe I did have a fever.

Through our salads, braised lamb for me and chicken parm for her, and our tiramisu desserts—hey, I could admit when I'd seen the error of my ways—we kept the conversation light and easy. She had two martinis and a glass of rosé, and I had two glasses of wine. Neither of us were drunk, just relaxed. Easy with each other, as we'd always been.

After the weirdness I'd introduced into our relationship with my contract, it was nice to be chill enough to laugh and tease each other as we usually did. My getting annoyed at her mention of a cute guy seated in her section of tables at the diner was new, but I chalked that up to thinking way too much about her reproductive organs lately. Thoughts in that direction tended to spread.

Kissing her senseless the other night—and being kissed back the exact same way—also probably didn't help.

I didn't actually care if she found another man "cute." Bully for her.

Okay, so I cared. A lot. And that might've been when I'd decided to go for that second glass when I usually stopped at one when I was driving. But we wouldn't be on the road for hours yet, since we intended to walk the shops that lined Main Street and head up the pier to check out the lake. If the freaking rain ever decided to stop screwing with our plans.

We had summer splendor to appreciate, goddammit.

Also rain meant Ally was more likely to make excuses about cutting the night short. I wasn't in any hurry for that to happen.

At least until we squabbled over splitting the bill. My insistence on paying added an extra sour note to the evening, but I pretended I didn't notice her dismay and headed up the street in the light drizzle as planned.

Eventually, she caught up with me, grumbling only a little.

"Cowboy boots probably weren't the best choice of footwear, though I do like how they make your legs look."

"You can't see my legs in this dress."

"Sure, I can."

"It's dark out."

"Your point?"

She blew out a breath and turned up the walk to one of the quaint old homes in our small town that served as a shop—in this case, a year-round Christmas store. "You can't see my legs and you have no reason to check them out in any case."

"I can see your ass too." I tilted my head as she climbed the stairs to the shop. "It's kinda perfect."

"I miss the old Seth who never said shit like this."

"Blind Seth who never noticed what was right in front of him?"

"Yes, Blind Seth was awesome." She rolled her eyes at me over her shoulder and opened the door before I could, slipping inside. She didn't hold the door for me, and even that made me grin.

Damn, I liked having our rhythm back. Even if it was now heavily laced with innuendoes, we were on track once again.

Mostly.

As always, Ally touched every trinket and ornament she came across. She was so tactile. Always had been. She claimed not to have a special affinity for any holiday, but she took every opportunity to visit this shop and pick up something small for Laurie. An ornament for the tree, or a little figurine she might like. She never stopped thinking about my little girl.

"She'd love this, don't you think?" Ally angled her head to study a tiny ballerina with a glittering tutu hanging from one of the higher branches of a Christmas tree. Her cowboy boots made her taller, but she still had to stretch to reach so I helped her by tugging the loop off the branch.

"She loves pink," I agreed. "We'll get this for her, and something for your new tree with Sage."

"Oh, Christmas is so far away."

"No further for you than it is for Laurie." I moved around the tree and picked up a shimmery silver arrow ornament, cupping it in my hand when she tried to get a peek. "It's a surprise."

She tugged on the sleeve of my suit jacket, but I kept my fingers in a tight fist. Shaking her head, she laughed. "You're a silly man."

"You haven't had nearly enough silly in your life for a damn long time." Something shifted through her expression and I leaned down to speak against her ear. "Let me give you some things you aren't used to tonight. We'll start with silly."

I grabbed a string of mini flamingo lights off a small tabletop tree and draped them around her neck without revealing the ornament hidden in my hand. It was difficult since she kept trying to get a glimpse of it, but I had big hands and stealth.

And long jacket sleeves I could slip it into.

After I'd paid—and insisted she wear the still blinking lights out of the store—Ally shook her head and aimed for the next shop. This time, we walked together. Our hands brushing back and forth, fingers colliding, wrists bumping. Neither of us making the grab.

Best friends didn't hold hands. God knows we never had before. But tonight, I wanted to. I wanted her fingers to clutch mine as I pulled her in close by that strand of madly blinking lights and met her smiling mouth with my own.

I'd give my right nut to keep that grin on her face. Pay any price. Risk anything.

Even us.

In the next store, she browsed the kitchen gadgets and cookbooks and household knickknacks with her typical curiosity. Her gaze touched every item before her hands followed suit. I swallowed hard, imagining what it would be like to be the object of all that fascination.

To be her sole focus, even for an hour. For a night.

She bought a cow salt and pepper set and some hot cocoa mix and we headed to the coffee shop where we studied rows of truffles through the glass cases and debated hot apple cider or cappuccino. She went for the cider and I chose black coffee with a shot of maple.

Maple like the golden-brown eyes that smirked at me when I gave in and dumped some cream into my coffee.

Getting to black only was a process for me, one she was sure I'd never manage. She thought I enjoyed my sweets too much.

If she only had a clue.

Outside the rain had started anew, so we ducked into another shop, this one with ship memorabilia and nautical apparel. I grabbed her a tote bag and tucked her flamingo lights and her surprise present and her kitchen shop purchases inside then threw it over my shoulder, ignoring her laughter at the picture I made in my business suit.

Whatever. It was only half a business suit, since I had jeans on with the shirt, jacket and tie as always.

Perk of owning my own business. Casual Fridays were every day of the damn week.

The next time we slipped outside, the rain had lessened, so we decided to take that walk on the pier. The long length of it was draped in white lights, and the tiny flickers bounced off the rippling expanse of dark water that stretched far in the distance. At the end of the pier, she stopped and leaned over the railing, her dark hair billowing behind her in the wind. Her flirty dress clung to the backs of her thighs and her ass, and the illicit glimpse I took of both probably had something to do with why I crowded her against the rail. I didn't move back as she stiffened and regained her full height, her ringed fingers suddenly clutching the rail.

"Personal space, Hamilton," she tossed back, but she didn't look me in the eye. "Ever heard of it?"

"I've been giving you all kinds of space." Testing us both, I gripped a handful of the fabric swishing around her thighs. Step one to touching her bare skin. "Doesn't seem like it's getting me anywhere."

"Since when is it supposed to? We're friends, remember?" There was no missing the thread of desperation in her tone, even with the wind kicking up and making it harder to hear her.

I didn't need to grasp every nuance in her voice to know how she felt. Her body was telling me with every rigid, unyielding curve. She was holding herself as far away from me as she could, practically leaning over the water.

Her reaction was a clear sign to back off. To steer clear.

Not interested, pal. Hate to break it to you.

I could almost hear her lobbing the words at me even in the heavy silence of the night. But it wasn't completely quiet. There was the wind, and the lapping water, and my heartbeat thudding crazily in my head. In the distance, people were laughing, and music was playing, and life went on.

Out here, it had stopped. Suspended in a moment we'd never get back.

As if she sensed me moving too close, she whirled around, nailing me in the gut with her elbow then pressing her spine to the railing. Her gaze never lifted above my Adam's apple. "Here we go. Should've known you'd try this. Always gotta close the deal, and so much for giving me space to make up my mind. Ha. Like you or Oliver ever give anyone a chance to say no. You cajole and wheedle and insist—"

I braced my hands on the rail on either side of her hips. "I haven't said a word about it tonight. You're the one who has it in your head every time you look at me." I dropped my voice. "Speaking of, why don't you try doing that?"

"How am I supposed to not think about it? You didn't ask me to go for takeout or on vacation. Hell, you didn't even ask me to have a crazy fling, as insane as that would be."

"Alison. Look at me."

Her eyes flickered up to mine and away, holding on some far-off spot while the lights danced along the gold of her irises. She might not be able to meet my gaze for long, but I was riveted on hers. On how she couldn't seem to take a full breath that didn't shudder out between her parted lips. I didn't look lower because I couldn't. One glimpse of those perfect tits straining the cotton bodice of her dress and I'd be a goner.

When she didn't make an effort to shift her focus to my face, I gripped her chin in fingers I deliberately kept gentle. I didn't want to scare her any more than she already was.

Hell, any more than I was too at this moment. So much hung in the balance, far more than contracts and deals and egg meets sperm.

"I'm not forcing your hand," I said quietly, staring at her eyes though she wouldn't look any higher than my mouth. "I told you what I want, what is important to me and why. Now the ball's in your court."

"You can't make a move like this based on the whims of a three-year-old. It's not logical. She wants a puppy too. Is that next?"

"Maybe, but puppies are easier to get my hands on than babies. And I'd rather like to see what a combination of our DNA would look like. Gold eyes, maybe, crazy temper, a slightly hysterical laugh? Should I invest in earplugs?"

"Ugh. You're impossible." She nudged me back, and I went, but only far enough for her to move to the opposite railing. "Laurie's going to change her mind, decide she doesn't want a sibling after all, and then what? My birth canal isn't the customer service counter at Macy's. You'll be stuck with the kid."

Though my temper jumped to life, I leaned back on the railing. Perhaps if I adopted a relaxed pose, the rest of me would follow suit. "Mind keeping your voice down? There's not many people out right now, but there's enough."

"Are you kidding me? It's storming. They can't hear us." As if she'd called down the rain, lightning forked through the sky and thunder rumbled in the distance.

"Okay, keep screaming. I'm cool with it. And guess what, Lawrence, I want the child too. To complete my family. Not that my family isn't complete now, but I want another baby. Is that so crazy? If I was a woman, no one would be questioning why I'm doing this."

"Wrong. Big time wrong. They'd be thinking you couldn't get a man and wanted a love substitute."

"Well, that's not entirely wrong. I can't get a man, but I have to admit I haven't tried."

Her lips twitched. "You're such a jackass."

"Yeah, and I can see why you're wary about crossing streams with me. Hamilton men aren't easy to take on. Why we all end up divorced and bitter, or in the case of my twin, just the bitter part." I moved toward Ally, boxing her in again neatly against the rail. Some part of me enjoyed doing that far too much. "Why I'm giving you an escape hatch. Do the deed, make the baby, escape while you can."

Her lips trembled. "That's not why at all. You just want the kid, not a woman."

"Oh, I can assure you that's not true, especially right now." I tipped up her chin. "God did me a favor by blinding me to your beauty all these years. Otherwise I would've had you under me before we made it out of high school."

She rolled her eyes. "Do these lines work on other women? Because gotta say, I'm not falling for them—"

My mouth covered hers just as thunder shook the sky one more time, but the crack wasn't enough to disguise her moan. She lifted her hands up to my chest and I didn't press for more, just kept my lips against hers, sucking down her staccato breaths while I gave her the moment to accede or shove me back.

Then her fingers curled into the fabric of my dress shirt and it was on.

I buried one hand in her hair, tilting her head back so I could have her the way I needed to. The sweetness from our tiramisu and her strawberry lip gloss battled in my head, setting off a furious pounding in my groin that had nothing to do with making a baby and everything to do with getting her naked.

Now.

Whatever it took.

I lowered my hands to her hips, fisting the cotton that barely hid her curves from my view, twisting it as our tongues touched and tangled. Without warning, I lifted her up on the railing and she gasped, wobbling, her hair streaming behind her as her honey eyes went wild and frightened.

"I've got you." Tightening my hold, I moved between her legs and ran kisses over her delicate collarbone, tracing the edge of the arrow necklace. Aiming lower, burying my face in her cleavage so that her frantic heartbeat seemed to throb in tandem with my own.

Turning my head, I nipped the side of her breast through the material, just to hear her broken moan. She didn't disappoint me. One hand gripped the railing and the other came up to grasp a handful of my hair as I lowered my mouth, making a wet path to where her nipple stood so tight and proud.

I couldn't breathe. Couldn't think past wanting her. My sanity was gone, blown away with the rising wind.

Hovering there, my breaths puffing out against the swelled flesh, I searched for words. Something to make this okay. Her legs trembled on either side of my hips, and I was holding onto her with every bit of strength I possessed. Her long dark hair blew against my face, tickling my skin, and I was helpless not to suck her nipple between my teeth, to scrape the edge of them over that sensitive tip.

A quick yank on my hair drew me closer, not away. *Thank fuck.*

Only half aware of the rain now pelting my back, soaking through my jacket and shirt to the skin, I sucked on her, already thinking about how I was going to get inside her. This wasn't the end. I couldn't have her walk away from me tonight like she had on Sunday.

Not if I wanted to survive it.

She bent forward, leaning over me, her hair surrounding us as I tugged at the fabric and the lacy bra beneath. A hint of pink gleamed wetly in the darkness before she covered herself, her long fingers caging in her nipple. Keeping it from my mouth.

Acute regret cleaved through me. I set her down on her feet, already fighting to shove myself back in line. My tongue buzzed from the taste of her, from the tang of my own needs. I couldn't go home and jack myself off again with her flavor on my lips. Jesus, I'd go mad.

"Sage is home," she said, and I stared at her, not understanding. "She doesn't usually go out on Friday nights." She pinned me in place with her stare and clutched her arrow necklace. "Your house is on the other side of the lake. The Inn. If there's a room, we'll do it and be done."

Joy coursed through my body, and I nearly freaking dropped to my knees in gratitude.

Then what she'd said sank in.

"Just do it and be done," I repeated. "Just like that."

"If there isn't a room, that means this is a mistake. Hell, it probably is anyway." She started hurrying away, her heeled boots clacking on the cobblestones of the pier. "But you're the big stud, Mr. Important, so see if they give you a suite. Text me the number if you get it. I'll find you."

"What the hell are you babbling about?" I caught up to her in a couple long strides, seizing her arm and spinning her to face me. "You'll find me? Where are you going?"

"You may not care about being discreet, but I do. I'll go back to my car, give it some time. Go up once it's not obvious we've gone frigging nuts. And we'll take care of this…issue."

"This issue? The one where I want to fuck you until you're hoarse from screaming my name?"

She nodded primly. "That one."

I didn't mention the baby plan. She didn't either. Okay, so we weren't going there. At least we were going somewhere that might lead to my balls getting some goddamn relief.

But that whole getting it over with thing? Was not happening. And she would soon realize that, too late for her to do anything but lie there and take every bit of what I dished out.

I tugged out my phone and hit the speed dial for my brother. Rock-hard dick or not, my little girl was my number one priority.

"Laurie?" I asked as soon as my twin answered, turning away so I didn't have to see the melting expression that overtook Ally's face.

"She's fine. Curled up with some rum and an episode of *Empire*."

"What?"

Oliver laughed. "Make that rum raisin ice cream and an episode of some Care Bears crap on Disney. So easy to rile, brother."

"How was the party?"

"Good. She was a hit. I collected numbers like it was my damn job. Now to sort through the prospects."

Christ, only my brother would use his three-year-old niece both as a way to ditch a party and as date bait. "Can you keep her tonight? I know it wasn't part of the deal—"

"Well, now, this is interesting. What happened to Ally?"

I swallowed and tried to come up with something that wasn't a lie. And also was absolutely not the truth. "Plans changed. Can you keep Laurie or not? I'll be there early to get her."

"Of course I can. This Care Bear shit isn't half bad, if you're practically wasted." Before I could question him, Oliver sighed. "I had two fingers of Scotch. Your child is perfectly safe."

"Thanks. I'll owe you. Tell her I love her?"

Out of the corner of my eye, Ally turned away, and if I wasn't mistaken, lifted her fist to her mouth.

"Will do. Whatever happened to your plans, hope it's good. Don't forget the condom this time, little brother." Oliver clicked off before I could toss something back, probably rude as hell.

Pocketing my phone, I dipped back my head. The relentless rain streaked down my face as I hauled in a breath that didn't do a damn thing to ease the constriction in my lungs.

Time to get this night moving. First, some insurance she wouldn't run.

"Ally," I rasped, sure she could hear me, rain or no rain.

She turned, studying me warily.

"Your panties. Give them to me."

"What?" Her mouth rounded.

I moved in closer and spoke against her hair, raising my voice just above the rain. "You want to be discreet. I do too. I also want to smell your pussy before we get in that hotel room. Take them off and give them to me." I eased back enough so our eyes were level. "Nice and slow."

Even with the weight of what we were about to do between us, it was good to see I could still shock her. Enough that she seemed to move as if she was in a trance, casting a quick glance around to discover what I already had—the driving rain had sent the few tourists still wandering about scurrying into pubs and the ice cream shop, seeking shelter from the storm.

Right fucking now, the storm was inside me, throbbing in my

head, my dick, my chest. Everywhere she'd touched and the places she still hadn't.

But she would.

She shifted closer to the railing, reaching out to use it for balance. And bent to whip off her panties, barely even glancing my way as she pressed them into my hand.

Warm. Even with the cool rain sluicing down my neck and face, there was no denying the heat I held in my palm.

Blinking the water out of my eyes, I held her gaze and lowered my head, drawing in a deep breath of Ally and rain, mixed together. Her excitement and the burnt ozone in the air, colliding together and somehow mixing. Sweetness layered over fire.

Helpless to resist, I buried my face in them and she watched me, hair streaming back from her face, lashes starred, mouth trembling and used from mine. The tip of my tongue touched the delicate fabric and she shuddered visibly, hauling her thin jacket in more tightly around her body.

We were both soaked to the core, but she'd had a goddamn head start.

Stepping in close again, I flexed my groin lightly against hers. Her breath hissed out. She was well aware of how she'd affected me. "I'll text you the room number. If you don't come to me, I'll find you."

She said nothing, her soft exhalations somehow loud in spite of the storm.

A finger under her chin brought her face up to mine. "Every moment you make me wait is one more I'll spend between your legs, making you beg." Cupping her panties in my fist, I stepped back. "The choice is yours."

7

ALLY

I COLLAPSED AGAINST MY SEAT AND SLAMMED THE DOOR CLOSED. Rain thrummed against the roof of my car. Again, I was sitting behind the wheel with decisions whirling in my head.

I'd walked away from him a few nights ago.

Okay, ran. I wasn't proud of it, but my self-preservation instincts had been in full effect. And I'd been able to ignore him for the last few days. Moving out of my house and into Sage's apartment had taken up some time. Falling on my face in exhaustion had been the only way to survive after Sunday.

Now I was right here again. Choices had been made. Panties had been surrendered.

I bounced my head against my headrest. I hadn't even blinked, just forked them over.

I wasn't that girl, dammit.

Or maybe I was.

I squirmed in my seat as rain and my own slickness soaked my dress and coated my inner thighs. The rain had activated the dryer crystals I'd splurged on and my entire car smelled like wet springtime and a hint of sex.

Harbingers of the night to come?

He'd promised to make me beg. And sweet Jesus, I believed him.

The pocket of my denim jacket buzzed against the side of my breast. I hissed out a breath and fumbled it out.

Just a single number.

SEVENTEEN.

Was it wrong that Winger immediately popped into my head? And right now, I felt like an illicit seventeen-year-old girl making crazy decisions. Of course, things would have been a lot easier if I had lost my virginity at seventeen like most of the girls I'd known in high school.

But no, had to tack on another decade for me. Late bloomer times one thousand.

A second later, another text came through.

COUNTDOWN BEGINS.

Trumpets were blaring in my brain. Europe's "The Final Countdown" was on repeat. God, I needed to get a grip.

I curled my fingers around my phone and stuffed it back into my pocket. I couldn't even come up with a pithy reply. All we did was swap barbs. That was what we did. And all I could think of replying was...

Okay.

Yeah, not even close to worldly. Just dumb. So I didn't reply at all. Part of me wanted to race inside and get it over with.

I hadn't been lying when I'd said that to him.

As insane as it would be to do this with Seth, I was so damn overdue that my ovaries and hormones would officially go on strike if I said no to this opportunity. I had a feeling my sanity would be added to that list as well.

I shouldered the door open and winced at the grinding metal on metal action of the hinge. Time to oil that one up again. I needed to make this car last a little longer.

The winters were rough on cars in this area of New York. Snow and salt were as stubborn and bitchy as my boss, Mitch.

And I was officially stalling in the worst way possible.

My phone buzzed again.

You're dangerously close to being carried in here, damn the consequences.

Yeah, no. That wouldn't do. I could walk—well, drive. I could just turn over the engine and drive home. He wouldn't follow.

Maybe.

The heat in his eyes had been as thrilling as it was terrifying. There was no turning back on tonight. Honestly, there'd been no turning back for me the moment he'd let me know he was interested in seeing me naked—babymaking or not.

I dashed out into the night and headed for the front door. I couldn't get in the side entrance since I didn't have a card key. Evidently, I hadn't thought this out very well.

I kept my head down and skirted around the edges of the lobby. My hair hung in wet, ropy ringlets down my back. Not an inch of me was dry.

And I do mean not an inch.

At any second, it felt like everyone in the room would be able to tell I was sans underwear. The cute yellow dress had been a nice idea when I'd left the house, but now it was the consistency of damp tissue paper.

Good thing I'd made sure all the important parts were nice and tidy.

God, what a thought. Could people see my little landing strip through the skirt of my dress?

Would Seth when I went upstairs?

I dragged the edges of my jacket together to cover up my nipples, which were definitely on display. I'd worn a sheer bra so it wouldn't show through the summery dress. Mistakes firing every-damn-where tonight.

I glanced up to get my bearings and the woman behind the counter made eye contact with me. I couldn't remember her name, but she'd been in the diner. Everyone in the damn town had been in the diner at one time or three.

Fuck.

Quickly, I looked away and sprinted for the elevator, holding my skirt down with the other hand as I darted through the doors.

I slapped the button for the second floor, desperately happy there was no one else in the elevator. I should have taken the stairs, but the possibility that my ass could be on display if my skirt flared up had nixed that idea before I could even slot it in my brain.

The doors opened onto the ornate floor. The hotel was high-end with an ornate brocade runner over a finely stitched ruby carpet. The walls were a textured cream with paintings and sconces giving it a rich, old world feel.

Rich was the name of the game. New England money with a side of stately age.

Outside my comfort zone by miles. Hell, again this one could be measured by galaxies. All of this was Seth's life, not mine.

Even his booty call couldn't be normal.

Thankfully, the hallway was empty and quiet. I sure as hell hoped it was soundproofed to go with the fancy-ass decor. I glanced at my watch.

Evidently, I would have some begging to do.

Why did I find that so hot?

The feminist residing in my chest should have been appalled. Or maybe she'd request equal rights all around.

A little tit-for-tat on the begging. He could start.

Maybe.

Oh, who was I kidding? I would be the one standing there like a deer in headlights, praying he wouldn't figure out just how much I sucked at this.

A fumbling accidental orgasm when I was nineteen was as close to experience as I had. And when I said accidental, it was the God's honest truth.

Enough friction could eventually give anyone an orgasm, even if it was a depressing and awkward trip to the finish line. It wasn't Craig Kimmel's fault—well, not entirely. We'd just had no chemistry.

I couldn't say the same about Seth. I'd felt the pull the very first day I'd laid eyes on him while I was making a mad dash for class. Seth had been amused at my graceless entry.

He'd also been—and still was—stupidly sexy.

I wasn't sure when I'd been slotted as the best friend. Maybe it had been that first day we'd met when I'd been wearing a shapeless sweatshirt over my pajama top and he'd instinctively saved me from a tardy slip on the second day of the school year.

Or maybe it had been when I'd laughed at him for checking out the chick in front of him as if her boobs were mana from heaven.

All I knew was I'd never had a chance before now.

And it was both hilarious and terrifying. I just wasn't sure which one was going to win out.

I slowly crept down the hall as the numbers increased. Seventeen was at the end of the hall. A suite, I'd guess, with a huge bed with sumptuous sheets and class. And I was a drowned rat on her way to get laid.

A testament of my life to date.

Before I could lift my hand to knock on the door, it flew open and Seth reached out to drag me into the suite. Good guess there. Everything was as high-end as the hallway, but right now, I didn't care.

Right now, there was only him and me and a flashing need in his eyes that mirrored my own. His gaze dropped to my dress and the naked excitement went dark as his brows lowered.

I looked down at myself. In the brightly lit living space, there was no denying the see-through nature of my dress was even worse than I'd feared. My nipples pushed at the thin material of my bra and right on through to the cotton dress.

"You walked through the hotel like this?"

I lifted my chin. "Someone kept me out in the rain."

He stalked to me and dragged my denim jacket off. My skin instantly flooded with chill-bumps, making my nipples even tighter.

His hands fisted at his sides and the muscle in his jaw pulsed. Didn't he like what he saw?

I crossed my arms over my breasts, but he pulled them back to my sides. "No, don't cover yourself."

"Then why do you look like you're about to go all T-Rex at the end of *Jurassic Park*?" My question became more a squeak when he spun me around to look at the back.

"Jesus fuck." He fell to his knees and I yelped as his fingers raked up the outside of my thighs. "This perfect ass was on complete display to everyone?"

I tried to turn around, but he held me still. "Well, someone demanded my panties." The reply ended in a growl of exasperation. I didn't understand him at all.

My skirt rose as his touch grew bolder. When the cool air of the room hit my over-sensitized flesh, I had to bite back a whole different kind of growl.

His fingers went from my thighs to the heavy curve of my ass. He lifted my dress higher and I tried to move away from him.

"I know I'm not perfect."

His grip intensified as his tongue flicked over the crease where my butt met thigh. I wobbled on my feet, but he held me still. "This ass is perfection." He filled his hands and I wanted to die.

I could only imagine how much flesh overflowed even his big hands. No matter how much running around I did, I had a butt for days. Probably because of my deep and abiding love for ice cream.

Living over an ice cream parlor definitely wasn't helping my affliction.

"Open your legs, Al."

"Seth, I don't need all this. I'm totally a sure thing."

"Then open your fucking legs."

My boots thudded on the carpet as I widened my stance. I felt ridiculous. On display in a way I'd never imagined.

He bunched up my skirt and maneuvered me until I was actually sticking out my ass. Before I could slap his hands away and smack him for being so ridiculous, his warm, wet tongue slid between my thighs and along my dripping pussy.

The little squeak became a moan as I dragged in all available oxygen in the room. I had no choice but to bend my knees or I'd topple onto my face.

He didn't let up. Didn't give an inch.

Or rather he gave me a lot more than I thought was possible with just his tongue and lips. He curled inside of me and carved out every space, every drop of wetness and I lost my balance as the room fuzzed.

I grabbed for something and found his wrist. He held my ass apart to get deeper. Leaving no part of me untouched. I didn't have time to be embarrassed.

There was nothing but his tongue and his hands, holding me open.

I gripped his wrist and his hand turned to lock onto my arm, then he did the same with the other until I was tethered to him. I should have had control at that point, but there was no controlling this man. There was only surviving.

And I wasn't entirely sure that was possible. His devil of a tongue slid between my folds and up to my clit then back until I was a mess.

God, I didn't have any resistance to this insidious level of seduction. He played my body like he played his piano late at night when he'd had too many glasses of whiskey.

He let one of my hands go and slowly slipped a finger inside of me.

I purred out his name and my body went tighter and tighter in reaction to his invasion. I was helpless against his mouth and the pressure of the pads of his fingers at my clit.

The first orgasm sucker-punched me. Somehow, I didn't even realize I'd coasted up and through the teasing and into the victory circle. My thighs shook and my scream ended in his name.

"Fuck, you're so damn tight." He pushed a second finger inside me and I arched to get away from him. My body was too sensitive as I soared and crashed in the space of thirty seconds.

"That's it, baby. Give me everything."

I tried to curl into myself, but he wouldn't let me go. My knees trembled and the heel of my boot tapped out the little aftershocks as my body tried to process this level of stimuli.

He stood up and buried his face in my neck as he turned his hand and fucked me with his fingers. I cried out as the pleasure twisted into pain. "Seth, wait."

He paused. "I'm sorry. Was I too rough? You soaked my face, so I thought you were with me." He made sweet hushing sounds against my ear. "I'm sorry. I got too into it."

I breathed through the invasion of just two of his thick fingers. How the hell was I going to take his cock?

God, I was so over my head.

"Don't tense up." He wrapped his other arm around my waist and fit his cock against my ass. "You're perfect. We're so good together, can't you feel it?"

I nodded, but I couldn't think around the invasion of his fingers.

He pulled out of me and went to my clit. "Sweet little circles until you're ready for me. I want inside you so bad I can't think straight, but I can wait. I've waited this long, right?" He laughed against my neck and I wanted to weep in reaction.

My stupid virginity was going to ruin everything.

"Where did you go?"

"Never mind."

His eyebrows snapped down and he pulled his fingers from between my thighs before turning me toward him. "No, not never mind. No matter how much I want you, if it's too soon, I'll survive. I promise."

I shook my head and wrapped my arms around his neck. "No. I want this more than you could ever know."

His fingers dug into my hips. "Thank God."

I stared at his chin and traced the bristles of his scruffy face. My fingertips went farther down to his neck, where his Adam's apple jumped under my touch.

The vibration of his growl made my skin prickle. Somehow, I'd thought I could just walk in and make this work. It wasn't as if I was a complete novice about sex. I hadn't actually had it, but I was a woman with needs. Some nights the only way I'd gotten to sleep with the stress and frustration of my life was to take care of myself.

But I'd been deluding myself that it compared to reality in any way.

He lowered his face until our gazes collided. "What?"

"I…"

"You…what?" He laughed. "You can tell me anything. You know that." His dark brows pinched together. "Has someone hurt you?"

"No! Oh, God, no." I blew out a breath. I was doing this all wrong. I slid out of his arms and paced the wide living space. "It's not that. In fact, quite the opposite."

He tunneled his fingers through his hair and gripped the back of his neck. His anger and heat had ignited a dangerous prickle of excitement in my bloodstream. That he'd been so upset on my behalf was only one of the reasons I was so head over heels about this idiot. "What does that mean?"

As a hint of something I couldn't read filled his eyes, suddenly it was Seth who was pacing the length of the room.

He tugged the tails of his shirt out of his jeans. "You aren't telling me what I think you're telling me."

I pushed a wild curl out of my face. My hair was finally drying and my curls were a little intense, thanks to the rain. "I mean, I know it's crazy, but look at it from my point of view. I'm always working, or I was always taking care of my mom. I didn't really have much time to date."

I couldn't spit out the word. I knew he needed it, but I just couldn't get it off my tongue. I blocked him from making another path across the Aubusson carpet.

"Seth."

"No. Don't you 'Seth' me." He grabbed me by the upper arms and lifted me onto my toes. "You spit it out right now."

"I've sort of never done this with a person before."

He dropped me back onto my feet and staggered back as he jammed his fingers into his hair again. He pulled until his thick near-black hair was as wild as mine. "No one has ever been inside you?"

I winced. It was kind of crazy when he put it like that. And I felt even more stupid. I folded my arms over my chest. "It's not a big deal."

He crossed to me and lifted me up, then crushed his mouth to mine.

Well, okay then. Guess that talk was over.

He curled my legs around his hips and walked me through the suite and kicked open the door to the bedroom. He set me on my feet at the end of the bed and lifted my dress over my head before I could say another word.

I crossed my arms over my chest again instinctively. My boobs were too big and my ass too shapely. I'd gotten my hourglass figure from someone in my family. My mother had been slight for as long as I could remember, but there were pictures.

Ones with her smiling on the shore of Crescent Cove in a bikini. We could have been twins once upon a time.

He pulled my arms away. "No one has ever touched you here?" He skimmed the back of his hand along the swells of my breasts. The bra was too flimsy to really hold me in, but it went with the dress. And like the dress, the sheer factor was very in his face at the moment. He circled his fingertip around my nipple. "No one has sucked on these?"

I swallowed as I swayed on my feet. "I'm not a complete nun."

He peeled back the nude colored nylon and hissed. "Did he know to touch you like this?" He tugged my nipple with his first two fingers until the skin stretched a twinge past pleasure into pain before he let it go.

My nipple tightened even more and the quick rush of blood under the dark rose flesh made me gasp. "No."

He reached around me and unsnapped the bra and eased it over my shoulders, then set it with my dress on the chair in the corner. He lifted each of my breasts until they filled his hands, and my nipples were trapped by his thumb and forefinger.

"No one has ever taken the time to find out just what you need?"

I tipped my head back and fought against the quick rush of tears that had come out of nowhere. "No," I said brokenly.

"I will. I'll make sure I know every inch of your precious body."

He released one of my breasts and his hand slid lower. He coasted over my waist to the soft skin just above my slit. "And no one has been here?"

I shook my head. "Just me."

His nostrils flared. "At night? In the dark?"

I swallowed. "Not often, but sometimes when the loneliness was too much."

"Show me."

I shook my head.

"Show me," he said more forcefully. "I want to make sure I'm doing it right."

"You are." My lower lip trembled. "Everything has been right."

"I was too rough."

"No. I just wasn't ready."

He led my hand to my pussy and made small circles. My cheeks burned at just how wet I was. No, definitely not like when I touched myself. I was fuller and more swollen. My body had reacted to the differences and made room for my fingers and his as I gasped.

"Like that?" His voice was like gravel and his eyes were a touch wild, along with being kind.

I didn't really want kind. I wanted the Seth who couldn't wait to get his hands on me. I wanted the man who was so hot for me he couldn't wait to touch me.

Hesitance was the last thing I wanted.

I slid my fingers out from under his and held him to my entrance. "You know what I need. I need you to trust that. *I* trust you with this." I lifted trembling fingers to the buttons of his shirt. "I trust you with me."

Swallowing hard, I pushed his shirt open and over his shoulders. We struggled with his cuffs and finally he was as bare as me from the waist up. I took a tentative step closer to him and had to take a slow breath when my breasts touched his chest. The soft hairs along his abs felt different than the more wiry ones between his pecs. Both of them were rather glorious.

I chased the wonder and hoped it would lead me away from the nerves multiplying in my belly and brain. I wanted this with everything inside of me. Even knowing things would change between on us on a fundamental level, I couldn't turn away from him any longer.

He kicked off his shoes and I did the same with my boots. His pants hit the floor next and we stood in front of each other nearly naked.

Me, completely, but I was sort of glad he'd left on his black boxer briefs. I wasn't sure I was ready to see just what my choices had led me to.

Especially with the bulge tenting under the snug cotton.

I lifted a shaking hand to his shoulder and he swept me up into his arms and deposited me on the mattress. "We're going to take this as slow as you need to, all right?"

"What if I want fast?" I scuttled toward the head of the bed.

He grabbed my ankle and widened my legs before fitting his shoulders between my thighs. "Oh, there's no way we're going fast." He grinned up at me and I was relieved to see the thrill in his eyes again.

Challenge accepted.

I could see the change building inside of him. I was pretty sure I was in a lot of damn trouble.

When he lowered his head, and slipped two fingers along my slit, I fell back against the pillows with a groan.

He looked up from between my thighs. "Let's just make sure you're ready for me. Now that I know I need to be a little more careful."

"Not too careful."

"It's not supposed to hurt."

"How many virgins have you deflowered, buddy?"

He twirled his tongue around my clit. "Just one."

When I tensed, he grinned. "This one."

"Oh."

"So it's technically a first time for both of us." He rolled his hips into the mattress and I was suddenly very jealous of the high thread count sheets and his cotton underwear.

I wanted him to roll those hips against me, dammit.

"I'm a big guy. I'm used to having to get a woman ready for me."

"Oh, that's very kind of you."

He grinned then dragged the flat of his tongue over my center. "Jealous?"

"How would you like it if I was talking about another cock inside me right now?"

His nostrils flared again. "I'll be the only one inside this pussy from now on."

"You don't own me or my pussy."

He dragged in a breath and slipped those two fingers in farther. I arched under him and groaned when he stretched me further. He went at my clit like a man possessed. I slapped the mattress and bowed up and pushed pillows out of the way as he drove me up and through another orgasm.

Not sweetly.

No, I'd asked for the sweet Seth to step aside and it seemed like that was exactly what I was getting.

Part of me wanted to tweak the demon out again, but I couldn't quite breathe yet. The lights of the bedroom were sparking and my thighs wouldn't stop quivering.

"Mine," he muttered and went in for another round.

I was weak and my elbow collapsed beneath me as I giggled my way through the band of hysteria around my chest. How many orgasms were too many?

He blew over my clit and I shuddered and tried to roll away from him. "Seth, please."

"I like when you say that word."

"Don't get used to it."

He inched up my body finally and settled his hips between my thighs. He pressed his cock against my pussy and I cried out. Christ, I might just come from that little touch.

Every nerve ending was firing and my synapses had crossed and recrossed until I was so wrung out, I was ready to flip him over and take care of things myself.

Too bad he was so goddamn tall. And the endless flexing muscles of his shoulders and thighs were deceptively heavy.

A perfect kind of heavy.

One I could become addicted to.

No. Don't go there, girl.

I sifted my fingers through his sweaty hair and gave him a long lazy kiss. He groaned against my lips and his hips shifted. God, yes. Finally.

"I need you inside me."

"I don't want to hurt you."

"It's not like you have a damn python in your pants." I stroked my fingers down the intricate tattoo along his left arm. I rarely got to see it since he was almost always dressed for business, but the white snow leopard was stunning. Using his skin tone and a deft hand, the artist had created a stunning animal that climbed up his arm and over part of his shoulder. I leaned over and licked the muscles that twitched and flowed under the art.

The cat's blue eyes were sharp and assessing, and the claws and jaw were in mid-attack. Just like him. Sleek and panther-like, with a bite that could surprise you when you weren't paying attention.

He finally lowered his boxer briefs and butted the head of his cock along my pussy. He leaned down and tugged at my lower lip. "Someday I want to watch these full lips widen around me. Take me deep."

I swallowed a shuddering breath. I wanted that too. I wanted everything.

He reached for the bedside table and a black wrapper sitting on the corner.

My eyebrows shot up. Everyone, even a virgin, knew what a black labeled condom meant. He slid the length of his cock along the outside of my lips until the flared head rested right above my slit.

Good grief, he wasn't being boastful with the Magnum condom.

I was a dead woman.

He leaned back until he was kneeling between my legs and I was suddenly worried that maybe I really wasn't ready for this. As he rolled the condom over his length, the almost angry hue of his cock made me wonder just how on edge he really was.

I looked a little closer at his face. Because, seriously, I needed to not look at that monster between his damn legs. Sweet merciful heaven. There was a tension around his eyes and his lips were pinched. He'd been giving me the royal treatment to make sure this night was amazing for me.

Now I'd have to figure out how to give some of that back.

I reached up to cover his hand at the base of his cock and pulled him back down over me. The tension I'd been trying to avoid suddenly didn't seem to so overwhelming. I guided him between my legs and he slowly slid inside. My body was never going to be ready for him, not to this level.

Not until he stretched me and made me his.

He paused and blew out a slow breath. I reached around him and gripped his ass to pull him deeper.

"Ally—" But he groaned and his head tipped back. His neck rippled with each swallow and the tendons raised in reaction.

I let out my own slow breath as I took him deeper, stretching, opening. But then he was just mine.

Just everything.

I wrapped myself around him and my hips lifted to meet him as he slowly withdrew and pushed forward. "God," he muttered against my neck.

I tightened my grip around his shoulders and my legs around his hips until we were moving as one. I wanted more. I wanted it harder. Some part of me was craving the stretch, but he kept each stroke measured.

He reached between us and suddenly, with a few flicks of his talented fingers, he tripped me back into the whirling pleasure. He'd truly primed me for this moment. He pumped inside of me a few more times, his rough movements just what I needed, and I cried out.

I wasn't ready to be done. But the orgasm slammed into me just the same, and the chain reaction seemed to pull him under too.

My name was a prayer on his tongue as he kissed me through the end of his release. I encircled his shoulders and held on as he shook over me, and there was an overwhelming sense of peace that flowed through his muscles.

He rolled off me and disposed of the condom with tissues from the bedside table. His eyes were so heavy, I wasn't sure he was actually still awake.

When he rolled me under him and threw a thigh over me, I knew he was half asleep. The actual confirmation came a moment later when he softly snored in my ear.

"Seriously?"

I tried to move him, but I was utterly pinned.

Afterglow, my ass. He had literally tapped out.

8

SETH

Holy fuck, I was dead.

No, wait, I was still alive. That was oxygen puffing out of my lips against the pillow under my cheek. There were definite scratches on my back from—

I jerked up in bed, gripping my head so it didn't revolve off my neck. I wasn't in my bedroom at home. Swanky suite. Friday night in the summer, all booked up, but I got a room for sex because I was old town money. So that meant I got to fuck a beautiful girl on the fly, since no one wanted to deny my dick a thing.

Sweet, really.

Christ, was I hungover? No. Fucked over. Completely. I'd had the best sex of my life, and now I was in an empty bed.

Eyes still half closed, I swung out and patted the sheets. Ice cold. She'd been gone for a while. Probably the moment I passed out.

And passed out about summed it up. I'd drained what was left of my smarts and my sense into that condom and gone to sleep quicker than a drunk at the tail end of a bender.

Wasn't completely my fault. I hadn't had a childless night for a while, and my little girl tended to have a few crappy dreams. Monsters with snapping teeth. Wild dogs. Demons in closets I had to dispel with wise words and hugs in the dark.

I wasn't even going to touch on exactly how long it had been since I'd had sex. Well, sex with someone other than myself. Self-created booty calls happened often, but with an actual flesh-and-blood woman? It had been a while. Hell, Ally was *the* woman, even if I hadn't fully realized it before I'd presented her with that contract. I'd been rocking a boner ever since.

So yeah, I'd been kind of pent-up. Exhaustion had claimed me swiftly, and it had been much preferable to fighting to stay awake to talk about…

Way too much.

No wonder she'd sneaked out on me. Supposed best friend, and I'd dirty-talked her and taken her virginity—which was *not* my fault, since she'd never seen fit to tell me that little fact until we were getting naked—then fallen asleep as if it was any old night.

Jesus, and I thought my brother was a douche? He had some stiff competition for the title.

Forcing my heavy eyelids open against the sun trying to carve my brain in two, I glanced around and wished for alcohol. Maybe there was something worthwhile in the mini bar.

Those days are over, pal. They ended right about when the condom slipped when you were banging Marjorie in the Mustang. Now you're a responsible father, remember?

I braced my head in my hands and sucked in a breath. Responsible, right. I had to pick up Laurie. It had to be mid-morning from the amount of sunlight, and I'd told Oliver I'd be there early.

Rubbing my eyes, I kicked off the sheets. And noticed a bright red splotch on the fitted sheet.

Christ. I'd tried to be careful, to take it slow, but I hadn't at first. I'd rammed my fingers into her like a damn bull, and she'd never—

Before I could argue with myself, I fumbled for my phone on the nightstand. I had to know she was okay. She could hate me, probably did, but I couldn't move from this room until I knew she was all right. She'd certainly come last night, and I was pretty sure she'd been right there with me for most of it, but she wasn't here now. She was alone, and I couldn't fucking bear it.

I typed out a quick text.

MISSED YOU THIS MORNING.

Oh yeah, that was how to demonstrate my concern. By couching it in a healthy streak of douche swagger.

She answered swiftly.

HAD AN EARLY SHIFT AT THE DINER. EGGS BENEDICT & BURNT COFFEE WAIT FOR NO MAN.

YOU DIDN'T EVEN LEAVE A NOTE.

Good lord, I might as well have taken out my tampon with that statement. She was probably laughing at my pathetic ass.

From her next reply, it was close.

WAS I SUPPOSED TO? DIDN'T REALIZE WE'D PROGRESSED BEYOND BOOTY CALL STATUS TO SOMETHING ELSE.

I gripped the back of my neck. Yeah, so she was annoyed. Whether it was because I'd fallen asleep right after or because we'd had sex in the first place was anyone's guess. Only way to find out for sure was to piss her off enough to be honest.

I KNOW YOU'RE CLEARLY UNFAMILIAR WITH BOOTY CALL PROTOCOL, BUT YEAH, IT'S GOOD TO LET THE DUDE KNOW YOU'RE LEAVING IN CASE HE WAKES UP WITH A HARD DICK AND WANTS ROUND TWO.

Her response was instantaneous.

SORRY, CHARLIE, THAT WAS A ONE-TIME EVENT. BUT GOOD LUCK FINDING A MORE SUITABLE PARTNER. I HEAR TINDER IS NICE.

Tinder, huh? You tried that? Is that why you couldn't find anyone to finish the job?

Thank God you came along. Willing prick and all. You're such a good Samaritan. When I can walk straight again, I'll send you a thank-you note.

Pride surged first. I was a man, after all, and fucking a hot chick until she couldn't move was pretty much every dude's dream. But she wasn't some random hot chick. This was Ally, and she wasn't just a conquest.

She'd been a virgin, for fuck's sake, and if she was hurting from my lack of finesse, I'd saw off my own dick. Okay, maybe take a swing or two at it at least.

Ah, to hell with it. I was asking, straight out.

Are you all right? Physically? I was rough.

Fine. Dandy. All good under the hood.

I didn't mean to fall asleep. Laurie wakes me up every night & super-charged O put me down for the count.

She took longer to reply.

Just as well. Talking makes stuff messy. We did it, it's done.

While I was pounding a dent in the mattress beside my hip, she texted again.

How's L?

Don't know. Haven't gone to get her yet. Just woke up. I should've checked with Oliver first, but I was worried.

Don't be. I'm perfect. Thanks for not making this weird, okay? Gotta go. Work calls. Give L a kiss for me.

Al, come over for dinner or something?

I waited a few minutes for her to answer. When it became clear she wouldn't, at least anytime soon, I headed into the bathroom and took care of business. The shower beckoned, but I wasn't in that much of a hurry to wash her off me. Especially since I was fairly certain this would never be happening again.

Forget making a baby. Our friendship was probably in shreds.

Never learn, do you? Last time you thought with your dick, you ended up married to a woman you hadn't even intended to keep dating.

Of course, that was entirely different, and out of that relationship had sprung the best thing to ever happen to me. Sure, I'd been divorced by the age of twenty-five, but eh, shit happened. Especially in my family. The key was getting out of a bad situation.

With Ally, I'd been thinking practically. The kid thing had been building for a while. Approaching her about it had only come about after I'd mulled it over from every direction. Sure, they were sticky parts. I'll admit I hadn't expected the sex thing to go down so well. I mean, she was beautiful, no denying that, but I didn't want to fuck every lovely woman I saw. And it was *Ally.*

So yeah, the lust had been a surprise. Even more so? The morning after, I wasn't regretting we'd done it so much as I was regretting we hadn't done it again before she split. And there had been no babymaking involved.

Just Ally and her soft, lilac-scented hair and rain-soaked skin. Her full lips and her curves and those perfect thighs, spreading for me...

Swallowing hard, I braced a fist on the sink. Maybe I'd better take an ice-cold shower so I didn't go to my brother's with a damn hard-on.

A quick glance at my phone made me curse. Almost noon. Laurie was probably wondering where I was. Oliver too. My brother didn't like his schedule being disrupted, so his lack of a phone call was surprising.

I texted him as I grabbed my jeans off the floor.

ON MY WAY. **S**ORRY. **S**HE OK?

WHO'S THIS? **N**OT MY DERELICT BROTHER WHO WAS PROBABLY GETTING LAID THIS ENTIRE TIME WHILE **I** DOTED ON HIS OFFSPRING.

In spite of my bleak mood, I grinned. Leave it to O.

I WISH ON THE GETTING LAID. **M**ORE LIKE SLEEPING IT OFF.

IT BEING PREVIOUS LAYING?

GENTLEMEN DON'T KISS **&** TELL.

WAITING…

ASSHOLE. **I'**LL BE THERE IN A FEW.

I finished dressing and went downstairs to check out. The woman behind the desk didn't wink or waggle her brows or do anything to indicate she knew I'd gotten a room for the purposes of sex, but it was pretty obvious. I lived on the other side of the lake. Sure, my excuse of having a few too many to drive home might hold water, but small towns and suspicious minds went together.

As long as no one had seen Ally enter the hotel too, all good. I didn't care what people thought of me.

"Thank you so much, Mr. Hamilton. Please come again. And give our best to Ms. Lawrence."

I stared at the concierge for so long that my vision blurred. Then I shook my head and strode toward the door.

Maybe she knew Ally and I were friends. Sure, she did. And maybe we'd be the hottest topic of gossip by lunch. Probably before then. I just hoped Ally didn't have to deal with shit at the diner.

The drive to Oliver's place didn't take long. He lived about a mile away from me, also on the lake. The Hamilton family home was about a mile away on the opposite side of Oliver's. We were like three points of a triangle of dysfunction with beautiful views of the water.

I pulled up behind Oliver's BMW and parked in the circular drive. To torment myself some more, I checked my silent phone. No response from Ally.

Surprise, surprise.

I jogged up the steep flight of stairs to the porch and went inside without knocking. I followed my little girl's laughter into the kitchen, already smiling. No matter what kind of shit brewed in my gut, hearing Laurie was the way to put me in a better mood.

Especially when she was covered in chocolate chip batter from making cookies with my not so stern, older-by-six-minutes brother.

"Well, look who it is, L-monster." Oliver swung Laurie up onto his hip and carted her over to me. He was all smiles, but his eyes were a little wild.

I knew that look well.

"Daddy!" Laurie said, already extending her arms to me and leaning half out of my brother's hold.

"Hiya, sweetie. Sorry I wasn't here sooner." I grinned and took her from Oliver, setting her on my hip as he had done.

Every now and then it occurred to me how similar our mannerisms were. Oliver didn't have any children, of course. I wasn't sure he ever would. He'd used my experience as reason to double and triple bag ever since. For all I knew, he could've gotten snipped, he'd been that freaked out about unplanned procreation.

But he was a damn good uncle, as evidenced by my little girl's giggles as she recounted her night with my brother.

"We watched movies. Poor Dory. And Hank. Unca O loved Hank." Laurie looked back at my brother for confirmation. "Didn't you?"

"I did. So much so that I decided I need Hank bedding for my Alaska King bed. I may have to get it handmade, but such sacrifices are made for love." Oliver ruffled Laurie's messy blond curls. "Right, baby girl?"

"Unca O has the biggest bed ever." Laurie held out her hands as far apart as she could, tilting precariously on my hip until I righted her.

"He said it has enough room for all his favorite big ladies to come over for sleepers."

"Sleepovers," Oliver corrected, winking at me before he turned away to clean up the cookie mess on the counter.

I narrowed my eyes at O's back. "That sounds fun. We should do that sometime. What do you think? You, me, and—"

"Ally! She'll come over for a sleeper. And her friend. The one with the bouncy hair." Laurie grinned. "Like Goldilocks."

"Your hair isn't too far from Goldilocks's hair yourself, princess." Oliver turned back to brush a kiss over Laurie's hair while mouthing the word "no" at me.

"That sounds fun. I'm not sure Ally and Sage could make it, but we should ask them. And we'll get lots of snacks. All your favorites. Cheetos, and caramel popcorn, and gummy worms. Wouldn't that be fun to eat all of that in Uncle Oliver's big special bed?"

"This is how you repay me," Oliver muttered, shaking his head as he swept the tray of cookies into the oven.

"Yes. So much fun. And we could get a puppy too." Laurie's big blue eyes glowed. "Puppies love sleepers. Right, Unca O?"

"Sure. Why the heck not? Might as well get a marching band in there too."

"I'm sure it could be arranged. I'll get back to you."

Oliver flipped me the bird behind Laurie's back and I swallowed a laugh.

Half an hour later, we were eating warm chocolate chip cookies while Laurie played on a blanket in the living room. Dory was on TV again and Laurie was babbling happily as she dressed the dolls Oliver had bought her to leave at his place.

And I was shoving cookies in my mouth faster than I could speak, so hopefully I wouldn't have to.

"Out with it. If I'm on overnight babysitting duty, you're at least going to tell me which townie is now off-limits."

I picked up a stray chocolate chip and popped it between my lips. "You have a filthy mind."

"Yeah, and you are long overdue for a reckless night. I hope it was worth me missing three hours of sleep because L kept waking up."

"Fuck, more nightmares? That's a new thing. Well, relatively new. The last six months or so. I chalked it up to her seeing a movie she shouldn't have."

"Yeah, some of those porn chicks have traumatized me too." Oliver gave a mock shudder, but I could tell from his furrowed brow that he was worried.

"How bad was it?"

"Not awful, but she was spooked, so I read to her and she eventually fell back asleep."

"Just once?"

Oliver shifted on his stool. "Three times."

"Ahh, fuck." I raked a hand through my hair, guilt swarming my belly like drunk locusts. While my little girl had been crying in her sleep, I'd been fucking Ally.

Father of the year material for sure. Jesus.

"I'm sure it's just a phase. Kids go through tons of them. Remember that year you wouldn't eat anything but bologna and cheese sandwiches?"

"It wasn't a year, more like three months, and this is a bit worse. I wonder if—"

Oliver held up a hand. "Don't even say it. If you mention that bitch, my good humor will be ruined."

I leaned forward. "Regardless, she's her mother. And maybe there's just no getting around that fact."

Hearing myself, I frowned. What business did I have trying to set up this arrangement with Ally? My needs—and even Laurie's—weren't all that mattered. I'd told myself I could be both parents to my children, but maybe that was crazy talk. I couldn't magically become the children's mother. And when it came to the baby I had with Ally, he or she would have a mother. The *best* mother. Even without seeing Ally have kids of her own yet, I knew that just from watching her with Laurie. So how could I ever consider Ally might want to have a baby and walk away?

Christ, I was a selfish fuck. No wonder Ally didn't want to talk to me. I'd thought up the most insane plan ever and I'd asked her to make the ultimate sacrifice for a few pennies. All right, a lot of them, but still. Exchanging a child for a college education was nuts.

Ally wasn't Marj, and asking her to make a deal like that proved that I didn't deserve a best friend like her.

I just fucking hoped she'd give me another chance.

"Seth?"

Shaking my head, I held up a finger at my brother and yanked out my phone. I texted Ally as fast as my fingers would work.

I'M SO FUCKING SORRY. MORE SORRY THAN YOU'LL EVER KNOW.

She didn't respond, and by now, I almost didn't expect her to. I couldn't have screwed up this situation any more if I'd tried.

I jerked to my feet and almost without thinking, tucked two cookies in my suit coat. Chocolate chip was Ally's favorite.

Oliver rose, clearly reading my intentions to split. "You're leaving? Just like that?"

"Yeah, I have shit to fix. I'm sorry, man. I really appreciate last night." I clapped him on the shoulder and went to talk to my daughter.

She wasn't in a hurry to go, of course, but I mentioned a possible hot fudge sundae at the diner in her future if she came without a fuss. More sugary snacks weren't the best idea, and I'd probably pay the price for the rest of the weekend, but desperate times.

Oliver shook his head before I carted Laurie and her bag of toys and clothes out the door. "Whatever you're up to, I hope it ends well."

"Me too. I'll call."

I was already halfway down the steps with Laurie, who was waving frantically at my brother. "Bye Unca O! Bye bye!"

"Bye sweetness. Be good for your daddy."

She wriggled in my arms, smelling of powder and chocolate. "We go see Ally?"

"Yep, we're going to see Ally. But Daddy needs to talk to her alone for a few minutes, so Aunty Sage will keep you company." If Sage was even working. And if Sage didn't hate me too for being a jackass and debauching her roommate, assuming Ally had told her what had happened. Part A and Part B.

Shit, I'd asked a virgin to have my baby. Not knowing she was a virgin didn't make it any better. Somehow, I should have known. Ally was a lockbox under the best of circumstances, but something like that…

Not to mention that I'd agonized more than once about her choice of dates over the years, imagining her going home with some of them and needing to drink to get the pictures out of my mind. I'd been certain it was just my streak of protectiveness in her direction kicking in, but what if?

What the fuck if?

I placed Laurie in her car seat and adjusted the belt, snapping it into place. "Extra sprinkles on your sundae if you're good for Aunty Sage."

"Sage has pretty hair. Yellow like mine." Laurie touched her curls.

"Yes, just like yours, though yours is the prettiest in all the land." I leaned forward to kiss the tip of her nose and she giggled.

A minute later, we were on the road to the diner. I debated giving Ally a head's up that I was stopping by, then decided a sneak attack was best. I wasn't trying to corner her or convince her of anything. All I wanted to do was look her in the eye and make sure she was okay. And to apologize. Possibly fifty times or so.

I parked up the street from the diner and released Laurie from her car seat prison. Setting her on my hip, I checked my jacket pocket to make sure the cookies were still intact. Laurie wasn't about to miss a chance for more sweets, however. She got one forbidden glimpse of them and screwed up her adorable face, her big blue eyes going shiny with unshed tears.

"For me?" she wailed. "For me?"

God save me from women. I truly wasn't equipped to deal with them. Every time I thought I could handle the task, new obstacles were thrown in my path.

I dug out one of the cookies and resigned myself to a sleepless night with my child. Just as well. God knows I had no other reasons not to sleep at night. Last night's event had been a one-off, certain to never be repeated again.

Virginity destroyer.

The little bell over the diner door dinged as I entered with a now contentedly munching Laurie. She was spewing crumbs all over my wrinkled dress shirt, but my attention snagged on all the faces that turned my way. It seemed like every patron in the place was staring at me and Laurie.

All but one person with a high, bouncy dark ponytail, and that was because she had her back to me. Luckily, she was talking loudly enough that I could hear her just fine.

"Oh, not you too, Sally Mae. As I was just telling Vern, I was just helping him with a problem. You know, as a friend."

Sally Mae was looking past Ally at me. She cleared her throat. "Uh, dear, I'm not sure—"

"Certain issues of a performance nature," Ally went on. "Any good friend would help. Now would you like eggs over easy like usual with red potatoes and a side of sausage? We have the summer fruit cup on special today. Comes free with any meal."

"Alison," I said in an undertone.

Ally's shoulders went tight in her uniform, but she didn't glance my way. Didn't acknowledge me at all.

"The fruit cup has blueberries, honeydew, pineapple, and slices of fresh strawberries. The first crop this year from Happy Acres Orchard, right down in Turnbull."

"Alison," I said again.

Laurie finished scarfing down her cookie and pulled her chocolatey fingers out of her mouth. "Ally!"

Yeah, my best friend might be able to ignore me, but she definitely couldn't ignore my little spitfire.

Ally turned, a genuine smile creasing her face and lighting up her honey eyes. "Hiya you. What're you doing here?" She moved forward and snatched Laurie out of my arms without acknowledging my presence. "Look at these cheeks, all covered in chocolate. What has your daddy been feeding you?"

"Cookies. Unca O and me made 'em. Daddy brought you one."

"Daddy actually brought you two, but a certain thief felt the need to sample more of the merchandise." I cupped my daughter's head, leaving my hand there until Ally had no choice but to meet my gaze.

"I texted you."

"Sorry, working."

"And gossiping. About problems of a performance nature." The diner was far too quiet around us, and I wasn't about to give the town anything more to chat about today. "Is Sage working?"

"Sure am." The cheerful blond crossed the restaurant with a tray full of dishes. "How can I help you?" Sage asked as she passed us, stopping to say something to Mrs. Negley in one of the booths.

They both giggled and glanced my way.

Fabulous.

"By the way," I said, raising my voice, focusing on Ally's face as it paled, "we both know my performance was just fine. Spectacular, in fact."

"Enough to knock you right out?" Sage asked, blinking innocently when I narrowed my eyes.

"Back room," Ally muttered, handing off Laurie to Sage without even waiting for my direction. Even with all this shit between us, we had a rhythm.

A damn fine one, in and out of bed. Fuck performance issues. Mine had been spot-on.

Sage hugged Laurie and carried her to an empty booth. "How about a nice cup of fruit while your daddy and Ally talk?"

"Ice scream. Daddy promised ice scream." Laurie glanced my way and banged a tiny fist on the table. "With sprinkles if I was good."

"Were you good?"

"Yeah, put a hot fudge sundae with sprinkles on my tab. A small one," I said out of the side of my mouth.

Sage nodded. "Will do."

Ally was already headed down the hall that led to the bathrooms, the break room, and the storage room, so I followed, figuring she'd aim for the break room. Instead she went right for the storage area.

The second I shut the door, she whirled on me.

"What was I supposed to say? Everyone knows, Seth. *Everyone.* Someone must've seen us at the hotel, or hell if I know."

I started to reply, but Ally wasn't finished.

"They asked me questions all shift. I had to make a joke out of it, so people didn't think you and I could—that we could ever be—"

"Had to make a joke out of me, you mean." I tucked my thumbs in the pockets of my jeans. "Think you got your wish. Probably half the town is now wondering how I even managed to make my daughter."

She bowed her head and her jaunty ponytail drooped over one shoulder. "I'm sorry. It was just a joke to save face and I guess I went too far."

"Save face why? Even if someone got the idea that we were together, why not just roll with it?"

"*Roll with it?* Are you crazy?"

"I must be, considering the last week." I stepped forward and forced the irritation from what she'd told people out of my head. When compared with my recent sins, it didn't really rank. "I texted you that I was sorry."

She tucked a stray curl behind her ear. "For what, exactly?"

"I never should have asked you to have my baby."

Ally's gaze shot to the door as if she expected it to blow open at any moment. "About time you realize that."

"It was completely unfair of me. I'm not enough to be both mom and dad to a new child. I mean, with Laurie, it just worked out that way, but to set up a situation where I'm the only one making all the decisions for another child isn't right. I'm simply not enough."

"What the hell are you talking about?" Ally stepped forward, going toe to toe with me. "Laurie is a happy, well-adjusted little girl. She adores you."

"I'm not her mother. I can never be her mother." I swallowed hard. "No matter how much I love her, it's not the same as—"

"You think a child knows the difference as long as they're treasured? Sure, they might wonder what if, but the lack comes from not being loved enough, not from whether the person who tucks them in at night was mommy or daddy. I didn't know my father, and I grew up just fine with only my mom. She was everything." Ally gripped my wrists and jerked my arms until my eyes snapped up to meet hers. "She was way more than enough."

"Your mother was amazing."

"You're right. She was. And so are you. Laurie couldn't be any luckier if she had two parents. No one could love that little girl more than you do. Just like you'd love that new baby. I never doubted for a second that you were enough. It wasn't that."

"I didn't know you were a virgin. If I'd known…"

"It's not about that either." Her nails scraped my wrists, and the bite of pain made my cock spring to life. I wasn't proud of it, but this woman was like a goddamn torch to my libido.

One taste of her hadn't been enough. Would never be enough.

"Then?" I asked softly, fighting the urge to cup her cheek so she had no choice but to look into my eyes. I hated that she never fully looked at me anymore. That was a new thing too.

So much of this was new, and she wasn't the only one struggling to keep her footing. With every step, I felt as if I was sinking in quicksand.

"You're the most important person in my life. If this goes sideways and I lose you—" she began.

"Not gonna happen." Even after the past week, I didn't have to fake the confidence in my voice. "We are solid. Always. No matter what."

"A baby would change things. You thought you'd make it easy on me, give me the chance to walk away. But I couldn't. Just like I can't turn my back on you or that little girl." Her face tipped up to mine and her pleading tone cut me to the quick. "Do you honestly think I could walk away from a child we'd made?"

"So do it with me."

Her mouth quivered. "What?"

"Have the baby with me and we'll raise it together. Why the hell not, right? We're both single, and we're friends. As close as could be before sex, and now that's obviously a go too, so why not?" I rushed on, the idea gaining speed. I didn't know all the logistics of what I was suggesting, but right now, I didn't care.

This way, we could both get what we wanted. And I wouldn't lose her. She wouldn't walk away from town for school, or if she did, she'd come back.

She'd always come back to me. To *us*.

Ally backed up and spun around, facing the stacks of boxes along the far wall. "What about Laurie?"

The question barely registered, because all I could think about was that she hadn't said no.

Hadn't said yes either, but she definitely hadn't said no.

"She wants another sibling. You know that."

"But if it's me you have the child with, won't it confuse her? We've spent years telling her we are just friends."

"She loves you. She'd be thrilled to have you around more. As would I." Unable to stay away a second longer, I wrapped my arms around her from behind.

She not only bristled, but she pulled her body not so subtly away from mine. Something else she was always doing lately. Now that I knew she was attracted to me too, it seemed like just one more confusion to pile onto the rest. But maybe she wasn't comfortable being attracted to me yet. In her mind, we were still off-limits. Still strictly friend-zoned.

"Hey," I said gently. "It's just me. Last night doesn't change all that came before." She let out a broken laugh and I swallowed over the dust in my throat. "Does it?"

She laughed again, weakly. "I know you're not a chick."

"Not so much, no."

"But yeah, for women, sex changes stuff. Probably not all women. I'm sure there are plenty who can do it and not overanalyze, but I'm not one of them. Not when it's you."

I stroked a hand over her arm. "Plus, it was your first—"

"God, don't." She buried her face in her hands. "So embarrassing."

"What is?"

"I'm almost thirty and I hadn't done it with anyone yet. I'm a freak with super-high expectations."

"Having super-high expectations makes you a freak? Good to know." Carefully, I turned her to face me and skimmed my thumb down the side of her throat. The skin was more than a little pink there, and my dick stirred again. My stubble had branded her as surely as my cock had.

Mine. I would always be her first. No matter what.

"I'm glad it was me," I said hoarsely, tightening my hold on her throat. That brief show of dominance had her glancing up warily, but she didn't back away. "That it was us. You gave me a gift I won't ever forget."

"Yeah, well, ditto, Hamilton." She took a breath and the next time she spoke, her voice was stronger. "It didn't quite compare to your Mustang exploits for your first time, but as far as first time fucks go, it probably wasn't too bad."

"Probably not." I brushed a kiss over her forehead and she softened in my arms, melting against me in a way that didn't make me want to stop kissing her. Or touching her.

Ever.

"Now we have time to perfect the technique," I added as lightly as possible when my vocal cords were squeezed as tight as my swollen cock in my jeans.

"Do we?"

"Oh yeah. If you want to." I wrapped my hand around her ponytail and tugged. "With or without a baby, I want you again. In every goddamn way possible."

Her chin trembled. "But the baby is important to you. You wouldn't have gone to a lawyer to draw up a contract if it wasn't. It wasn't a lark."

I was tempted to deny what she'd said, but I couldn't. She was the only person I'd always been honest with.

Her and my little girl.

"Yeah, it matters. Not just because Laurie's asked for one. That might be a passing whim, who knows." I shuffled my feet, feeling idiotic. Still, telling the truth was important. "Growing up without my mom around for more than random holidays was rough. Not because my dad raised us, but because he wasn't into it. He cared more about his work. And yeah, I know I have the tendency to get caught up too, so I want some insurance Laurie has what I did."

"Your twin," Ally whispered.

"Yeah. We always had each other. Even when he stole my Legos or hid the second Xbox controller or put rice in my socks, the little fucker." I had to grin. "She should have that too, and soon, before the age difference is too much. She's already almost four, and it's not like there's anyone special in my life." I sucked in a breath. "Except you."

She shifted out of my arms, but not before the wetness in her eyes stole the oxygen right back out of my chest. "Ally—"

"Give me a few days, okay? Some time to work through all of this, to figure out how I feel."

I wanted to argue. To try another tack. That was what I did. I negotiated for new angles, new perks to throw into the deal. Whatever it took to close the sale.

And she deserved so much more than that.

"Okay." I nodded and shoved all the jagged edges inside me back in line. "As long as you need."

She glanced back, surprise erasing the raw emotion on her face. "Seriously? Maybe I wasn't the only one who needed to get laid."

I laughed, shocking us both before I leaned forward to press my lips to her forehead again. "Definitely not."

Though it about killed me to walk away from her, I headed for the door. I placed my hand on the knob and looked back, memorizing the way the lone overhead bulb gave her dark hair an angelic glow. But those deep brown eyes were temptation unparalleled.

"If people ask what we did in here, don't suppose you could say you found out my little problem was miraculously solved?"

Her lips twitched. "Never said it was a little problem, Hamilton. All your problems," she cleared her throat, "are huge."

I grinned and stepped out, shutting the door behind me. Now I just had to wait.

A peal of girlish laughter flowed down the hall and my grin widened.

And eat ice cream with my baby girl.

9

SETH

"No, Bart, I don't foresee any additional holdups with the check. Like I told you yesterday, we're just waiting on the bank to—"

"Fucking bureaucrats," Bart Jenkins mumbled. "I don't have time for their bullshit. Maybe if I golfed more often with old man Chandler, I'd get better service."

"Doubtful. I've heard his swing is killer. He'd probably annihilate you."

Bart huffed out a laugh. "You know, Hamilton, you're the oddball in your family, aren't you? Your father and Oliver, they're the serious ones. The sharks. You just make jokes and amble through life, smiling at everyone while you quietly pile up your assets."

"Some of my friends would debate the quiet label, but yeah. That's me in a nutshell." I smiled and kicked back in my chair, crossing my legs at the ankle on the edge of the desk. It was almost lunchtime, and I was starving.

Maybe I'd meander over to the diner and—

Nope. With a side of hell no.

Ally had asked me for space to make up her mind, and I was going to give it to her even if it drove me crazy. I was already more than halfway there, so it wouldn't take long.

"All right, I'll check in again tomorrow." Bart sighed. "I hate fucking waiting."

"You and me both," I said under my breath as I hung up.

Phone in my hand, I debated my lunch choices. If I wasn't heading to the diner, I needed some sustenance. Maybe I'd ask Shelly to pick me up a sub when she was down at the bank, since Thursday was payday.

Thursday already. I hadn't talked to Ally since Saturday afternoon. Almost a freaking week.

But who was keeping score? Not me. I scarcely had even noticed that we never went this long without talking. Even after the kiss following Laurie's bathtub adventure, we'd bumped into each other at the diner midweek.

Bumped into meaning I'd gone over there intentionally because her blueberry pie was the best on the planet, but whatever. I wasn't going to do that this time. Even if it meant I starved to death.

I reached for my office phone just as the button for the receptionist's line lit up. I grinned. That woman was a godsend. "Hey, Shell, can you stop by Jersey Angel's while you're out at lunch?"

"Sure. Pastrami on rye, light mayo, extra Russian, leaf lettuce, not shredded, tomatoes, extra peppers and onions?"

"You're the best. And a brownie. Cheesecake if they have it." Damn sweet tooth.

"Of course. Grape soda?"

In front of anyone else, I would be slightly embarrassed about my pedestrian food choices. Shelly, however, had worked for the family business for more than a decade. She knew my weaknesses.

Even those that came in purple cans.

"Yes, please. Thanks so much."

"No problem. One more thing, sir."

"Ahh, Christ, not the fucking sir shit—" I broke off as the door to my office swung open and Ally stepped inside carrying a Hamilton Realty folder.

The one that probably contained the contract I'd had drawn up.

I swallowed deeply enough that Shelly probably heard it. Maybe Ally too. Fuck, had she always been this beautiful?

Probably. I'd just been blind. A complete fool.

"Sorry to interrupt," Ally said tentatively, gripping the folder until it dented.

Good sign? Bad sign? Impossible to say for sure. She might've returned the signed version, or she could be plotting to throw it in my face. With Ally, one was never certain.

Just another thing I loved about her. Platonically loved. Like a friend I had sex with.

Great sex.

"You're not interrupting," I said to Ally. "You know you have a standing invitation. Just a second."

I returned to my phone call. "Thanks so much, Shell. Gotta go." I clicked off without finding out if Shell's one thing was to announce Ally's impending arrival.

It didn't matter. I'd deal with anything else later. Like next year.

"It's the middle of the workday. I should've called first, but—"

"No need. Standing invitation," I repeated, rising and coming around the desk. I met her at the door and closed it, using the wood for support as I indulged in a nice long look at her. "You look incredible."

It wasn't an exaggeration. Her dark hair had been left long and loose, flowing down her bare back. She had on a red sundress type thing that showed off her breasts and narrow waist, not to mention her long legs that went on forever and ended in strappy red sandals.

Even her toenails were a dark, vampish red. My tongue tingled. I'd never been one for sucking on feet, but for her, I just might start.

Her cheeks reddened. Seeing Ally blush was a new thing. I liked it. A lot.

"Thanks. Had the day off today, so I figured I'd wear something fun." She walked toward the windows, checking out the view from this floor as she always did.

The building that contained Hamilton Realty had a primo view of the lake, and today the sunshine was dappling the restless water. It was breezy today, and the whitecaps proved it.

"Day off? Imagine such a thing." Feigning nonchalance, I sat on the edge of my desk.

No part of me was nonchalant around her, not anymore. Not after we'd had the most amazing sex of my life and all I wanted was to do it again. And again.

Oh, and maybe to have a baby with her.

But at the moment, even that want paled in comparison to fucking her. The insistent pressure in my cock was making *everything* pale in comparison to sex.

Sex with my incredible, smart, funny best friend who also happened to be hot as hell.

I was a lucky man.

"Then Jean called off and Sage is probably going to get stuck working a double, but she was insistent she needed the money," Ally continued, happily oblivious to my sex-starved mental meandering.

"I thought she was set financially from her parents. The Hummingbird's Nest always did well. They certainly got a nice check from the sale of the property."

I frowned. Why did I care? Sage was a nice girl, and I didn't want her to struggle financially, but her family wasn't exactly poor. Her parents had sold their B&B and retired to the west coast, leaving their sheltered only daughter on her own.

Working at a diner. Hmm. So yeah, maybe they hadn't left her as much as I thought. Not my business though.

Ally shifted away from the window, standing sideways so she was framed in sunlight. "It did, but Sage wants to make her own way. A loft on the lake doesn't come cheap."

"I should know," I said drily, "seeing as I brokered the sale."

"Yes, real estate guy extraordinaire." She fingered her arrow necklace. "Is your father back yet?"

"Later today supposedly. Al, why are you here?"

A wrinkle formed between her brows. "I thought you said I had a standing invitation."

"You do, always. But you're fidgeting and you're holding that folder and c'mon, you don't really care where my dad is. You've never liked him."

"More like he never liked me. I wasn't good enough to be friends with you."

I frowned. "He never said that. Not once."

At least not to me. He wouldn't dare. He better not have dared to say it to her either.

"But it was heavily implied. And of course he'd wonder what you saw in me. Our worlds couldn't be more different. We just happened to land in the same classroom in the same high school and somehow we ended up here."

I pushed off the desk and stalked closer. Somehow now that I'd been inside her, even having a room's distance between us seemed like too much. "Right here." I brushed my hand down her hair and she shuddered, and fuck if that didn't make me harder than steel. "My father hasn't mentioned you in years."

She rolled her eyes. "Probably hoping if he denies my existence in your life, I'll disappear."

"I don't give a shit what my father thinks, and you shouldn't either."

"Sorry to say, I'm not as good at going with the flow as you are."

"Just takes practice. I'd be happy to demonstrate anything you'd like."

"Mmm-hmm, I just bet." Her lips twitched with the beginnings of a smile, then she pushed the folder at my chest. "Okay."

I took the folder with suddenly boneless fingers, but I didn't open it. "Okay?"

"Okay, I'll do it. I'll have a ba—"

"Fuck yes." Threading my hand into her hair, I tugged her against me and dragged her lower lip between my teeth. Her pupils flared wide and I did it again, making her moan. "Say it again."

"You didn't—" She paused to drag in air. "You didn't let me say it the first time."

"Sorry. Say it now."

"Bossy." She smiled as she stroked a hand down my tie, and I swear she might as well have stroked my dick. "It may be the craziest thing I've ever done, but I'll have a baby with you."

I slanted my mouth over hers, slipping my tongue inside. She curled hers around mine, all heat and need, as she rose up to her tiptoes and tightened her grip on my tie. Pulling me closer, sinking deeper into the kiss. I dropped my hand from her hair to her ass, palming it brazenly, hauling her against me so that she could feel the rigid outline in my pants. She gasped, her eyes popping wide, and I relinquished her mouth long enough to fumble for her hand and drag her around my desk. I opened the top drawer and threw the folder inside without looking at the contents, then pointed at my chair. "Wait here."

I opened the door and leaned into the hallway until I caught Shelly's eye. She had the phone cradled against her ear. "Hold all my calls until further notice."

She nodded and waved me off. It didn't look like she'd be going out for lunch just quite yet, which might be awkward if I gave a shit.

I stepped back inside my office and shut the door, locking it. Then I glanced toward my desk.

Ally was not sitting. She had her arrow necklace up to her mouth, between her teeth, sucking on it as I hadn't seen her do in a million years. Nervous habit 101.

"What're you doing?" she asked as I skirted the desk. Coming toward her like a damn panther scenting his mate.

Because she was. She would be. Again and again until we accomplished our aim.

Not just mine. Ours now. That it was a joint mission made it more important. This would be the biggest thing we'd ever done together. The absolute best. A little of her, a little of me. Combined into a little person with all their own hopes and dreams and wants.

It was scary as fuck to do this again. To make the choice this time. The circumstances weren't perfect, and most people— including the members of my own family—would think I was loco for posing the suggestion. They would think she was equally nuts for agreeing.

But in my gut, this felt right. Being with Ally had felt right since the very first day. Nothing else in my life had ever felt this natural. This perfect.

I picked up my desk phone and set it on the floor. Then I did the same with my iMac, power strip, and various peripherals. Overkill, perhaps, but I wanted us to have space.

"Seth…" God, that tremulous tone of hers was making my balls throb.

Once I'd gotten the tech stuff out of the way, I leaned over the desk and swept everything to the floor, blotter included. Ally screeched and jumped back, sending the desk chair rolling away across the hardwood floor. Worked for me. I needed room to move.

"I didn't mean right now," she said as I approached. "Like right this instant."

"You didn't, but I did."

"You're at work." She took a step back, then another, finally bumping into the wall. "Clients are coming and going. Oliver is on the other side of this wall."

"In the field," I said easily, drawing her purse strap down her arm before setting the small, weathered bag aside and caging her in with my arms against the wall. "But I wouldn't care if he was standing in the hallway. Let the jealous bastard listen." At her gasp, I dropped my mouth to her ear. "I can't walk out of here until I've had you again."

"You're insatiable. I never guessed."

"Did you think about me in bed?" I trailed my finger underneath her jaw and down along the tops of her cleavage. She fought not to shiver and to hold my gaze, but she was on the verge of losing it, I could tell. "I thought of you."

"Liar. You did not."

"Only when you went out on dates with assholes," I admitted. "And it was entirely unwitting. I tried to stop it. To not see you in my mind naked and writhing on their sheets, mainly because no one was ever good enough for you."

She lifted her chin in challenge. "But you are?"

The question stopped me in my tracks. A tremor went through my hand and she must've noticed, because she gripped it and held it against her cheek. "This is where you say yes. That you're everything I could ever ask for in a guy. More than. And you fuck like a goddamn champ, even though technically, I don't know the difference. Just roll with it."

The laugh started in my gut, spilling out of me with a freedom that had never occurred with anyone but her. I buried my face in her hair, pulling in deep breaths of her summery scent. It centered me, just as it always did. She was the embodiment of the lake and the town that had been my home for my entire life.

I eased back to study her. Memories of the long summer days we'd spent chilling with a picnic basket by the lake—or doing way riskier stuff like joyriding in my dad's Porsche when he was away—stretched out in my mind, somehow reflected in her eyes.

She was safety, and home, and family in a way no one else had ever been except my brother. And now she was so much more. That fresh-air-in-a-bottle scent of hers was capable of making my dick hard in an instant. The way she'd tied off her sundress so neatly behind her neck drove me wild, making me imagine the strapless bra she had on underneath.

Or nothing. I was voting for nothing.

Fuck, I had to see. But first…first, I had to make sure.

Sucking in a breath, I turned around and braced my hands flat on my now-bare desk.

"What's—what's wrong?" Her tremulous question nearly broke me.

I didn't want her to ever doubt the effect she had on me for a moment. I'd already fucked up so much with my stupid contract and crazy scheme to have a kid when if I'd just talked to her, explained where my head was at, maybe we could've made some decisions together. I'd caused her to think that any attraction I might have in her direction was just based on my wanting to knock her up.

Truth was, I'd been trying my goddamn hardest not to notice her that way for years.

Now I didn't have to shove those errant thoughts away. We were both single. There was no reason we couldn't do the family thing our own way. With sex and kids and our own rules.

Love wasn't a necessary component. At least romantic love. I didn't see her that way. Of course not. I mean, I loved her, but to love her romantically would be taking a huge fucking risk.

The biggest of them all.

"Hey." She stepped forward and stroked my back, and even in that single touch, she conveyed her growing confidence. Not in general, but in this particular space with me. "You're running hot and cold."

I laughed. "Far from it. I'm so hot right now that I'm amazed I haven't torn a hole in my pants yet."

"So why did you pull back?"

For fuck's sake, I knew she was blushing just from that little breathy catch in her voice. I knew so much about her, and instead of that making this boring, almost routine, it made every moment better. Bigger. I wanted to find out everything I didn't know. How her eyes hazed over as she came, the tremble of her lips just before she went over. The way she'd soak my dick with her release.

Without a condom between us this time.

I pressed my palms into the desk, searching for clarity. For restraint. "Every time, it feels like I'm pushing you."

I expected her to argue. That's what she did—what we did.

Instead she reached around me and stroked my cock through my pants, so slowly that I hissed air between my teeth. "Mmm. You weren't lying."

Christ, that little purr in her throat? Gonna be the death of me.

She didn't wait for my affirmation. Her first task was to undo my belt and toss it on the desk, where it hung half off like a waiting snake. The metallic sound of her undoing my zipper seemed loud in my head, competing with the throb of my heartbeat. She dipped her fingers inside, grabbing my shaft through my boxers. I was so hard that just her light grip had my balls drawing up, full and tight.

I might not plant a baby in her this afternoon, but it wouldn't be from lack of coming. Holy shit. It was going to happen whether or not I wanted it to if she kept touching me like that.

As if she heard my thoughts, she pushed down my pants and my boxers and turned me around to face her before going to her knees. I didn't breathe. Didn't make a sound. Just watched and waited as she stroked my dick from root to tip and flicked her gaze from mine to my length, over and over.

It fucking grew in her hand, and she laughed. Softly. Like a damn vixen.

"Some magic trick," she whispered a moment before her lips engulfed the tip.

I grasped the edge of the desk and threw back my head, fighting not to command. It would be so easy to grab a handful of her hair and pull her down my erection, but she probably wasn't ready for that. Her tentative licks and sucks were working a magic all their own.

"Undo your top," I rasped. "Let me see you."

She kept me in her mouth while she reached up with one hand to undo the tie behind her neck. The red straps fell and my breath caught.

Holy fuck, her gorgeous bare tits had been pushing against the material all along.

"You went out like this." I reached down to twist her hard pink nipple and she gasped around my shaft. "Showing off all this perfection." I gave her other nipple a twist and swore I could feel pre-cum pulsing onto her tongue.

She eased back and licked her lips. Naughty vixen. "It's only for you."

"Again." Already her mouth was full of me again, precluding talking, but I didn't care. As much as I was dying for her to suck my cock until I spilled myself in her throat, I had to hear her say it. "Say it again," I demanded, hooking my hands under her arms. She barely had an instant to release my dick before I drew her to feet. "Say it," I repeated, latching my mouth onto her tight little nipple and pulling it between my teeth.

Her moan made my erection lurch into the softness of her belly. But I didn't stop working her nipple, using teeth and tongue. She writhed against me as I pressed my hand between her legs, right through her dress. "Gonna walk out of here with a wet spot so everyone knows?"

Her hips pulsed, driving her covered pussy against my hand. I couldn't wait another second. I dragged the dress down her body, letting it pool on the floor around her red sandals. She wore only a scrap of white panties, and yes, they had a telltale wet spot right in the center.

I growled. All for me.

It was my turn to drop to my knees. Locking my gaze on hers, I licked that damp spot again and again, groaning as her taste filtered through the fabric. Sweet. So sweet. Peeling the material away from her swollen lips, I flicked her clit with just the tip of my tongue. She whimpered, swaying on her heeled sandals until I banded an arm around the backs of her thighs to keep her still. Taking off her panties would require too much time, but I had to have her. Opening my mouth over her pussy, I ate at her like the starved man I was. The man she made me. Her legs trembled so I hauled her closer. Impatiently, I yanked at the thin material, almost as shocked as she was when it gave way. I shot her a glance and her wide eyes tore a laugh from my chest as I tossed the strips aside.

That laughter ended in her moan as I resumed my task.

When the angle wasn't good enough, I rose and picked her up, setting her on the desk. I kissed her, slanting my mouth over hers as I yanked up her legs, placing her heeled feet on the edge. Spread open obscenely in front of me, the tatters of her panties still guarding part of her pussy, she shivered. And I looked my fill, drawing my fingertip through the wetness she was making for me.

"Say it again," I said as her dazed eyes lifted to mine. "Tell me who this belongs to."

"Seth, please." She bit her lower lip. "God, it's you. It's always been you. Okay?"

Her breathless, annoyed words slashed through the roar of blood in my head. Always.

Yes, fucking always.

I dipped my head and cupped her breast in my hand, squeezing it so the nipple stood taut and proud. Then I licked my way around it as she dropped her head back, her long dark hair trailing over the desk. Brushing my knuckles over her soaked slit, I found her clit, so hard and full and pulsing lightly under my touch. I circled it again and again while I sucked on her breasts, switching my attention from one to the other. Her whimpers grew and I slipped my fingers lower, pushing them inside. All the way in. She lifted her hips off the desk, her thighs falling open even wider.

A sterling invitation.

I bent to lick her, sealing my lips around her pulsing clit as I rocked my fingers in and out. She grabbed my hair in her hands, pulling me against her without shame. That just turned me on more. Barely aware of it, I fisted my throbbing cock in one hand as I lapped at her pussy and she gasped, making me lift my head.

She was watching me jerk my cock, honey eyes wide. Fuck.

"Like this?" Regretfully, I slid my coated fingers out of her pussy, swallowing a groan at the way her body clutched at me. I slicked those wet fingers over the side of my dick, making it jump. Ally's eyes ate up the wet trails I left behind. "So wet. Gonna get even wetter before I get inside you."

"Not possible." She was staring at my hands, watching me work my length. "You look bigger in daylight."

"Thanks. I think." I had to laugh again, even if it hurt. Christ, even that movement had my erection stretching farther up my stomach.

"Oh, it's definitely a compliment." She licked her lips and my balls tightened. "Your cock is beautiful."

"Beautiful, huh?" I undid my shirt and dumped it on my chair before following instinct and grabbing her hand and bringing it back to my cock.

She didn't balk. Far from it. Together, we stroked my erection until I was panting. "Fuck, I gotta have your pussy. But first..."

Holding her gaze, I grasped her fingers firmly in mine and brought them back between her legs. She pulled back slightly but I kept my hold steady until she relaxed again. Slowly, I rubbed her clit with our joined fingers. Her wetness seeped between them and she let out a few broken breaths, not quite moans but almost. Her thighs shook. "Seth," she whispered.

Already I was learning her tells. "Yes. Come on our fingers."

She licked her lips and dropped her head forward, her long hair tumbling over her gorgeous tits as her chest rose and fell. Without my prompting, her fingers sped up and she lifted her head, her pupils flaring before she closed her eyes and her hips rose from the desk.

She came silently, her body shuddering and her pussy contracting beneath our fingers. And it wasn't enough. I needed more.

Before she'd even stopped spasming, I gripped my cock and lined it up with her slit. She registered the movement and opened her eyes, letting out a gasp at the nearness of my erection to her pussy.

Bare. No condom this time. I was going to spill myself inside her, intentionally.

Fuck, my dick was rock-hard just imagining it.

"You're sure?" I murmured. "You want me to come inside you naked. Want me to fill you up with my cum." It was probably cheating to stroke my cock, knowing how it affected her, but she couldn't nod fast enough.

"God, yes. Want all of that...inside me." She rubbed her damp fingers over her mouth and I lurched in my fist. "Please."

"Suck them," I said, and she edged the tip of one inside. That red nail dipping just past her lips as her lashes fluttered and her tongue sneaked out. "Taste your pussy like I did. So fucking sweet."

She whimpered and drew the finger deeper. Then I gripped her wrist and brought her hand to my mouth, tasting the finger she hadn't yet, savoring her flavor as I pulled back and drove deep.

Goddammit, she felt good. So fucking good.

Her broken moan—tinged with pain—made me still and relinquish her finger with a wet little pop.

"You're so goddamn tight. Are you okay?"

Eyes wild, she nodded. "Yes. So full." She pushed against me and I threw back my head, searching for strength. "Seth, please fuck me. *Please*."

She didn't need to ask again.

I pressed her hand to the desk. "Better reach back and hold on."

She did as I requested and I slid my hand up her leg, gripping her thigh to drag her closer. Hooking her ankle over my shoulder, I wrapped her other leg around my waist. Swiveling my hips, I let her get used to the feel of me inside her for another moment—bare, finally bare—before I drew back and slammed home, rocking the desk on the floor. She gripped the edge of the desk with one hand and pressed the wrist of the other against her mouth to stifle her sounds as I pulled back and drove forward again, over and over.

Dammit, she was going to end me. Right here and now.

Grinding my pubic bone against her clit, I smacked her hand away so I could smother her cries with my mouth as I fucked her until she was shaking with the need to come again.

I was way fucking past that point.

She gripped me like a fist, squeezing me past my endurance until I had to switch positions or end this right now.

I shifted her opposite leg to my waist and picked her up, holding her on me, lifting her up and down with every thrust. She clung to me, her kisses biting, her moans spilling out like the liquid coating my cock. I could hear each stroke. Smell the scent of us together like the sweetest, dirtiest perfume.

Ours.

Hating to break our connection for even a second, I withdrew and set her on her feet before spinning her around so she faced the desk. I pushed her down and cupped her perfect ass in my hands, tracing that silky pucker between her cheeks while she bit her knuckles to keep from crying out.

And I plunged.

There was no hiding her moan this time. It seemed to fill the office, or maybe it was just my head. Either way, as I pulled back and drove home again, that sound spurred me on. I needed to hear it again when she soaked my dick. Hell, while we soaked my desk. I wanted every dirty drop inside her, but I wanted the proof on the place I worked every day too so I could never forget.

She was mine. Had always been mine. And now I was going to fill her up with my release.

Scooping her up, I reached around her to rub her clit. Hard, fast. She scrabbled to hold onto the desk and bucked back against me, her ass bouncing. "Come with me," I grated out.

"Going to." Her ragged response had me hauling back and shoving deep as I circled her clit.

She splintered apart around me, and I couldn't hold on. I managed to pull out once more and sank home while she was still coming, her relentless ripples milking my cock. I turned my head and bit her shoulder, sinking my teeth into her flesh as my hips flexed and I squeezed out every drop into her giving pussy.

Then I collapsed onto her, trying like hell not to crush her before I got to fuck her again.

"Oh shit." She slapped the desk once, twice. "Tapping out."

Groaning out a laugh, I pulled out of her. "Don't move."

"Not gonna. Can't."

As carefully as possible, I turned her over and eased her back on the desk, hoisting her legs high. She gaped at me.

"What the hell are you doing?"

"Keeping my cum inside you."

She threw an arm over her eyes, chest still heaving. Her tits were distracting as fuck, and my supposedly used up dick was already waking again. "That's not necessary, is it?"

"Can't be too careful."

"Good to the last drop," she muttered, and I laughed.

10

ALLY

I'D JUST LET A GUY COME INSIDE ME, AND HE WAS NOW OUT IN the hall, discussing lunch with his secretary.

He had a secretary. The guy I'd just fucked to make a baby.

A baby, for God's sake, when I wasn't even entirely sure how to make Eggs Benedict. That logic didn't fully track, but it did for me. I had cum running down my thighs—*so much for your legs up trick, Hamilton*—and the dude I'd banged like a drum was ordering me a salami sub. Sweet, really, since it was my favorite.

Holy crap, I had to get out of here. First, I had to get to a bathroom.

My gaze swung wildly around the office. Spotting a closed door, I let out a breath. Of course he had a private bathroom, though I'd never had the need to make use of it before.

I bent to gather my discarded dress. Not panties, since they were destroyed. The shreds were scooped up and thrown in the trash. Good thing they were a Walmart special and not La Perla. Not that I actually owned any La Perla, but—

Panic babbling had officially overtaken my brain. I wasn't as weirded out by this whole thing as I was the first time we'd had sex—

God, we were on multiples now—but the addition of procreation followed by shared salami was definitely upping the strange factor.

I needed to get cleaned up and get out so I could think without those sexy chocolate brown eyes unraveling me. Was that so much to ask?

After tugging up my dress and tying the straps behind my neck, I reached for my purse and cleaned up as quickly as I could with the single tiny tissue—fine, cocktail napkin—inside. Then I carefully walked on my tiptoes to the bathroom, more to remain as tidy as possible than to hide my escape. Tiptoeing wasn't particularly easy in heeled sandals, but I was used to a number of foot tricks to distract myself from long hours waiting on tables. Prancing sideways to that closed door like a polo pony, however, was a new one.

I grabbed the doorknob and ducked inside, shutting my eyes on a grateful breath. Even having another door between us was a relief. Harder for him to work his magic on me through multiple layers of wood.

Then I opened my eyes and discovered the supposed bathroom was a dusty storage closet.

"Shit."

No private bathroom meant I had to leave the office and slip down the hall. Which might not have been so bad if Shelly wasn't at her desk, but since he'd been talking to someone out there, chances were good it was her. And oh my Lord, the humiliation. She had to have heard everything Seth and I had done. We weren't exactly quiet. I'd tried to be, but this was all new to me and I guess good sex meant making a lot of noise. Then again, maybe it was just as Seth had said—he didn't mind if others heard. Was that his kink?

The depositing-his-cum-inside-me thing definitely seemed like another one, even if it did have an established end purpose. Still, did he have to relish it quite so much?

I rubbed my forehead. Okay, time to think. I still needed a bathroom, and I wanted some air, and I was also hungry, according to the roar currently emanating from my stomach.

Oh, lookie there, that window led to the fire escape. Score. Of course, there was the small matter of my still slightly damp thighs, but delicate steps.

Forget the walk of shame. I'd patent the matching tiptoe.

I crossed the room, dodging boxes and miscellaneous paper goods, and stopped at the window. The fire escape snaked down the side of the building. Perfect. I could slip around Barb's Bakery and into the alley, then cross the street and cover the short distance to the diner.

Where I would finish cleaning up, fold up this beautiful dress, and put on the spare uniform in my locker so I could get to work. Day off or no day off, I needed some normalcy in my life. Routine. A way to keep my hands and my mind occupied.

My spine prickled and I gripped the window, pausing long enough to haul in a breath. Maybe I shouldn't do this. I couldn't keep running out on the guy. Though this wasn't that, precisely. I just needed to work. To figure out why I'd had sex with my best friend twice and was now trying to have a baby with him, without happening to mention the pesky fact that oh, I'd been in love with him forever.

No big.

That wasn't all that relevant anyway. We were having sex, weren't we? I'd never even expected to have that much with him. Any last flickers of hope in that direction, small and rare as they were, had been stomped out when he'd married Marj. Even after they'd divorced, that hope hadn't returned. I was nothing if not pragmatic, and Seth and I worked as friends. Lovers were something else entirely.

But we seemed to be working there too. At least physically. Though that was pretty much a key-in-lock situation.

I shoved up the window. Yeah, I had to get out of here.

Gingerly, I climbed out, adjusting my dress as I went, and turned to push the window back down. I hurried down the surprisingly sturdy metal steps, sure everyone in town could see my midday flight. At the bottom of the steps, I realized I didn't have my purse. Fuck. I'd just have to come back for it later. There was no way Seth wasn't back in the office now. Besides, I lived with Sage and she would have a key. There was nothing I needed urgently in my purse. I rarely used my cell phone and I'd walked over to Seth's from the loft so my car keys were still in our apartment. Other than a spare tampon, breath mints, and my wallet that contained a slim ten singles, my emergency credit card, and driver's license, the bag was empty.

And I wasn't risking running into Seth again right now, whether or not that made me a coward.

Now I was a coward who was ducking my head and rushing across the busy street to the safety of the tree-lined opposite side. Tall, stately buildings shielded me as I jog-walked to the diner, smiling at people as I passed, still walking as if I was carrying a glass time bomb between my jittery thighs.

Nah, not a time bomb, just Seth Hamilton's possible progeny.

The diner was like an oasis in the center of Main Street. I slipped inside and immediately aimed right for the back, tossing smiles and hellos as if they were confetti. But the second that swinging door shut behind me, I closed my eyes and breathed. Just breathed.

Made it.

My state of euphoria was short-lived.

"What the hell are you doing here?"

Swallowing a sigh, I lifted one eyelid and faced my best friend. The other one, with cherub blond curls and green eyes that didn't miss a trick. "I work here, last I knew."

"Today is your day off," Sage said as if I'd forgotten. "You're all dressed up and everything. Love the shoes, by the way."

"Thanks. My favorite pair." I almost said my *only* dressy summer pair, but she already knew that, living with me and all. She'd seen the pathetic lack of nice clothes and shoes in my closet.

I sucked at girling.

"Yet you sneaked in here, all spy-like. So what's up? I want details." Sage crossed her arms over her ample breasts. I'd been envious of her rack a time or two, until Seth had shown such appreciation for my set. Now it was hard to want any others.

Nope, I didn't have it bad or anything. Badder, since I'd been sunk over him to begin with.

I grasped Sage's arm and towed her along with me past the kitchen and out the door to the back hall and on to the storage room where I'd had that confab with Seth almost a week ago. A week where I'd spent more nights tossing and turning than sleeping.

I'd nearly confided in Sage about Seth's latest suggestion, but I hadn't because I didn't know what she'd say. Would she tell me he'd clearly gone off his rocker and to run while I still could? Or would the diehard romantic inside her insist I throw all caution to the wind and have a baby with the man I'd loved for so long?

So what if he wasn't suggesting a real relationship? Those were so 2016. Besides, it wasn't like I'd ever had one that lasted more than the change of a calendar from one month to another. A few dates, a few makeout sessions and things always petered out.

A therapist would probably say I drove men away and had too high expectations. I'd say that I spent so many years being a caregiver to a woman I owed everything to and loved so much that I was too tired to waste emotional energy on dating. I'd already used up so much on just getting through every damn day.

But being with Seth didn't require that whole getting-to-know-you dance. Even sex with him had been surprisingly effortless. We had a rhythm, even when he scared me shitless with his hidden dominant side and dirty talk.

Dirty talk, for God's sake. From Seth. To me. The girl whose hair he'd held back after the prom when I lost every bit of the tequila I'd loaded up on to try to have a good time and get wasted with my friends. I'd never been skilled at cutting loose. As proven by the fact that the first time I had sex, it was with a man who wanted to impregnate me, so obviously, I made weird choices.

And now I was going to have to admit them. Out loud.

I opened the storage room door and pulled Sage inside with me, shutting the door safely behind us. "You have to swear not to breathe a word of this to anyone. You have to promise me."

Sage slapped her hands on her hips. "You think you need to ask? Of course your secrets are safe with me." She held out a hand, pinky extended, and I smiled a little as I hooked mine with hers. "To the grave," she said solemnly, and my smile turned into a slightly misty grin.

"To the grave," I echoed.

"Did you make love with him again? Tell me." Her eyes gleamed and she leaned closer, reminding me of a nosy news reporter. Her face was a few inches below mine but it didn't lessen the invasive factor. "Was it amazing? The first time isn't supposed to be, but the second…" She sighed dreamily. "Were their sparks?"

I slid away from the door so she couldn't hem me in. She was like a pug—adorable, pushy, and relentless. "Don't call it making love. That's creepy. We fucked. Both times."

"I knew it. I knew you had that sex flush going on. You're the same color as your dress. Was it incredible? Was it all you hoped for? Did he give you a climax?"

"More creepiness. No, he didn't *give* me a climax. He helped me to get there but I'd like to think I had a lot to do with it myself. The mind is the biggest sex organ, you know."

"But it was better this time. It had to be better because you're barely answering my questions."

I gripped my shoulders, turning away to stare at a dusty corner of the storage room. I'd run from Seth's right to this one, and my flight was weighing on me now. He'd been so incredible, so careful to make sure I was right there every step of the way, and I'd repaid him by taking off.

Again.

"It was more than I ever imagined," I said softly, swallowing over the grit in my throat. "He was almost desperate to have me. I never fathomed that could be real. That he could want me the way I always—"

"The same way you want him."

"Yeah."

"But he did. Oh Ally, that's so awesome." She stroked my arm, but didn't try to get me to turn around. Under her relentlessness was a heart of pure platinum. "Did he take a long lunch break or something and bring you back to his house? Handy living so close."

Heat blasted my face. "Um, no."

"Don't tell me he went for a room at the Inn again. Is he just trying to make tongues wag?"

"Not that either." I cleared my throat. "We did it in his office."

"You did it in his office?" she screeched and I winced and covered my face with my hands.

If there was anyone left in town who didn't know that Seth and I were slapping skin, there wouldn't be after this conversation.

"Yes. Please keep your voice down."

"Like where, on the floor?"

I shook my head.

"Against the wall?" Sage lowered her voice about a quarter of a decibel. "On the—on the desk?"

The sheer scandalization in her tone made me laugh. "It's not that shocking. People have office sex all the time. There's even a category on porn sites."

"Huh. Anyway, on the desk. Really." She whistled. "Wow."

I cleared my throat again. "Yeah, it was fairly wow. I didn't expect that when I went there, by the way. I just came over to tell him all systems were a go, and he surprised the hell out of me by—"

"You said yes? Oh, my God." Sage let out an excited peal of laughter and darted in front of me before pulling my hands off my shoulders to grip them. "So you could be pregnant, like right now? Oh God, I need to prepare. We'll need to have a shower. Are you planning on finding out the sex? We can go neutral themed for the party."

"Sage." I huffed out a laugh. "The first time, he used a condom."

"But this time he didn't, right?" Sage demanded. "So you could be with child this very instant."

11

ALLY

Those words made my brain chug to a stop. Though they were funny as hell, especially when combined with Sage's expression.

I swear to God, hearts swam out of my best friend's eyes and aimed for the ceiling. Imagining exactly that only made me laugh harder.

And distracted me from thinking about the reality bomb she'd just laid on me.

"With child? Really? What are you, a nun?" I wiped my eyes and found Sage's smile had vanished, along with her bubbly excitement.

"Yeah, guess I kind of am." She tucked a strand of hair behind her ear. "I should get back to work. I didn't let Jean know I was taking a break."

My stomach clenched and I grabbed her arm. "Wait. That didn't come out right. It wasn't a virginity dig. Hello, I'm barely not one myself anymore."

"There's no barely not a virgin. Either you've ma—fucked or you haven't. And you have. Twice."

"Yeah." I wanted to smile, and it so wasn't the time. "The nun comment wasn't referring to that though. I meant you make it sound so spiritual. So holy. Sometimes people just lean over a desk and get plowed into from behind."

She forgot to be mad at me long enough for her eyes to go wide. "That sounds hot."

"It was. Extremely."

"And he didn't use a condom this time."

"No." Since Sage's imminent flight risk seemed to have passed, I released her to rub my throat. I was having Seth coming flashbacks, and the heat between my legs was swiftly outpacing the flush in my cheeks. "He did not."

"Did it feel different? Like you know, no condom vs condom."

"Yes. It felt very different. The biggest difference was when he…" I couldn't tell her this. I couldn't tell anyone this.

Dear God, I had to tell someone.

"After he, um, let go inside me, he did this thing. He, ah, lifted my legs up. Straight in the air. So—"

"So the ejaculate didn't run down your legs." Sage fanned herself. "Lordy, I'm about to blow."

I laughed again. "Skip using the word ejaculate, because ick, but yeah, me too. It shouldn't have been hot. It freaked me out more than a little. But it was hot. Everything he does is hot, and now I might be pregnant, and I should be running the other direction. Instead, even though it's insanely premature to even think this way, I can't help wondering what if I can't do this for him. What happens then."

"If you can't do what?"

"If I can't give him a baby." Just saying it sounded ridiculous, so I laughed again, right on cue. I wasn't prone to fits of tears all that often. Hysterical laughter was another story. "I'm untried in that area, you know? I could have fertility issues. We could be a mismatch. So many reasons why this might not work, and that's not even why I'm wigging the most."

Sage just waited.

"I loved the guy before we got naked," I whispered. "Now I can't imagine life on the other side. Where he gets where he wants or he doesn't, but he can move on."

"What if he can't? What if he feels exactly the same way as you but, I don't know, concocted this elaborate ruse so he doesn't have to put anything on the line?"

"Oh please. Seth Hamilton? Do you not know the guy? He oozes confidence. He could have any woman he wants, and—"

"And he wanted you. Not just you, but to have a baby with you. A lifetime bond, Ally. Do you get that? You have a kid with someone, you're not walking away. Even if you think you can, there's always that tie. That piece of you linked."

Shaking my head, I rubbed at the sudden moisture in my eyes and looked away. Anywhere but at her. "He wanted to pay me off for my egg, basically. Send me away and raise the kid on his own. He might not think I'm a bad risk DNA-wise—and even that's a crapshoot with my family's history—but he didn't even want me involved much at first."

"At first?" She inched up on her tiptoes and got right in my face. "Lawrence, you're holding out on me."

I sniffled. Stupid allergies. "After I bailed on him after we did it, when he found me here at the diner the next day, he apologized for coming up with such a crazy plan. And he suggested we do it together instead. I don't know, it could've just been his new way of getting me to say yes."

"Have it together. Raise it together."

"Yeah."

Sage let out a laugh. "Girl, I might be the virgin, but you're the dummy. He so wants to put you on lockdown. Forget put a ring on it. He wants to put a baby in it."

"You're being silly. He just wants to have a kid for Laurie, so she has a sibling like he did before they're too far apart in age."

"You just said he could have any woman. Does that or does that not include their wombs as well?" She propped a hand under her chin. "I wonder what the average woman would say if a man like Seth Hamilton asked them to have his baby. He's a wonderful, devoted father already, and he's rich, smart, suave, kind-hearted, and judging from today's office performance, a near stallion in the bedroom Olympics. Sure, he has his jackass tendencies as well, but I'm sure he'd get few takers."

"He didn't ask them, did he? He asked me." Hearing myself, I shut my eyes. "He offered me money, Sage. As if I was a common—"

"As if he wanted to make things easier for you and knew you'd never accept the help any other way." Sage's voice turned soft. "Honey, you don't always make it easy for people to love you. Me, I make it so easy people aren't interested." She laughed weakly and my eyes popped open. "There's a fine line between playing hard to get and being impossible to get. You're practically a fortress, and Seth's the only man brave enough to try to find a way in."

"He was always in, and he never even knew it." And now my shitty drugstore mascara was running from the heat in that stuffy room. Never buying that brand again. Nope.

"Al, after he put your legs up," she paused to fan herself again, "what happened next?"

"We talked for a minute or two then he went to speak to his secretary about lunch." I gripped my stomach. The hole inside it was growing vaster by the second. "Wonder if I can grab a hamburger before my shift. I'm starving."

"His secretary was right there the whole time while..." Sage blinked and swallowed. "Stallion," she said reverently, and I had to laugh or flush forty shades of red.

I probably did both, but I was laughing too much to care.

"What happened after that? You're talking hamburgers, so what, you didn't like lunch?"

"I didn't stay." My laughter fell off quickly. "I left."

"With his knowledge? Or did you run away again like last time while the poor guy wasn't even aware." When I glared at her, she lifted her hands, palms out. "Just calling 'em like I see 'em. You ditched the dude at a sensitive moment. Question is, was it once...or twice?"

"It wasn't like that." I paced away from her and pushed a hand through my hair. And inhaled such a strong whiff of Seth's cologne that he might as well have been standing in the room with us.

Because he was all over you. Up against you. Inside you.

Christ.

"If you say so."

"It was awkward with Shelly right outside. She probably heard, and this is all new to me, and God, it's still so strange to face him after having him—" I exhaled. "It's so intimate. I don't know how to do intimate. My leaving is actually doing him a favor, saving him from all the awkward."

"I'm sure he appreciates it."

"Jerk." I turned to smack her, but she darted away and reached for the doorknob.

"I gotta get back. But it's your day off. You should probably take it. Run home, take a bubble bath."

"Oh, God." Her mention of bathing reminded me that yeah, I could use some serious bathroom time. "Yes, let me go take a quick shower. I'll be back in half an hour. Can I borrow your key? I forgot my purse."

She rolled her eyes and pulled the lanyard with her keys over her head. "So that means he'll have to chase after you. Unless that was exactly what you hoped." She handed me the lanyard. "If it was, I have to say good move. I never think that clearly in the heat of the moment."

"One second you think I'm a skank for ditching him." I shook my head, running my thumb over the battered edge of the key to our loft. "Then I'm the chick with all the moves, and let's face it, I so am not."

"You're the one who has hottie Seth all tied up in a knot. I'd say you have a lot more going for you than you know." She winked and ducked out the door, closing it behind her.

A second later, the door opened again and she stuck her head inside. "Oh, and start thinking about that shower. I'll come up with a theme, but a gender would really help my design."

"Get out of here."

"Gone. And I'll make sure that hamburger is waiting for you at your preferred table in back once you've showered." She winked. "A mother-to-be needs her calories."

She shot back out the door before I could screech.

In spite of everything, I grinned. And glanced down at my mostly flat belly, hating that she was making me wonder. It was too soon. It couldn't be a thing already. I'd know, wouldn't I? Maybe even the instant it happened. How could you not? Something that incredible, that special, taking place inside you…

Dear Lord, I was sounding as woo-woo as Sage.

I shook my head and aimed for the door. I needed to run down the street to our loft and get cleaned up. Then I'd come back and eat my hamburger—oh God, so hungry—and read a book on my day off, instead of panic-working. I could totally handle all of this.

Maybe I'd take that meal to go and eat on a bench near the lake. A picnic for one. Yay.

Not.

Half an hour later, I was freshly showered and changed into a pair of capri jeans and a tank top. I felt like me again. Dresses were fun, but I'd always be a jeans and T-shirt sort of woman. Reason twelve-hundred-fifty I'd assumed Seth could never see me as more than a friend. He preferred the uber feminine type. Or at least he had.

I wasn't sure what he preferred anymore.

The bell dinged as I stepped into the diner, and this time, I didn't hunch my shoulders. I wasn't running away from anyone or anything. I was…taking a pause. There. That sounded better. Mature.

Of course, that maturity fell away the instant I glimpsed dark hair shot through with silver and a twin version of the man I'd just had sex with seated at the booth beside the one I always selected. Awesome.

I plastered on a smile and went right up to their table. This was Seth's family, after all. I'd just say hello and escape to my booth while clinging to my gratitude that they hopefully hadn't overheard Sexathon 2017.

"Alison," Mr. Hamilton said before I could speak. "You're not working today?" he asked, taking in my attire.

I was probably imagining the faint sneer in his voice. Had to be. He'd never been warm to me, but he usually wasn't rude either. Militantly civil was a more accurate description.

"Nope, day off," I said as cheerfully as I could manage. "Nice to see you're back in town. Successful trip?"

"Of course." He went back to his menu, signaling our brief exchange was over.

Okay then.

I shifted to glance at Seth's twin. As always, their similarities nearly knocked me off my feet, especially when I could still smell Seth's scent on my skin no matter how much soap I'd used. "Hi, Oliver."

"Al," he said, smiling thinly. "Haven't seen much of you lately."

"Oh, I've been around." I gripped Sage's lanyard hanging out of my jeans pocket. "Well, I won't disrupt your lunch—"

"Did you and Seth have a falling out?"

I frowned, unsure if I'd heard Oliver correctly. "What?"

"Are you and Seth beefing?" His lips twitched and for a second, I almost smiled too. Seth was the lighthearted twin, but occasionally, the normally uptight Oliver let loose with a sarcastic remark or a joke.

"No." I tucked my hair behind my ear and hoped my embarrassment didn't show on my face. The inferno inflaming my cheeks didn't give me much hope. "I'm fine. We're fine. Why would you ask?"

"Just haven't seen you two together lately." Oliver smoothed a manicured hand over the laminated menu he had to have memorized by now. The diner wasn't his typical hangout as it was Seth's—and it definitely wasn't Mr. Hamilton's—but it was almost impossible to live in Crescent Cove without patronizing it now and then. "You're usually glued at the hip. The only other time you weren't was when he was married, and even that was a brief interruption. Marjorie couldn't compete with you." The corner of his mouth ticked up. "Not sure any woman can."

The hum of conversation around us had nothing on the buzz in my brain. "What are you talking about?"

He adjusted his tie, stroking it as if he was already bored with the conversation. "Nothing. Nothing at all."

"Why, Alison, you didn't know Oliver introduced Marjorie to Seth? He thought she was just the sort of woman his brother was—" Mr. Hamilton fell silent, and when the heavy beat of approaching footsteps cut through the chaos in my head, I understood why.

"Oliver was as dense then as he is now. Hey, Dad. Good trip?" Before his father could answer, Seth rested his hand on my lower back. The weight of his stare seared the side of my neck. "Hey, you."

"And the natural world order is restored," Oliver said, glancing pointedly between me and Seth before flashing me an I-told-you-so smile. "I was afraid you must've been dead in a gutter somewhere if Al was left alone for more than a moment or two. Oh, and love your new accessory. It's so you."

I glanced down and bit my lip at the sight of my bright red patent leather dressy purse in Seth's big hand. He didn't relinquish it, and I didn't ask.

"Such a comedian." With his free hand, Seth brushed my hair away from my cheek and I bristled. We were affectionate in public, but not to this level. "Did you eat?" he asked in a way that didn't befit a guy who a, had just been ditched post-sex for the second time or b, was my purely platonic friend.

Rather than reply, I jerked my chin at the burger at the next table. My stomach promptly grumbled, making Seth laugh and steer me in that direction. "Lunchtime. See you later."

"You don't want to eat with your family?" I asked out of the side of my mouth.

"I work with them every day. I don't have to eat every lunch with them too." So much for being polite.

"Nice to see you, Mr. Hamilton." No matter what Seth did, I never forgot my manners.

"What, not nice to see me?" Oliver smirked and wiggled his fingers.

"No," Seth responded before I could, guiding me to one side of the booth.

I pried out the well-worn paperback I'd shoved in the back pocket of my capris before sitting down. Seth dropped on the bench on the other side. I frowned at him, well aware we couldn't have anything resembling a semblance of a normal conversation. He simply slid my purse across the table and lifted a brow at the book I still clutched.

"The Sun Also Rises?"

"So? I enjoy the classics." I picked up my burger and bit in, letting out a moan. Sage had made the burger just the way I loved them— medium rare, extra mushrooms and pickles, light on the ketchup and mayo, heavy on the cheese. I was so into it that I didn't glance at Seth again until I'd taken another bite, chewed, and swallowed.

He seemed to be short on air. He was breathing too fast, and he'd grabbed a napkin to lay across his lap.

Not because he was afraid of a flying pickle either, I was willing to bet.

I giggled. Honest to God giggled like a high school girl. And risked his family overhearing me as I leaned forward and whispered, "You can't be."

He nodded frantically and I laughed harder.

"You think it's funny."

"What was your first clue?" I bit in again and deliberately did a Meg Ryan style eyes-rolling-back expression just to make him lose his mind.

"Payback is a bitch." His low, intimidating tone had me wiping my mouth with my napkin and reaching for my nonexistent glass of water. Guess Sage hadn't thought of everything.

"Hey Jean," he said to my passing coworker before I could find my voice. "Mind getting the lady a glass of water? She seems parched."

"Seth. Didn't see you sneak in here." Jean smiled so widely that I was amazed Seth didn't get sunstroke. She was sixty if she was a day, but he had that effect on women. All women.

Even me.

Especially me.

"Jean, it's okay. I can go get it myself." I started to rise from the booth, but Seth held out a hand, stopping me.

"Day off. Sit."

I was too surprised by his authoritative tone to argue. More dominance from him, this time outside the bedroom. Just like that night he'd ordered for both of us at the Sherman Inn. It wasn't as if I didn't want my voice to be heard, but something about him occasionally taking charge worked for me.

Lord, I was fucked.

"It's no trouble. Be right back." Jean bustled toward the kitchen.

A moment later, Sage returned with my water, not Jean. She made a big production of setting it on the table and smiling at both of us, making enough small talk to set my teeth on edge.

"And look at that, didn't realize y'all had come in too," she said to Oliver and Mr. Hamilton at the next table. "Is Jean taking good care of you?"

"Not as good of care as you would, I'm sure." I wasn't positive, but I got the feeling Oliver winked at her, because she blushed twenty shades of red.

"Hamilton men are charmers. Why, they'd charm the panties off a woman before she knew otherwise."

"You don't wear panties. C'mon now."

Mr. Hamilton cleared his throat and lifted his menu like a shield as he leaned forward to talk to Oliver. His son's smile dimmed, but only slightly.

Sage was still beet-red. "I do so wear panties. Not thongs either. Thongs ride up your crack. Ask Ally."

Mid-picking off a slice of pickle to eat, I paused. I did not look at Seth. "Sage."

"Just saying. Anyway, I gotta get back. Call me if you need anything."

"Not fucking likely," I said under my breath.

The moment she was gone, Seth leaned forward and mouthed, "You wear thongs?" Then he cocked his head, as if he was imagining what I had on under my denim capris.

I ignored him and popped my pickle into my mouth.

"Laurie's birthday is next Saturday," he said after a few moments of charged silence had passed between us. Oliver and their father were laughing quietly in the next booth, and Seth was eye-fucking me with enough force to have my clit pounding. It was kind of impressive, if I didn't want him to stop.

Right now. This instant.

Okay, maybe tomorrow.

"She's going to be four," he added, as if I didn't have the date circled and red-starred in my planner. "I want to have a big party. Will you help?"

"You want to have a big party in a little over a week. Have you planned any of it yet? Figured out a guest list, sent invitations?"

He bit the tip of his thumb and shook his head. "No, not exactly."

"What does that mean?"

"I haven't planned it at all yet."

I sighed, the joy from my orgasmic burger already fading. "People need more notice than a week. It's almost summer. Little kids have activities and family stuff going on."

"I know, and I should have done it forever ago, but I got busy at work. Laurie's counting on it." His dark eyes silently pleaded with me.

I pointed. "That look is getting you nowhere."

His lips curved and he mouthed, "Already did."

I pried off the last pickle round on my plate just for the pleasure of tossing it at his smug, laughing face. "I don't have my planner with me here, but we need to figure some stuff out."

"So I'll come over tonight." The way he tucked his tongue in the corner of his mouth didn't make me think he had party planning in mind.

More like he was envisioning how many spots in my loft he could desecrate.

"Your child," I reminded him.

"So you can come over," he said.

"I have work early."

"So come over tomorrow." He leaned forward and skimmed his fingers over the back of my hand. "Come every day."

"Incorrigible, and no. We can do this via Skype."

He did that tongue in the corner of his mouth thing again. "I can work with Skype."

I reached for my purse and pulled out the pen and small notepad tucked in my wallet. He had to spring this on me the one day I didn't bring my planner.

Before I could begin my list of what we needed to accomplish, he grabbed the pad and my stubby pen. He scribbled something and turned the pad my way.

Why do you have a condom in your purse?

I glared at him and wrote a quick reply.

You went through my purse, you bastard?

He took back the pad.

You ditched me again, your fault I had to look for clues.

I snatched the notepad.

I just needed time to myself. To process.

He eyed me suspiciously and grasped the pad.

Girl thing?

I nodded. It was a little insulting, but hell, lesser of two evils. Then I returned to an earlier point of contention.

You were looking for clues that include condoms?

He snatched it back.

Condoms? Is there more than one?

In spite of myself, I laughed. He was so ridiculous sometimes. I took the notepad and wrote what I felt was a reasonable reply.

No. Just the one.

Which I'd gotten free at a bar some time ago, but whatever.

I thought it was good to be prepared. Wasn't sure if you'd want to go for the gold yet. Thought you might want to practice first.

The look he gave me after reading my words sent a jolt of pure arousal through me. Especially since he didn't look away as he wrote out his response.

Oh, I want to practice. Over and over. But every time I want to be dripping out of you like I was this afternoon.

I clutched the pen and breathed. Honestly, that was all I was capable of for about thirty seconds.

You're saying that stuff with your dad and brother two feet away? Don't you have any shame?

I nudged the pad at him and he grabbed it up fast enough that he tore the edge of the page.

Oh yeah, I do. Notice I haven't thrown you on this table yet and fucked you right here? Trust me, that's a feat.

He started to push the notepad back then took it again before I could.

You keep licking your lips and looking at me and looking away, and I know what all those signs mean. You want it too. Want me.

I read his words and debated a comeback. They were what we exchanged. Always, over everything. Rarely serious, always messing around and antagonizing each other. That was our way.

Telling the truth was so much harder.

Duh.

Okay, I didn't say it was a reveal worthy of Dr. Phil, just that it resembled honesty. Hesitantly, I slid the pad back to him.

He laughed. Just sat there laughing at me, or with me—hell, maybe at us—and I laughed too, because he wasn't the only one who was ridiculous. We both were.

For a moment, he just stroked the pen. That shouldn't have been sensual, but somehow it was. When he started to write, I inched forward on my seat, too eager to see his message to wait until he passed it back.

Skype tonight?

I nodded and he wrote more.

Naked Skype?

I shook my head, smiling faintly.

Maybe a still or two?

I bit my lip, pretending to think it over.

For sustenance during toddler party planning.

"Maybe," I mouthed, knowing I'd probably send him any naughty pictures he wanted. Even if I blushed the whole time.

This was Seth. I didn't have to worry he'd upload the pictures on the internet or do anything sketchy with them. We could have the world's biggest fight and never speak to each other again and I'd never have to worry about that. He was a decent, honorable guy.

So why I had been so sure he just wanted me for my eggs? It was as if I'd read that stupid contract and forgotten everything that had come before.

But God, I couldn't forget what had come since.

He smiled and scribbled a single word on the pad before nudging it back.

Tonight.

He kissed his fingertip and pressed it to the back of my hand before sliding out of the booth. The gesture was so sweet, I sat there dazed while he said goodbye to his family and loped out of the diner, every one of his long-legged strides doing something funny to my belly.

Oliver got up to go to the bathroom and I tucked away my notepad. Might as well wait to take notes when I spoke to Seth. I grabbed my book and my purse and was about to take off when Mr.

Hamilton turned in the booth to smile at me. But it was the expression of a shark who scented blood.

Mine.

"It's never going to happen, you know." He stretched his arm along the back of the booth. "You've played a long game, but he'll never settle down with you."

My spine locked and I gripped my well-loved book until the pages crinkled. "I think you have me confused with your son's ex-wife. I don't play games."

Except wasn't that exactly what I was doing? Pretending I wasn't in love with Seth. That I could have a baby with him and we'd still be friends and everything would be hunky-dory.

Having a baby together was a life changer. A friendship changer. What would our new reality look like on the other side?

"No? I bet Laurie's mother would have something to say about that."

Not Seth's ex-wife. Laurie's mother. Another reality I didn't like to face. That little girl didn't just belong to him. She had a mother out there, and whether or not she'd been paid to split—and had accepted that payment—she could come back anytime. Rules were made to be broken. Contracts made to be ripped up.

Bonds meant to be rebuilt.

"Laurie's mother's feelings have nothing to do with me. Now if you'll excuse me…"

"No? She knew you would always be between her and her husband and she grew tired of second place." Mr. Hamilton shifted back to face forward, adding over his shoulder, "Laurie not having her mother around is on you."

Oliver approached the table as I stared at the back of his father's head. Seth's twin hadn't returned to his own table, he'd come to mine.

"Hey, Al, you know next time you don't have to whisper—" Oliver stopped and frowned. "Are you all right? You're shaking."

"Fine. I'm fine." I started to slide out of the booth, but he halted my movement with a hand on my arm. "Don't touch me," I snapped.

He immediately drew back. "Okay. I won't touch you. Do you need a ride somewhere?"

"Oliver," Mr. Hamilton barked, but his son didn't pay him any mind.

"I'm fine. Really. I just need some air. I think I'm getting the flu or something." I attempted to get out of the booth and this time, Oliver let me pass.

My mistake was glancing up into his dark eyes, so familiar and so foreign at the same time. They matched Seth's in color and shape, though not in feeling. Not in humor or mischief.

No one was like Seth. And maybe that did make me a game-player, because I'd been lying all this time. To myself most of all.

Now I wasn't the only one without a mother. Laurie was too. I wasn't dumb enough to completely believe what Mr. Hamilton had said, but if any part of it was true, it was too much.

Swallowing hard, I sidestepped Oliver and hurried out of the diner.

12

SETH

My day was going to consist of chaperoning twenty-plus four-year-olds—and a three-year-old or two—and instead of drinking beforehand as any other intelligent father would be doing, I was again trying to bathe my daughter. Without success.

"I thought boys were the ones who didn't like to take baths," I muttered as Laurie gripped the edge of the bathroom door with both hands so she couldn't be nudged any farther into the bathroom.

"Ally," she said again. At this point, it was starting to become a chant.

"She'll be here in a little while. Wouldn't you like to be all dressed in your pretty party dress for her? She's so excited to see it on you."

Since the only reason Laurie even had a new party dress to wear was because of Ally taking pity on us and coming shopping with us last weekend, I'd wanted Laurie to be ready when Ally showed up. But naturally, my willful child was not having that. God forbid I demonstrate my competency at parenting even once per month.

Hell, per year at this rate.

"Wait for her." Laurie changed tact and decided to push the door shut, effectively shoving me into the hallway. I slammed a hand on the wood, halting her efforts. It wasn't much of a victory, considering she was four and all, but hey.

"If you want to take a bath by yourself, fine. I'll wait out here. But you have to start now. Your friends will be coming over soon and we can't wait for Ally. She might be late."

Or not come at all.

I didn't truly think she'd bail on Laurie's party. There was no denying Ally had been weird lately. Our Skype session had definitely gone in a surprising direction, though she'd still helped to plan Laurie's party.

Forget helped. She'd asked all the questions and made most of the phone calls to make it happen. That was my girl. She got things done.

Even if she didn't have nearly as much to say to me anymore.

Ever since I'd presented her with that contract—that was now collecting dust in my desk drawer where it belonged—she'd been…off. That was probably understandable, since it involved a big life change. And seeing her best friend in a different light, yadda, yadda. Then there was the girl processing thing she'd mentioned.

And she'd been a virgin.

Fuck, I'd been the only man to ever have her. Still couldn't believe it.

I shut my eyes. I was not getting an erection right now. Just was not gonna happen.

Moving on.

We'd been on a damn rollercoaster since that day. Having sex definitely represented the highs. We'd been together another two times over the past week, which wasn't exactly optimal for pregnancy-achievement, but I was rolling with her schedule. She claimed she was busy. That was the same reason she gave for never staying for more than a few minutes afterward. A couple of nights ago, I'd made the mistake of falling asleep after we'd christened the couch.

Unsurprisingly, I'd awakened alone.

Most of the time, she was oddly quiet and not as eager to toss back her usual zingers. The one place she was uninhibited was in bed. Or against the wall, since that seemed to be our favored spot. We hadn't actually done it in a bed again since the first time. I also hadn't been able to lift her legs in the air again. That was all right. I was just as happy keeping my cock inside her until she squirmed. I was all about improvising.

"You stay out." A thud against the door indicated my little girl was leaning against it. Apparently, shoving me into the hall wasn't enough of a signal. She wanted me to get the message loud and clear.

Ally—awesome.

Daddy—major suck.

"The door needs to stay cracked if you're getting in the tub. And you are getting in the tub, Lauren Elizabeth."

The cry on the other side of the door surprised me less than the windy sigh and tap of heels. "This again?"

I turned to see Ally marching down the hall toward me, once again in heels, her hair up in some complicated knot thing and her dress…

Fuck, her dress was like sheer gauze or something. A pale lilac wrap that hugged her curves and made me harder than the wood my daughter was currently pounding against.

"Front door was unlocked."

"Mmm." I couldn't currently speak, and from Ally's little smirk, she knew what her outfit was doing to me. This wearing dresses thing of hers was all new.

I fucking loved it.

"Down, boy," she said, pressing her knuckles against my chest as she grabbed the bathroom doorknob with her other hand. "Laurie, honey, it's Ally. Can I come in?"

Moving quickly, I snaked my hand into the back of her hair and yanked her mouth to mine. I had to. There wasn't any conscious thought involved. She drove me to a point no other woman had before.

Some kind of fruity lip gloss mixed with cherry cola hit my senses and I slipped my tongue inside, already desperate for more. She moaned, her hand curling in to fist my shirt.

And Laurie opened the door.

Gotta say one thing about my daughter catching me kissing Ally—it stopped her tears. Immediately. Instead, she started to giggle. She slapped her hands over her face as I drew back, not looking at Ally because I knew she'd be giving me that accusatory glare she'd patented in tenth grade.

Nice job, Hamilton. You fucked up again.

I cleared my throat. "Ally's here."

Laurie giggled more.

Ally swept in the bathroom and lifted Laurie onto her hip. That caused the wrap dress to shift and bunch in ways that had me shifting and bunching like a motherfucker.

I turned away. Christ. I'd need a cold shower myself if I didn't find a distraction.

Watching Ally with my kid wasn't going to work either. It might slow my roll sexually, but seeing them together churned me up in a different way altogether. Made me think impossible things. Like maybe we didn't have to be friends who had a baby. Maybe we could be more. A couple. For real. With two children, instead of one.

A fucking family.

"Were you giving your dad a hard time again?" Ally swept Laurie's sweaty blond hair back from her brow. "Today's your big party. You don't want the birthday fairy to hide all your presents."

I winced. Laurie was half and half on believing such things. If she decided you weren't telling the truth, she was apt to call you a big fat liar.

Delicate, my child was not.

"Birthday fairy?" Laurie screwed up her mouth and looked at me. "Daddy?"

I pointed at myself. "Are you asking if I'm the birthday fairy? Or asking if I know the birthday fairy?"

"Both. Real?" she demanded.

Ally sent me a secret smile over Laurie's head and I would've sworn this was her form of payback for having the softest, fullest lips I'd ever kissed.

"Ally is the birthday fairy, know why?" I took advantage of Laurie's curiosity to once again step foot into the bathroom. "She's the one who made your party as magical as it's going to be today. But you won't get to enjoy it if you're not clean. Dirty girls don't get to play with their friends."

Laurie sighed and tugged on one of Ally's brown curls that had come loose from her updo. In the light from the window, all the red highlights in her hair made it look as if it were streaked with fire.

Christ, I was barely a dude anymore. Anytime now, I'd whip out paper that curled at the edges and start composing sonnets about the wonder of a summer's morn.

Or Ally's pussy, which probably meant I wasn't quite ready to give up my man card yet.

"You do my bath?" she asked.

Ally stroked Laurie's hair. "You sure you don't want Daddy to do it? Or he can stay with us. How about that?"

Laurie shook her head and stuck out her lower lip, her most common expression these days.

I sighed. "I have to get the grill started anyway. Whose idea was it for me to feed hamburgers and hot dogs and veggie burgers to twenty kids and their parents, anyway?"

"Yours. I mentioned catering. You said you could handle a little grilling. That it was your manly duty." Ally hid her smile in Laurie's blond hair.

"I said nothing about my manly duty. Just that I like grilling."

"So go grill then. We've got it under control." Ally shifted Laurie in her arms, tipping her upside down until she squealed. "Don't we, shortcake?"

"Yes!"

"Okay then. I can tell when I'm not wanted." I turned in the doorway. "No bubbles this time though. It has to be a quick bath. Your friends will be here soon, and you don't want me entertaining them."

"Why not? You're so good at playing horse."

I narrowed my eyes at Ally. "Yeah, and if I throw out my back, guess who'll be rubbing it later?"

Ally took long enough to reply that I wondered if what I'd said was more sexually explicit than I'd intended. Especially since Laurie was glancing between us as if we were the most fascinating people ever.

She'd definitely never seen us kiss before. A hug here or there, a playful shove, sure. But anything resembling making out, absolutely not.

"That's what you think," Ally finally responded. "I'd suggest you invest in some Icy Hot, pal."

"I'm going to start the grill," I muttered, deciding my best place was far away from where I could somehow scar my impressionable daughter. I might be tempted to kiss Ally's smart mouth again and then Laurie might end up in psychotherapy years later because I couldn't control my hormones.

When they finally came downstairs, the first wave of dogs and patties were on the grill and I'd already fielded two phone calls from crazed parents who were having issues of their own rounding up their kids. One of Laurie's preschool classmates and her little brother were both attending the party, and their frantic Mom had called to commiserate about trying to get them ready. I'd figured she was just explaining why they'd be late until she asked me out after making a DILF joke.

I wasn't an idiot. I knew that among many women of childbearing age, I was considered something of a prize. An employed man who was willingly parenting his child singlehandedly—though not necessarily with any skill—was basically a unicorn, except my horn was in my pants. And many of them wanted to ride it.

Usually, I managed to divert conversations away from the topic of dates, or finding a good woman to settle down with. I must've been off my game today because this one had broadsided me and I'd ended up fumbling through an excuse and basically hanging up on her.

I didn't have an answer why I couldn't go out with her. Technically, Ally and I had no rules. No arrangement that precluded either of us from seeing anyone else. We were friends who were fucking and trying to have a baby. There was no box to tick on Facebook for that one. Even "it's complicated" didn't begin to touch the reality of our existence.

But I didn't want to date anyone else. And I sure as fuck didn't want Ally to. Ever.

"There's Daddy. Wait 'til he sees you in your pretty, sparkly dress." Ally's voice carried out to me.

When she stepped out on the deck, carting my daughter in her arms, the inane thoughts in my head spewed out. "What does your Facebook status say?" I demanded, as if it was the most important question in the world.

Ally shifted Laurie in her arms. "What? Look at her dress," she commanded.

Laurie's grin tilted precariously. And her big blue eyes filled with tears.

Ah, fuck.

"Look at you in your beautiful dress," I said, setting down my spatula to step toward them. I reached for Laurie but she pushed out a hand, nudging me back. With her other hand, she clung to Ally's neck and buried her face in her chest.

The look Ally gave me was mutinous.

I stroked a hand over Laurie's curling wet hair. She burrowed more into Ally. "You look like a princess, honey. All these purple sparkles."

She didn't reply. Ally just glared.

"What do you say you open one of your presents before your friends get here?" I wasn't above bribery. Besides, I was keeping a pretty big secret about the party. But hell, it was supposed to rain, and how else could we entertain twenty kids indoors?

Laurie lifted her head and knuckled one of her eyes.

"Let's go to the family room." I checked the food on the grill, making sure I could leave it for a moment or two. "You want to man the grill while I take her downstairs?"

Ally stuck out her chin and her hand. "I can do it."

"Thanks. We'll be right back." I exchanged the spatula for my daughter and had to swallow a chuckle as Ally poked at the simmering meat. Even after all these years of working at the diner, she still wasn't very adept at making food, with a few notable exceptions.

Laurie poked me in the chest. "Down."

Sure, Ally could carry her all over, but me? Not gonna happen.

Swallowing a sigh, I set her on her feet and she immediately took off down the hall, reaching up for the doorknob that led into the basement. She couldn't quite turn it herself so I helped, and she rushed down the stairs. And stopped at the bottom, still gripping the railing.

Saying absolutely nothing.

I descended the steps behind her and taking advantage of her surprise, swooped her up again and set her on my hip. "It's a giant sandbox." I walked around the edges of the mostly contained mounds of sand I'd had trucked in on a whim yesterday while Laurie was at Pre-K. I'd had to pay outrageously for it, as well as call in a few favors, but I now was the proud owner of a shit-ton of sand that would be hauled out tomorrow at great personal expense. Not to mention all the furniture in this room had been shoved into the spare room and would need to be brought back out again.

Too bad Laurie was frowning at the giant, cool-as-fuck sandbox as if she didn't get what it was.

"See, look." I put her down outside the sand and bent to grab one of the oversized beach balls. I tossed it and it got stuck in a little valley, so I leaned forward to grab it—

And my mischievous child saw fit to push me into the sand, letting out a huge squeal of laughter.

"Think that's funny, huh? You rascal." I darted forward on my knees and snatched her up, lifting her sideways and holding her over a big mound of sand. "Maybe I should push you into it too."

"No, no, Daddy, no!"

The door upstairs opened and closed and footsteps sounded on the stairs. I turned, still holding my squirming kid, to see both Ally and the mother who'd asked me out on the phone, Tina, gaping at me.

"You filled your entire family room with sand?" Incredulously, Ally hurried down the rest of the stairs and hiked up her dress to pick her way around the sandbox. "You do realize how impractical that is? You're never going to manage to get every grain out, and it's going to embed in the floorboards."

"There's safety rubber underneath." I glanced past her at Tina. "Hi there. Is anyone manning my grill by any chance?"

"Yes, Mr. Robinson from down the street took over. Tina was worried about you. Said you guys were in the midst of setting up a date when the phone disconnected."

Oh fuck.

"Al—"

"Then we heard squealing and hurried down here." Ally bent gingerly to push one of the inflatable beach balls across the sand. "I can't believe you did this."

I had a feeling I'd be hearing that a lot today.

I righted Laurie in my arms and gave her a quick hug before setting her on her feet. "Your friends are here. Why don't you go back upstairs with Mrs. Johnson while I talk to Ally?"

"Okay." She scampered off, scattering sand.

I'd just made it to my feet when she spun back around and charged up to me again, gripping me around the legs. "Thank you, Daddy."

It came out sounding a little like *Tank Eww, Dabby,* but close enough.

Though Tina held out a hand for Laurie, she was staring fixedly at me. "I hope we can continue that conversation later, Seth."

"Actually, it's probably good if we don't." I smiled at her to soften the blow. "I'm committed to someone right now. But thank you for your interest."

It was a toss-up which one of the women gave me a more scathing glance.

"C'mon, Laurie," Tina said. "Let's go upstairs so you can say hi to everyone in your pretty dress!"

Laurie trotted along after her, chattering happily.

The door shut behind them, and Ally kicked one of the beach balls hard enough that it nearly took out the TV on the other side of the room.

"Committed right now? Like this instant? You should've given her an end date. Don't want her to get discouraged and give up too soon." Ally aimed for the other beach ball and did the same thing, this time nearly missing the one lamp we'd left behind because it was also on the opposite side of the space. Lawrence had some serious leg power.

Which wasn't hot at all.

Not even a little bit.

I scratched the back of my neck. It wouldn't do to seem pleased by this recent turn of events. Being stupidly overjoyed that she was jealous was simply not appropriate. I should be ashamed.

I might be tomorrow.

Or next year.

"I'm getting the feeling you're angry."

"Oh, are you? Are you now? What was your first clue?" She crouched to pick up the plastic bucket and slotted scoop, and I quickly rushed over to take them out of her hands before they left a dent in my wall. "Don't crowd me."

"I wouldn't dream of it." I tossed the toys aside and hooked my fingers in the bodice of her dress, hauling her against me. "You know, I thought this purple was my favorite color on you, but I was wrong." I bit down on her lower lip, tugging it between my teeth. "It's green."

She shoved at my chest and moved her face away from mine. "You think this is funny?"

"More like ridiculous."

"I don't know what idea you had about this whole impregnate-my-bestie scenario, but while this is going on, you're not going to be hitting on other chicks."

"Noted."

"And if I actually do get knocked up, you're not going to be bumping uglies with anyone while I'm waddling around in muumuus. It's not going to happen."

"Also noted. Will you be barefoot while walking in muumuus? I'll probably need pictures if so."

She poked me in the side. "This isn't a joke. I get that you just can't help being so damn sexy that women throw themselves at you right and left, but you better freaking try."

I cocked a brow and framed her cheeks between my hands. "I'm going to need you to repeat that. All of that. Like twenty times. Feel free to add some heavy breathing around the sexy part for effect."

Her lips almost twitched into a smile, but she wouldn't meet my gaze.

"Hey."

Nothing.

"Ally Cat," I said softly, and she looked up at me, her golden-brown eyes wary. "I'm not interested in that woman. In any woman, for that matter, except the one standing in front of me."

"I didn't say you had to lie. Just while you're dipping your wick in this pot, you're not going to in any other. All I'm saying."

"Your pot is all I need or want." I nearly added more. So much more. Every hour that passed, I had more inside me for her, and I was just beginning to untangle what that might mean.

But she wouldn't have believed me anyway. Not now. Maybe not ever.

The corner of her mouth ticked up. "You do have your own form of sweet talking, gotta give you that."

"I have my own form of many things, as you're learning." I brushed a kiss over her ear. "I asked you what your Facebook relationship status was. I think we need to come up with one for this."

"Oh, we do, do we? Because being Facebook official is very important."

"It is." I reached down and cupped her ass through her thin dress, swallowing a groan at the barely there outline of her panties beneath. Would they be white lace? Blush pink? Maybe some other nearly translucent color that would never be enough to hide her swollen pussy from my gaze. "If another guy comes near you, even looks at you, I may rip his eyes out. Just fair warning."

"Is that so?" Her breathless question had me tightening behind the zipper of my pants.

"So you might want to consider a Facebook status as a humanitarian gesture. A warning sign to save other men from a fate worse than death."

"I've never seen you get violent. Or jealous. For that matter, I'm simply not the kind of woman men go batty for." She shrugged and shifted her feet. "I think it's because I'm missing the feminine gene. I'm wearing this dress right now, and all I want to do is take it off and get back into my jeans."

"You think dresses are what make you feminine?" I looped a couple of strands of her hair around my fingers and tugged. "I'd say what makes you feminine is that you're the bravest, smartest, most kickass woman I've ever known." I lowered my voice. "And the way you purr deep in your throat when you come. That too."

"What am I, a cat?" But there was no mistaking the pleasure in her voice.

Pleasure I'd put there, just by telling the truth.

My reply was smothered by her placing her hand over my mouth. "No pussy jokes. We have to get back upstairs."

"Mmm-hmm." I nudged her hand aside and squeezed her perfect ass one more time. "Don't suppose you'd be willing to play sex-on-the-beach later? I don't have an ocean nearby, but I do have this nice pile of sand…" I gestured.

"The sand thing was really sweet. Laurie will always have these memories."

"Not sure she likes it any more than you do."

"Sure she does. Wait until all her friends come down here and see this. It's like a kid's dream come true."

"Yeah, yeah, they'll love it. Now back to sex."

She grinned. "As nice as this sand is, you also have a nice big bed." She patted my stomach and my cock jumped visibly enough that she laughed, her eyes dancing. "Thumbs up?"

"All the way up." I cupped my hand around her neck and brought her mouth to mine, sinking into a kiss that was equal parts need and want and relief that she was still mine.

This hadn't ended yet. She'd be in my bed tonight, and if I was lucky, again and again after that.

For as many tomorrows as I could beg, borrow, and steal.

Our tongues tangled and she moaned as I cupped her cheek, tilting her head so I could take more. Always more. Her body curved into mine and I hooked my foot through hers, desperate to feel every part of her flush against me.

The sound of someone clearing his throat jerked us apart. I blinked away the Ally haze and shifted my gaze toward the stairs, somehow not surprised that my cat-quiet brother was standing there with one eyebrow winged up. Then he glanced around the family room, his frown deepening.

"If that's truly sand, your contractor deserves a bad review on Yelp."

13

ALLY

"ARE YOU DADDY'S GIRLFRIEND NOW?"

I stilled the backyard swing with my foot and turned toward Laurie. It was the end of a long day of children running, and laughing, and occasionally crying, usually after tripping on a toy or being denied something vitally important.

Like a second hot dog. Or a Transformer. Or for one little boy, not being allowed to take home the bunny we'd seen scampering through the yard.

That had led to Laurie once again asking for a puppy. Seth had said no, as he always did, but he was definitely weakening.

Softie.

I smiled and stopped fingering the ends of Laurie's curls long enough to remember her question. Not the best time to zone out and think about Seth and floppy-eared puppies.

A quick glance at the back door told me Seth still wasn't on his way back outside. He was probably eating a scoop of ice cream for every one he put in our bowls. We'd had cake earlier, of course, but the man had a sweet tooth for days.

Not that I could talk. I was starving. Again.

And I still hadn't answered Laurie's question.

"I'm still exactly what I always was to him, and to you." I pushed off with my foot and the swing kicked into motion again. "Unless you don't like what you saw today," I said carefully, hoping I was just referring to that aborted kiss she'd witnessed outside the bathroom.

It certainly hadn't been the only incidents of kissing or touching today. Seth couldn't keep his hands off me for long. I wasn't much better, especially when Tina sashayed past, her attention still far too focused on him. I'd had a lot of years of toning down my jealousy where Seth was concerned, but sleeping with him must've toggled off that switch because I'd found myself cleaving to his side more than once. Maybe it was the way he smiled down at me or brushed his hand over my hair or whispered something for my ears only. He'd always treated me as if I were special, and now that we were sleeping together, his attention was even more potent.

Even more dangerous.

Laurie fluffed out her sparkly purple skirt, her forehead wrinkled. I had a feeling she had something she wanted to say, but maybe didn't know how.

I understood far too well, because I did too. Ever since Mr. Hamilton had put that stuff in my head about driving away Marjorie, I'd been full of guilt. I tried to dismiss it as just his way of getting me out of his son's hair—and his bed. But maybe there was a kernel of truth.

"Honey, I hope you understand I'm not trying to take your mother's place. I wouldn't do that. You have your daddy, and he loves you so much, and I love you too, but—"

"But not like my mom." Her chin wobbled and I shifted toward her, my chest tightening until I couldn't breathe.

"No, no, that's not what I meant at all. I just meant I would never try to take her spot, to try to pretend I'm your mom, even though I'd like nothing better." I swallowed over the lump in my throat and reached for her small, chubby, popsicle-stained hand, squeezing it tightly. "Being your mom would have to be the best thing in the world."

She stared hard at me, that wrinkle deepening and reminding me so much of Seth. "Then, why can't you?"

Such a simple question, with such hard answers. The last thing I wanted to do was to give her false hope that her mom might come back into her life. From what I understood, that wasn't going to happen. I also didn't want to indicate I could fill that role. I didn't know how to be a parent, which probably made this whole situation that much crazier. I so didn't feel equipped to take care of anyone. Not even myself sometimes. After the years of caring for my mother, my reserves were low. I wasn't sure I could provide for anyone else.

If we had a baby together, I'd be in that caretaking role all over again in a much more formal role than what I had now with Laurie. Did I want that?

Even as I asked the question, the answer came through loud and clear.

Yes.

Yes, I wanted a child. But rarely dating tended to limit one's chances on finding someone to make that happen with.

Someone *else* anyway.

I'd found my someone early, and he'd found others while I waited. And that was exactly what I'd done. Waited for years for a bus that might've never stopped for me.

Before I'd found more with Seth—stumbled into via his idiotic baby contract—I'd found a strong, pure love for his little girl. One that would never go away.

"I will always be here for you, no matter what," I whispered, making her a promise in my head. My heart. Whatever happened with Seth, Laurie would always have me in her life. "I might not be your biological mom, but I love you just as much." I stroked a hand down her hair. "So if there's ever anything that bothers you, or you want to talk about, I'm here. Okay?"

Laurie didn't say anything for a long time. Then she hurled herself into my arms, clinging tight. Just when I was sure she'd move back and run across the lawn, she glanced up at me. "Can you marry my Daddy?"

Panic wrapped around my throat and squeezed. "Um."

Laurie nodded enthusiastically. "I could wear this." She pulled at her skirts, her smile wide. "Please?"

It sounded like *pweese*, and my heart broke a little that she actually wanted that.

She wasn't the only one.

"Maybe someday," I murmured, hoping like hell I wasn't cursing the situation just by saying that much. In my world, wishing for more got you less. It was so much easier not to hope.

Or dream.

The back door opened and Oliver and Seth stepped outside, carting bowls of ice cream. They were so different despite looking alike. Oliver's hair was shorter and straighter, cropped close to his head. Seth's tended to get shaggy when he wasn't paying attention. Seth had scruff, Oliver was militantly clean-shaven. Seth wore jeans and a raggedy T-shirt, and Oliver had on a dark suit sans tie, his idea of casual wear.

I was pretty sure every single woman in town—and some not—spent a good chunk of their time trying to figure out how to land one of them. Some industrious types might've imagined snagging both for a night or three of fun. Not that they did stuff like that, at least that I knew about. And I would have, because Seth had never been quiet about his hookups.

Killing me a little with every damn one.

"Who wants ice cream?" Seth called, rushing down the steps with Oliver at his heels.

Oliver hadn't said a word about what he'd witnessed before the party. I'd expected him to make some snarky remark about the kiss, but he'd just slanted me a knowing smile now and then, as if we were sharing some private joke.

I'd expected more surprise from him. Unless maybe others had seen something between me and Seth I never had.

Mainly because I'd been so afraid to wish. Wanting was bad enough.

"Me, me, me! I want ice cream," Laurie said, pitching sideways off my lap and nearly tumbling to the ground. I caught her just before she went flying, and Seth shot me a panty-wetting grin.

"Nice save, Lawrence." He sat on the swing and held out a small bowl of ice cream for his daughter. "Neapolitan for Princess Laurie," he said formally, making her giggle as she settled between us and dug in with her spoon.

"Why, isn't this cozy," Oliver said, passing Seth the bowl of ice cream he carried after Seth gave me his.

"Isn't it?" Seth returned before I could reply. "Don't you have stuff to do at home?"

I gasped. "Seth, don't be rude."

"He wants some alone time with his ladies." Oliver winked at Laurie. "Especially Princess Laurie, who was the most beautiful girl at the party."

Laurie giggled and fumbled with her spoon, getting more of the ice cream on her face than in her mouth. I immediately turned to help her, and looked up to catch Seth watching me far too closely.

"Okay, I'm outta here." Oliver leaned forward to brush a kiss over Laurie's head. "See ya, squirt. Sleepover on Friday night?"

"Yes!"

"Great. Bet your daddy will enjoy his sleepover too," Oliver added out of the side of his mouth when Laurie went back to attacking her rapidly melting ice cream.

Seth flipped his brother a discreet cheek middle finger, and Oliver backed away, laughing. "Goodbye, Alison."

I was flushing, I just knew it, so I decided to just wave a few fingers while I shoveled in ice cream.

We stayed outside, eating ice cream and swinging and talking, until it was nearly twilight. By then, a full Laurie had burned off her sugar high by racing around the yard in pursuit of one of the balloons that hung from every tree and post. There was a lot of clean-up left to be done—even beyond Seth's giant sand pit in the family room—but when I stood to see to it, Seth pulled me back down, so close that our thighs rubbed together.

"You've done enough today. Time to relax."

Oh yeah, like I could do that when he was stroking my hip through my flimsy dress. All the while, I made sure Laurie was still occupied with her balloon and not watching us.

"We can't just leave everything out here. If it rains tonight—"

"So stuff will get wet. No big deal. They're folding tables and cheap tablecloths. Easy to replace."

"But that all costs money. No reason to—what are you doing?" I asked breathlessly as he inched up my dress to caress my bare skin.

"Not nearly enough." He turned his face into my hair. "Next time, don't wear panties. I want easier access."

I snorted out a laugh. "Dude, you want me to go commando at a children's party? I was running around all day. Pretty sure a random kid doesn't need to see my muff and be scarred for life."

Seth chuckled and tugged at the edge of my panties. "I'd love to see your muff." He dropped his voice until it was barely a whisper over my skin. "Actually, I've been fantasizing all day about going down on my knees between these pretty pale thighs and licking your pussy until you come all over my chin."

My fingers slid off the condensation on my empty bowl of ice cream. "Hi, little ears nearby."

"She's not paying attention." He tipped up my chin with his thumb. Sometimes he seemed to have ten hands and he knew exactly how to use all of them. "Stay over tonight."

Arguments formed in my head. It had been a long day, and I wanted my bed. Needed that space to myself to regroup after the confusing feelings being with Laurie and her friends had stirred up in me. I'd enjoyed playing with them and keeping them from getting into too much mischief. It was tiring, sure, but it was rewarding too.

Add in Laurie's questions and the whole Tina thing that morning and the conversation with Seth that had come afterward, and I was seriously in want of some alone time.

But then I glanced over at Laurie, babbling to herself as she sat on the grass and poked at her Sleeping Beauty balloon, and absorbed the warm muscles pressed against my outer thigh and I absolutely didn't want to leave. My loft with Sage was fine. I liked it well enough, and maybe someday it could be a home.

This place—and these two people—had been home for me since the day Seth bought the house, right after his divorce.

"Okay."

Seth frowned, his expression so like his daughter's when she was trying to puzzle out something. "Seriously?"

I fought not to smile. "Seriously."

"Babycakes, it's bedtime."

Laurie glanced up and pouted. "No."

I had to laugh. He was about as transparent as glass. "How about a story first?"

"She needs a bath too," I added under my breath.

"Another one?" Seth asked, sounding as petulant as his child. "Twice in one day? A little soil never hurt anybody."

Laurie picked that moment to stand up, revealing the streak of dirt all the way down one leg, ending in a glob on her frilly white sock. I glanced pointedly at Seth.

"Not it," he said under his breath.

"I'll do it." Chuckling, I pressed my bowl into his rock-hard belly and rose to go scoop up Laurie off the ground, balloon and all. "Bath first, then a story. Can even have bubbles tonight."

"Yay." Laurie wrapped her arm around my neck and pushed the balloon in my face. "Here."

"Thanks." I grinned over my shoulder at Seth, and he was doing that way too intent watching thing again. It made my knees tremble and my belly do somersaults. Especially since he was smiling, his eyes warm and brown like melted chocolate.

He liked seeing me with Laurie, almost as much as I enjoyed taking care of her.

Maybe my reserves for taking care of others weren't nearly as low as I'd believed. Somehow taking care of her—and of Seth—filled me up in other ways.

"You coming in?"

He stretched out his legs, still holding the empty bowls of ice cream. Just the shift of his pose widened his legs enough for me to see exactly what was going on in his jeans—and the late day sun definitely wasn't creating any shadows. That gloriousness was all Seth.

I wet my lips and looked up into his eyes. He did the same, except on him the gesture was lazy and lion-like. A king surveying his backyard kingdom, and I was one of his belongings. That should've set my hackles up, but instead, all it gave me was a flutter, way down low.

"I'll be right in," he said.

Nodding, I juggled his daughter in my arms and smiled. "You ready for bath time and a story? Maybe *Mr. Peppermint and the Pushy Poodles?*"

"Yes!" She gave me a loud smacking kiss right on the mouth. "Love you, Ally."

It didn't matter that "love you, Ally" sounded like *lub eww, Awee.* It was probably the sweetest moment of my life.

Sucking in a breath, I tipped my head down to hers. "Love you right back."

The rustle of grass behind me gave me a second to regroup before Seth pulsed his hips against my ass. He truly didn't care that he was harder than wood and just the feel of him against me was enough to soak my panties. In fact, he'd probably done that intentionally.

Casually, he looped his arm around my waist and caught his fingers in the unused belt loops of my dress. "My two favorite girls," he murmured, his breath warm on the nape of my neck.

More flutters, by the dozen this time.

I passed Laurie's balloon to Seth and watched as he tied it to a chair. Then we trooped together toward the back porch stairs. "In we go."

"Not you, Daddy," Laurie said, and Seth gave a big sigh.

"Yes, I know, banned from my own bathroom. Or am I now exiled from the house too?"

Laurie clutched her balloon and stuck out her lower lip while she thought. "Come in."

"Thank you, Princess Laurie." Seth ate up the steps with his long-legged strides and opened the back door just in time to let us pass. "After you, Princess Ally Cat."

"Cat?" Laurie's head came up and she grinned toothily. "I like cats." She turned her head and stared hard at her father. "My little sissy wants a cat."

I lifted my brows. I'd heard much talk about how Laurie wanted another sibling, and supposedly it had spurned Seth's crazy

176

babymaking idea. But I'd never heard Laurie actually talk about the sibling as if she was real—one who could make pet requests, no less.

"Your little sissy?" I asked through the cotton in my throat. "Did you fill out an order form?"

Laurie giggled and dangled from my neck, stretching her arm out as far as she could so she could encompass her father. "Boys suck."

"Nice, kiddo." Seth sighed and tweaked her nose, meeting my gaze over her head. "My child has very specific requests. They seem to get more specific by the day."

The way he was looking at me again… God, it was as if he could see inside my womb and plant a kid there—a girl, because hey, ask and ye shall receive—from the sheer force of his stare alone.

He could definitely get me in the mood to practice, that was for sure.

"Or a dog," Laurie added. "My sissy likes dogs too."

It was so weird to laugh about something that potentially had a big effect on my life too. If she got that sissy she wanted, it'd be via my girl parts. And I didn't mind that thought.

One bit.

"Good to know." I brushed a kiss over Laurie's forehead and sneaked a glance at Seth. "We'll see how that whole ordering thing works out."

It was a dangerous thing to say. To pretend we were a little happy family. A happy, *normal* family, who wasn't playing house for the sole purpose of procreation.

But right now, with Seth's gaze hot on mine, and his hand on the small of my back, it certainly didn't feel like we were playing.

Nor did it when we tucked a freshly clean Laurie in her bed—Seth had waited in his bedroom, as requested—and she asked me to read her story. I figured she'd want her dad to read it to her since he was right there, but nope, she pushed the book into my hand then patted both sides of her bed so we could sit on either side.

My voice was trembling as I started to read about Mr. Peppermint's pushy poodles. The story was lighthearted and fun, and Laurie giggled as the pushiest puppy fell face-first in a puddle. But by the time the puppy was plopped in the kitchen sink to get cleaned up,

Laurie had fallen asleep, her cheek smushed adorably into the pillow and her damp ringlets draping like spun gold across her face.

Gently, I stroked her curls, unable to keep from touching her.

"You love her too," Seth said, and there was more than certainty in his voice. There was awe. Gratitude.

Even relief.

I nodded. "Yes. Didn't you know that?"

His Adam's apple bobbed as he adjusted her thin blanket. He wouldn't look at me. "Different seeing it."

He brushed his hand over her hair, nearly bumping my hand. The ink that swirled up his forearm caught my eye, and following the path higher to where it disappeared under the sleeve of his T-shirt was an imperative. I'd studied his tattoos so many times. The snow leopard one, and most of the others too. Hell, I'd been there as he added to the collection over the years. But it was so much different when I could touch them.

Touch *him*.

"Different seeing this too," he added huskily. I didn't need an explanation of what he meant.

He was reading my desire as plainly as I was feeling it. Because he could read me. He'd always been able to, and I'd finally dropped my shields when it came to wanting him. Now he was getting the whole story.

Or a lot closer to it.

In silent agreement, we eased back from Laurie and rose, trooping silently out of her pink bedroom. Seth stopped to turn out her Winnie the Pooh light, leaving her cheerful carousel nightlights to illuminate the room in case she had a nightmare. He never wanted her to wake in the dark.

He quietly shut the door behind us, then he reached for me. Hands grasping my face, he brought his mouth down hard on mine. Lips that were soft in contrast to his rough touch teased me into responding. Encouraging me to keep up. I went up on my tiptoes, clutching his shirt, my nails digging into his skin. He made a hungry noise in his throat and nudged me into the wall, hiking up my leg to wrap around his hips. He shoved my panties aside and slipped his fingers inside, burying my moan under his insistent kisses. His daughter was feet away from us, safe behind the door, but God, his bedroom was just down the hall.

We couldn't wait. Just could not.

We'd spent so many years stuck in the space between friends and more, and now that we'd moved forward, there was no slowing this train. It was ride it or...

There were no *ors* left. I wanted to ride.

I reached up to tangle my fingers in his hair as he pushed his fingers deeper into my pussy. I couldn't keep from crying out and he kissed me harder, so hard that I couldn't breathe. My head was spinning from lack of oxygen and I was wet, so wet. His thumb brushed my clit over and over while his fingers pumped, and God, I was shameless about rocking into his movements. I couldn't get enough.

When he moved his head, I chased his mouth, my teeth scraping his lips, our noses bumping as I sought his tongue. I needed it almost as much as his touch. He was turning me inside out, owning the parts of me only he knew. They were his.

I was his.

"Goddammit, not like this. Not this time." Abruptly, he yanked back his hand and I whimpered, dropping my head to his shoulder to breathe. I was so close. A heartbeat away. I was throbbing so hard, and I could hear him licking his fingers. Jesus. Then he fisted his other hand in my hair and tugged my head back, offering me his fingers while his wild eyes settled on mine in the dim light of the hall. "In my bed. Not against another wall. Not again."

Consumed with my taste on his skin, I nearly didn't hear him. He watched me suck on him and growled, backing me into the wall again. Bending his knees, he drove upward and the rigid column in his jeans rubbing against my clit was almost enough to push me over.

Almost. I gasped, dizzy, still holding onto his hand as I licked his fingers. I couldn't stop.

He thrust up against me again with only the thin barriers of my panties and his jeans between us, hitting the angle just right. So good.

I dropped my head back, closing my eyes as flashes of light went off at the edges of my vision.

It wasn't an orgasm but it was the next best thing. I couldn't stop shaking. If he'd shoved me down on my knees and told me to deep-throat his cock, I would've done it without blinking. Anything he wanted.

I wanted it too. Any way he could give it to me.

"Christ, you're so fucking hot," he mumbled, buzzing his scruff along my cleavage, on the verge of popping out of the top of my dress. "How did I miss it?"

"Asshole." Indignation fought its way through the heavy lust pulsing in my lower belly. In my breasts. Hell, everywhere. I bit his palm, making him laugh.

He dropped my leg and swooped me up in one smooth move. Epically smooth, since I started to screech and he caught my mouth with his before I could. If I hadn't been more than a little off-center from my near-miss orgasm and being hauled into the air, I wouldn't have kissed him back. Probably. But damn, he was good at it. He kept me thoroughly distracted as he carried me down the hall and backed into his room, kicking the door shut gently behind us.

His next move was to flip on the lights. I expected to be tossed onto the bed like a sugar sack, but he placed me on his messy comforter carefully, as if I was made of porcelain. "Never know," he whispered, reading my thoughts as he drew his fingertip down my belly.

I was still reeling from that when he stepped back and reached behind his head to drag his T-shirt off. Golden abs covered in swirling dark ink rippled, and I swallowed hard, suddenly riveted by the slash of his navel above his jeans. He undid the button teasingly, leaving it gaping while he stepped toward me again where I was spread out on the bed like his feast.

Quaking, wet, needy. All for him.

I still wasn't through kicking his ass for his missing my hotness—though come on, my hotness was debatable anyway—but he was already peeling off my dress as if it served as wrapping for his very favorite present. He touched me reverently, pulling the fabric aside to bare my bra and tiny panties before dispatching those too. Lowering his head, he licked one tight nipple, his gaze locked with mine. Every minute movement made me clench inside, tighter and wetter than I'd ever been. I splayed my legs wider so he could move between them, already writhing against the soft spread under my back.

"Tell me what you want."

I shook my head and shut my eyes. Dammit, he was supposed to know. Wasn't that his job? Best friend and all, for fuck's sake. He was supposed to know I was dying for him to keep doing that to my breasts while he fingered me and made me come. Then he was supposed to move down my body and—

"That's it. Tell me. Every dirty word."

I blinked. Had I spoken? Oh, that wasn't good. Except maybe it was, because he was doing all of that. His big hand covered my pussy, rubbing gently before he parted my swollen lips and stroked my clit in circles. Over and over so that I had to grind myself wildly against his palm. He released my achy nipple with a pop and slid down my body, his intended target clear. Instead of closing my eyes again, I leaned up on my elbows and licked my lips, ready to watch every lewd moment—

"Daddy!"

14

ALLY

THE CRY FROM DOWN THE HALL HAD SETH SCRAMBLING BACK SO fast that I nearly fell off the bed. I grabbed hold of the bedding and tried to haul myself up, but all the build-up without a finish for a second time was giving me one hell of a head rush.

Almost in slow-motion, the doorknob started to turn. Seth flung himself at it while I scrambled for my dress, for a corner of the comforter, hell, even for a damn shoe to cover my nakedness. I settled for Seth's T-shirt where he'd tossed it on the footboard and yanked it over my head just as Seth blocked Laurie's flight into the bedroom.

"What's the matter, sweetheart? Come here." He scooped her up in his arms and cupped her head, holding it to his shoulder while he pivoted and ascertained I wasn't flashing any T and A at his young daughter.

I was already ruing not making a grab for my dress, because what was I supposed to do to cover my lower half? Lace panties were not adequate. But without any alternatives, I tugged the comforter halfway over me and tried to unobtrusively tug them on.

And Laurie was crying, and it just did not matter. Nothing did but making her feel better.

As soon as I'd yanked them up my ass, I flung off the comforter and scrambled toward Seth and Laurie. "What's wrong, honey?"

She cried harder and clung to her father, and for the first time in a long time, I felt as if I didn't belong. As if I didn't have a right to intrude. This was a private moment between them and I wasn't her mother.

I stepped back, pushing my messy hair away from my face, and would've aimed for the bathroom—possibly to have a good cry, though I was even sure why—if Seth's voice hadn't stopped me.

"Ally, c'mere."

Frowning, I looked back to see Laurie knuckling her red eyes with one fist and reaching for me with the other.

I moved toward them and took her chubby hand. Seth shifted to slide his free arm around my waist. "Let's go back to your room." His voice was low and soothing. "We'll read you the rest of the story from earlier."

Laurie curled into his chest while I rubbed my thumb over her soft skin. "Spend the night?" she asked me, peering out from underneath her father's chin. Her lashes were starred with tears.

Seth answered before I had a chance to think of an answer. "Yes, Ally's spending the night. She's going to be spending the night a lot more often from now on. Okay?"

Laurie nodded and stretched out her other arm to me so I could take her. I glanced at Seth, and he held her out to me as if she was mine too.

Eyes scratchy all over again, I pulled her into my arms and buried my face in her still damp hair.

"Story time," Seth murmured, and I nodded.

Together, we walked down the hall to Laurie's bedroom. Gently, I unwrapped her from her ferocious hold on me and set her back on her bed, taking my spot again on the side as if I belonged there. Seth sat on the opposite one. We took turns reading the story, with Seth playing the part of Mr. Peppermint while I played Mr. Peppermint's nosy neighbor. By the end, Laurie was laughing at our exaggerated play-acting, but her eyes were heavy with fatigue.

"We'll stay until you sleep," I said, fussing with her sheet.

Seth nodded.

It didn't take long, maybe ten minutes. We waited another fifteen beyond that, making sure she was out. Then we tiptoed back down the hall to his room and carefully closed the door behind us.

"I like this on you," he said, fingering the hem of the shirt that brushed my thighs. I still hadn't felt comfortable wearing it without pants in front of Laurie, but at least it had covered everything. Mostly.

I started to shrug off the compliment. My emotions were raw and jagged and all over the place. I was still horny yet I wanted to sniffle. So much was changing, and even trying to hold on to what I knew was impossible. Nothing was the same. Not Seth.

Not even me.

"I like wearing it," I said instead, turning my cheek against the worn cotton and taking a nice big sniff of Seth's sugar sex cologne.

"So don't take it off." He grabbed my hips and pulled me close. "I can do what I need to do over, under and through it."

"That sounds promising. And filthy."

"Filthy promises are the best, baby."

The affectionate term made me cock my head at him. I was still Ally, he was still Seth. We fucked, but 'baby' was new.

He took that moment to grip my chin and haul my mouth to his. And like always, his lips were tender when everything else about him was hard.

Especially the stiff cock trapped in his jeans between us.

"I want you so much," he said between kisses, and I nodded, because I got it. Every part of me was trembling to be with him again. Craving that instant when he'd slide inside of me and fill me up.

"But Laurie—"

"Might wake up," I finished.

"Come to bed." He gave me a quick smack on the ass, making me laugh.

I skirted around the bed and got in while he quickly shed his jeans, boxers, and sneakers and followed suit.

Now what? Move toward him? Cuddle with my pillow? Wait for

him to be bowled over by the sight of my collarbone revealed by the saggy collar of his T-shirt?

He didn't suffer from such indecision, however. He just hooked his arm around my waist and dragged me closer, covering my mouth with his before I could so much as sigh.

"I need you," he said, and I couldn't argue. I needed him too. So much.

"Will do better later, promise," he said, anchoring my leg over his hips. I wasn't fully sure what he was apologizing for until the damp head of his cock rubbed against my slit. I bit my lip as he slid all the way in, relishing that stretch even as I winced.

"All right?" He frowned.

"You're big."

"God, I love virgins."

"Not a virgin anymore, wise ass." Slugging him in the chest while his cock was inside me was a new thing, but it fit us somehow.

As did him gripping my thigh and shifting me slightly on my back so he could thrust in and out, over and over, until I couldn't do anything but dig my nails into his shoulders and try to hold on.

"Damn straight you aren't a virgin." He cupped my breast through his T-shirt, rolling the nipple between his thumb and forefinger. "Goddamn, woman, I love fucking you. If only I'd known."

So many things nearly sprung from my tongue.

I knew. I always knew. At least I wished it could be like this with us.

But I didn't say anything, just savored the way he was moving inside me. The rhythm he was building, stroke by stroke.

"Now this pussy is mine. This too." His hand spanned over my belly and shock and pleasure and fear twined inside me, each fighting for dominance. "All fucking mine," he said, staring straight into my eyes as he pulled back and sank home, deeper than before. He braced on one hand, rising above me, his muscled, tattooed chest glistening with sweat in the faint moonlight. "I'm gonna come inside you. So fucking deep."

Part of me, the side that stayed safe behind a wall of sarcasm, shouted out a mental insult.

Yeah, yeah, so do it already so I can finally come too.

186

But the me who yearned to belong to him only nodded and moaned, scraping his back, jerking my hips to prod him to go harder, faster.

"God, Ally." Desperately, he sucked on my breast through his T-shirt, getting the material all wet. My pussy throbbed in tandem with the nipple between his teeth. "You feel so damn amazing. Wanna fuck you over and over, fill you up with my kid. God, I want that."

I tried to swallow over the dust in my throat, to blink away the haze in my eyes. I was so twisted up, so hot and achy all over. All I needed was to come. Then I could think again.

His movements stimulated my clit with every pass, and I'd been so long denied now that probably a strong breeze could've set me off. I cried out, turning my head to bite the pillow.

"Yeah, yeah, that's it." He leaned over me, speeding up until his sweat dripped on my lips. And God, even that was hot. The salt burned where he'd bitten me through our crazy kisses. "Fucking come on me. Now."

It wasn't instantaneous. Maybe later I could take pride in that. But straining toward that peak and not getting there made me frustrated enough to drag my nails down his arm, ripping a groan from him that sure as hell didn't sound like pain. Especially since his cock started to jerk and spurt inside me.

And that was what did it. Not his breathless demands. Just feeling him let go so far inside me, that sticky warmth making me feel so full. It didn't matter if I was imagining I could feel it or not. Just knowing he was coming inside me bare was enough to make me give in too, my hips rising and falling against the mattress as I relished every pulse. I couldn't stop moaning, and this time, he didn't try to cover up my sounds.

We were both too far gone.

He grunted and kept pounding into me with his half-hard dick until we were broken and sweaty and panting.

Then he dropped his head to my breast. I stroked his hair, the words on my lips.

Finally, the truth would be out there between us. No more secrets. *I love you.*

But in the end, I couldn't ruin the perfection of this moment. I couldn't ask for more when he'd already given me so much. More than I'd ever thought could be possible between us.

Maybe we'd even have a baby together. Our own kind of family.

Our own kind of miracle.

15

ALLY

I DIDN'T REALIZE I'D DOZED OFF IN HIS ARMS UNTIL I TRIED TO move. The watery fingers of early morning light peeked through the edges of his dark curtains. He'd pinned me between him and the mattress with his leg and arm. I tried to be annoyed. It would've been easier if I was, but I couldn't work through the molasses-thick emotions threatening to choke me.

Love.

Greed.

Need.

I wanted to belong to him so very badly. Almost as overwhelming was the equal need for him to belong to me.

And that was so very dangerous.

I wiggled out from under his arm and he moaned into my ear. "Where are you going? You said you'd stay tonight."

"And I did. It's morning."

"No." The word was more of a moan and rumbled through his chest and along my back. "I missed the whole thing?"

"We were a little tired."

"There were many little boys and girls, and a very excited one who didn't want to go to sleep last night. Then...a nightmare." He curled his arm under me and danced his fingertips over my inner thigh. "There was also another not-so-little girl who tired me out."

"You wouldn't be calling me fat, would you?"

"God, no. Perfect." He skimmed his finger over my thigh to my hip and cupped my ass to shift us even closer. "You fit me in every way."

I bit back a moan. "Sex is easy, Seth. We're good at that."

"Yeah, we are. It's more than that and you know it."

I stiffened and tried to wiggle free again. I didn't want to hear this now. Not when he was all soft and rumbly with sleep. When he could say things he didn't really mean.

I longed to hear them so badly, and it was way too easy to believe him while my shields were down. Exactly why I didn't want to stay the night with him.

Pillow talk was dangerous. Recriminations were even worse.

He rolled me over and nudged my thighs open.

"Seth." I wasn't sure I could resist him and he must have heard the warning in my voice. He settled down until I couldn't move, but he didn't slip inside.

He could have.

He was hard and I was weak when it came to this part of us.

Instead, he cupped my face. "I love that you slept with me all night. That you allowed me to fill you up and hold you close. That even now we may have a family growing between us. But that's not all this is about. It hasn't been for a damn long time."

I closed my eyes.

I couldn't face those dark eyes. I knew he loved me in his way. The hugeness of our history would always be full of complicated emotions. But there had been so many changes around us and between us.

"Ally."

His voice was low and patient.

I tried to move my hips a little. Maybe I could distract him.

He groaned and buried his face in my neck. "No fair. And I'm not letting you distract me. Open your eyes, babe."

The different endearment startled me enough for my eyes to pop open. Yesterday he'd called me baby. Now babe.

The couple vibes were everywhere, but I didn't dare believe them. If I did and he was just being affectionate—like he might with a friend he loved but wasn't in love with and liked banging—I wasn't sure I could survive it.

"There you are. Don't shut me out. I don't like it. That's not what we're about. We've always had each other's back."

"I know." I hated that my voice was so tentative and shaky. He was right. I was the one changing things, not him. Well, minus his insane idea that had started all of this in the first place. But I was the one who couldn't box up my emotions when it came to him any longer. "Things are different now."

"Not for me."

Well, they sure as hell were for me. Could he really not see that? Was this ever going to work between us if I had to pretend every day?

I leaned up to kiss him. To distract him so I could finally get some much-needed space, but he turned away from me. "Distracting me again. I don't just want this. I love this part of us, but the family we're creating is even more important."

"For Laurie," I said on an unsteady breath.

"Not just Laurie. For us. We both came from families that were a hot mess. I want Laurie to have an amazing mom as well as a sister. That's because of you."

I swallowed hard. Deep down, I'd never truly believed I would have the opportunity to be a mom. His little girl was more than I could've ever wished for. And if I couldn't have all of Seth, at least I'd have a part of him.

A child between us could be enough. I hoped.

"I learned from the best." I blinked away the rush of tears.

"You sure did. I wanted your mom to adopt me. One of the many reasons I want you in Laurie's life. Can't you see how perfect this is? How we are?"

"I'm so not my mother."

"You're even better."

I tried to shift him off me. "Stop. I don't need you to butter me up. I already said yes."

"That's not what this is." He let me up, but didn't move away. In fact, he reached for me, gripping my hair and dragging my gaze up to meet his. "I couldn't imagine anyone else being the mother of my child. I wish you really were Laurie's mother too, but I can't wish away her mother because she's part of Laurie. And Laurie is perfect just the way she is."

"Yes, she is."

"But the fact you love her so completely makes up for the rest."

The rest. Aka his brief, shitty marriage.

My chest tightened. It really was my fault Marj had left. He'd practically admitted as much.

I wanted to roll into a ball. I was the reason that little girl didn't have a mother.

He lowered his mouth to mine. "Don't cry, baby. I know you miss your mom."

I clung tighter to him, letting him believe the grief living inside me was because of my mother. I missed her desperately, but I also knew she was at peace.

And she hadn't been for a long, long time.

My tears mixed with his soft, sweet kisses. Because I didn't have it in me to say no. And because I needed this as much as I needed oxygen, I melted into him.

Soft and gentle as rain. Maybe, just maybe…as healing.

I strained under him as we moved together faster. As the morning light streamed over our bed, with Seth braced over me, I wound my legs and arms around him as if I'd never let go.

When he came inside me, I held nothing back.

He nearly shouted out his release when I lifted my mouth to swallow it down inside me. I held that too. I held every piece of him close. I trailed my fingers up his back until his breathing evened.

I liked the stillness of the morning and my brain was too wired to drift off again no matter how tired I was. I sifted my fingers through his shaggy hair. The dark curls twined and teased my skin. Even in sleep, he was hard to ignore.

A thud from out in the hallway made him jump. "Laurie?"

I kissed his temple and slid out from under him. "I'll get her. Go back to sleep."

"Are you sure?" His dark eyes were blurry and unfocused, but the father in him was ready to get up and take care of his little girl. It melted my heart even more.

"Yes. We'll make some breakfast."

He curled his arm under the pillow and slid the rest of the way off me with a low groan. "That sounds amazing. I'll be down in just a few…" He didn't even finish the sentence.

I laughed and pulled the sheet over his distractible ass. I slipped out of his bed and darted for the bathroom. I'd fallen asleep wearing his T-shirt, but it was hopelessly wrinkled. I tossed it into the hamper and glanced at the huge glass shower. Those jets would probably feel amazing.

A second thump from down the hall and Laurie's exaggerated shush put an end to that fantasy. I cleaned up as best I could before rummaging in Seth's drawers for something to wear. I hadn't packed an overnight bag, so a pair of boxers and T-shirt would have to do.

I darted out the door, closing it quietly behind me. Down the hall, Laurie's door was open and her dolls and Care Bears were arranged around a white table. A plastic tea set from one of her friends was set up ever so carefully. Except for the teapot that had somehow ended up under Laurie's bed.

Laurie's tousled blond hair was a halo of snarls around her head. She was searching around the room, picking up toys and discarding them.

"Under your bed."

"Ally!" Her huge blue eyes went wide and she slapped her mouth shut. "Shhh," she said through her fingers.

I tried not to laugh. "Nothing's going to wake up your dad right now. But if you're looking for your teapot, it somehow got under your bed."

"Share Bear was very rude." It came out more like *berry rood*, but she was too adorable to correct.

She was a super smart kid and often spoke in a manner that seemed far beyond her years. But sometimes she was just a four-ycar-old.

"Well, that's not good. Why don't you grab it and we'll go down and make some breakfast for Daddy?"

Laurie crawled across her rainbow rug to the ruffle of her bed. "There you is."

"You are," I corrected.

"That's what I said."

I snorted. She picked up her teapot and set it on the table then proceeded to take each of her stuffed animals off the table.

"You can bring down one of your friends."

She looked up at me with her arms full of Care Bears. "But Ally."

"We're going to make pancakes. It gets too..." I trailed off when she dropped three out of the four in her arms and ran for the door. "Sticky." I crossed my arms. "Laurie?"

She halted. "Yes?"

"Is that how you treat your toys?"

She scrunched up her face and hugged Share Bear tighter. "Um, yes?"

"I don't think so."

She sighed dramatically. "Okay, but only because I should put my friends on my bed." She set Grumpy Bear and Leo on the bed. "There, just like Daddy."

"Grumpy?"

"No. Friends in bed. All snuggled like you and Daddy."

My eyes widened and I choked. "Uh, let's go downstairs, okay?"

"Okay. Can we have chocolate chip pancakes?"

"How about banana?"

She put Share Bear in a headlock as we neared the stairs. "Ohh. I've never had those before."

"Never? We need to fix that ASAP. How about banana with peanut butter?"

She squinted up at me. "I don't know. That sounds gross."

"Banana and Nutella?"

"Now we're talking."

I laughed and took her hand as we went down the stairs. "Sounds like a plan."

When we got downstairs, I pulled out the ingredients for pancakes.

I'd been with Seth when he picked out all the things for his kitchen. I knew where almost everything was.

Well, except the cinnamon evidently.

I opened doors and backtracked to the pantry.

"What are you looking for?"

"Cinnamon."

"Oh." Laurie zoomed out of the kitchen into the hallway. She came back with a white bag full of supplies. She couldn't quite lift it, so she dragged it along the floor. "Daddy went to the store for cookies stuff."

"Thank goodness for Daddy," I murmured as I moved forward to reach for the bag.

"I got it."

I held up my hands in surrender. "All right." Still watching her, I pulled down the cast iron skillet and started the bacon.

She huffed and I prayed the bag wouldn't explode as she dragged it over the threshold and over every grout line of tile. When she stopped in front of me with the biggest smile ever, I decided right then and there I'd have cleaned up five pounds of flour and sugar for her without complaint.

"When did you get to be such a big girl?"

"I'm four, silly."

"You sure are."

She looked up at me with the bag straining from her fingers. "Okay, you can have it now."

I lifted the bag onto the island counter. "In fact, you're such a big girl, I'm going to make you help me with the mixer."

"You are?"

"Yep. Where's your chair?"

She zipped away again to get the little chair Seth had bought so she could help him cook. How many times had we cooked dinner with her? A dozen. More?

Had to be more.

And yet Laurie seemed even taller now. She was growing out of her baby face and chubby legs and arms. My eyes misted. She wasn't even mine, but I was mourning the loss of the baby I'd helped raise.

The nights when Seth was beside himself with worry, the triumphs, and even the meltdowns. I'd been here with him more than not.

Until my mom had taken a turn for the worse. There had been little room for anything other than her at the end and I'd missed out on a lot with Laurie. I didn't realize how much I'd missed this little girl until now.

She pushed the chair beside me and climbed up on it, then held up her hand. "Oh. Forgots."

She clambered down and I had to stop myself from helping her as her feet dangled before she dropped to the floor. Instead, I busied myself with flipping the bacon and pulling off more strips from the package.

I tightened my hold on the tongs when she skimmed too close to the counter. She was so very independent. Allowing her to do things for herself was one of the hardest things I'd had to learn. She made a beeline for the far wall. There were two adult height hooks with a black and a white apron on each, then a shorter one adorned with fairy wings that held a smock and two child-sized aprons. One purple with yellow flowers and a hot pink one with white butterflies.

Laurie went right for the pink.

I grinned and followed her. "Think your Daddy would mind if I borrowed his?"

"No. Just don't touch Unca Ollie's black ones. He no like people touching his stuff."

I grabbed one of the white ones and looped it over my head. Seth was quite a few inches taller than me, so I had to tuck it up a little higher before wrapping the strings around my waist.

Laurie pulled the pink strap over her head and twisted around in circles to try and get the ties around the back. After she made three rotations, she finally huffed. "Can you help me?"

I laughed and crouched down in front of her. "Of course. Turn around."

She spun around and lifted her hair out of the way. She smelled of baby shampoo and watermelon. I dragged her in for a quick squeeze and tickle. She giggled until I lifted her to set her on the chair.

"I can do it!"

"I know you can, but I need to get you in front of the mixer real quick. Your dad is going come down as soon as he smells bacon and coffee." I reached for the coffeemaker that was always full and ready to go in the morning. One thing Seth never skimped on was his java.

Laurie wrinkled her nose. "Coffee is gross."

"Coffee is heaven, but it's not for little girls."

"I'm a big girl."

"Yes, but not quite big enough for coffee."

She made a little humming sound. "I don't want it anyway."

"Coffee is mana from heaven."

The deep voice behind me made my skin instantly flush. Seth slipped his arms around my waist and dragged me back against him. He tucked his chin into my neck. "I thought I liked the T-shirt, but those boxers are giving me ideas."

Right then, I was very glad I had an apron on. I elbowed him and Laurie giggled.

"Hi, Daddy."

"Hi, Munchkin. What are you making?"

"We're gonna make nana pancakes," she said.

"Banana pancakes? I could go for those." He flicked his finger under the apron and stroked across my belly. "Are you having a craving maybe?"

I rolled my eyes and slipped out of his arms. I felt weird cuddling with him in front of Laurie. Weird because I wanted it so very badly.

Her eyes tracked over us and a lopsided smile tugged at her lips. "Daddy has scruffles."

I slid my palm over my neck. "He does."

"You have red marks all over. Did Daddy play tickle monster with you?"

Seth snorted and covered his laugh by turning toward the bacon on the stove.

"Don't eat all of the bacon." I glanced over my shoulder and sure enough he had a piece in his mouth.

"Just one."

I moved to Laurie and poured flour and cinnamon into the mixer.

"I can do it!"

I winced. "Sorry, kiddo. You can crack the eggs. Hang onto your chair."

"M'kay."

I swung over to the fridge for supplies and with my arms full, I couldn't avoid Seth's ambush. He cupped my face and settled a soft kiss on my lips. He tasted like toothpaste and bacon and all of that was wrapped in his toasted sugar scent.

"Daddy!" Laurie's giggle filled the room.

"Sorry." He turned and did the same to his daughter, you know, without the tongue part though.

My system had little time to readjust from the highest highs of touching him, and sleeping with him all night, and now to domesticity. It was all so jarring. I'd been careful not to allow our interactions in front of Laurie to be too familiar and now it seemed like every boundary was gone.

Was it just my imagination? Or maybe I just wanted it that way.

"Ally, hungry."

"Right." I blinked out of my stupid overthinking moment and grabbed the bananas on my way by. I dumped all the fixings on the counter and went to work teaching Laurie how to make banana pancakes.

By the time we were done, we were covered in flour and my arms were dusted in cinnamon. The three of us soon figured out a system for the pour, flip, and finish of each silver dollar pancake.

Seth stole a kiss when I passed him the cup of Nutella.

"Hey. None of that."

He leaned down with a smile and nibbled at the corner of my mouth. "Was just getting the bit of chocolate there."

"Uh huh." I flicked out my tongue to find he'd actually been telling the truth.

"Don't tease a man. I have other things I want to do with that tongue."

My stomach jittered and my heart pounded. Before he could lean down again—and God, did I want him to—Laurie yelled from the dining room for the chocolate spread.

"Coming," Seth said against my mouth.

"Not yet."

His smile slid from sweet to calculating. "Oh, I'll fix that soon enough."

"Daddy!"

I laid my hand against his chest. "Go on. We'll finish later."

"Oh, you will. Again and again."

I swallowed as he backed through the swinging door. I quickly washed my sticky hands and grabbed the bacon to follow him when I caught the telltale colors of our high school on an envelope stuffed in the napkin holder on the counter.

I set the bacon down and slid the card out. Seth's bold checkmark was the first thing I saw. I scanned upward and my stomach pitched.

Reunion.

God, how could it be ten years already?

Ten years and I'd done absolutely nothing.

I dropped the invitation and had to curl my fingers into my palm. For God's sake, they were shaking.

Seth pushed his way back into the kitchen. "What's taking you so long? Your pancakes are going to be ice-cold."

I looked up at him.

"Hey. Are you okay?" He rushed forward and slid his hand along my hip.

"Fine. Just gotta get the bacon."

He frowned down at me. "I know that fake smile. That's the one you give Patty Duncan when she's gossiping."

"It's nothing."

His gaze slid down to the counter. "I forgot, I was going to mention that to you. I wasn't sure if they were forwarding mail to your new place. I gave Jill your new address, but I wasn't sure if you got the invite." He stroked his thumb over the raised type on the card. "I'm excited to see everyone."

"Yeah, definitely." My voice was flat, and I had to tamp down my astonished laugh. No way did I want to go back and see those people.

High school held a lot of crappy memories for me. My mom being sick on and off, along with generally just feeling as if I didn't fit in. I'd never really come to terms with being the best friend of one of the most popular guys in school. Not that Seth tried to win over people. He just attracted them without effort.

Basically, he was the anti-me in so many ways.

He picked up the bacon. "Yeah, Brad and JT texted me. They're coming in from California. The Three Musketeers ride again. Come on, let's eat."

"Right." I followed him and tried to shake off the dread filling my chest.

Seth set the bacon down as he filched another piece. "Hey, Munchkin. Did I ever tell you that Ally and I went to school together?"

Laurie was nibbling around a misshapen pancake on her fork. A ring of chocolate stained her lips. "Mmm. Big kid's school? Or like me."

"Half-day pre-K is almost big kid's school." I smiled. "We went to high school together. You'll go to high school in about forty years."

Laurie's mouth rounded and I laughed.

"Not quite forty, but close. Don't want you to grow up too fast, munchkin." He took a bite from his plate and popped another piece of bacon in his mouth. "These are really good." Then he pushed his chair in so he could round the table to go to the hutch.

My stomach dropped as he licked his fingers and pulled out the yearbook standing beside his senior picture. He still loved looking back on those glory days.

"God, you still have that?"

He grinned and sat down at the table. He pushed plates out of the way and flipped pages. "Of course I do." He spun the book to show his daughter. "Do you remember Daddy's friends? Brad and JT?"

Laurie cocked her head. "I don't think so."

He was grinning down at the picture of the lacrosse team. I remembered how amazing he looked on the field. All those muscles and aggression wrapped in a boy becoming a man.

And now he was so much more than the cocky kid on the field.

And me? Not so much. I was stuck in the same place as if ten years hadn't gone by at all.

Before I could stop it, I blurted out my disbelief. "You really want to see all of them again? All those judgy people."

He laughed and looked up from the pages. "Well, most of them are still in town with us. Not like it's a big deal. Besides, let them judge me. I have everything I could want." He swiped his hand over Laurie's head then tickled behind her ear.

Laurie grinned around a slice of banana.

I stabbed at my pancake and forced down a few bites. Of course he did. All the things he wanted were right in front of him.

And me? I was looking in on the world again. The almost family behind glass. I was good enough to make a baby with him, and to help take care of his daughter, but I wasn't part of them. Not really.

He flipped the page. "Oh, man. Remember those letters we had to write to our future selves? God. I don't even remember what I wrote."

I certainly did and it made everything worse.

I pushed back from the table and picked up empty plates. I'd barely eaten, but my stomach was twisting so much I couldn't choke down any more. "Done, sweetie?"

Laurie was poking at the banana on her plate instead of eating. She set her fork on her plate with a nod.

Seth didn't look up from the glossy pages. "I got it. You cooked. I can clean up."

I nodded. "Okay. I need to go upstairs and get dressed."

"What?" He stood, closing the book. "Why? I thought we were going to hang out today."

"I didn't agree to that. I have to work. As it is, I'll probably catch he—um, heck—for being late."

He glanced down at his watch. "You don't usually go in until ten."

I swallowed. I couldn't be around him right now. Too many memories were bumping into my pathetic reality. "I need a shower and to get ready."

He sighed. "Are you sure you can't call in?"

"Some of us don't have that luxury."

Seth blew out a breath. "Dammit, you know I didn't mean it that way."

"Dollar to the swear jar!" Laurie chirped happily.

I wiped my fingers on my napkin and pressed a kiss on top of Laurie's head. "You tell him, kiddo. Thanks for helping me cook this morning."

She grinned up at me with chocolate smeared all over her face. "Thankie, Ally."

"Daddy will wash your face." I gave him a pointed look and escaped.

Not that I got too much of a head start. Five minutes later, he was bounding upstairs with *The Care Bears* blaring from the living room.

I'd slipped into my dress from the night before. *Hello, walk of shame.*

"Do you really have to go?"

"I do." I didn't want to turn and look at him. He was too good at making me forget just what this was between us. I had to remind myself that we weren't a happy little family.

No matter how much I wanted it to be so.

He crossed to me. "Can you come back tonight?"

"I'm tired, Seth."

He tugged me close and linked his arms around me. "We have babymaking to accomplish."

One more reminder. *Thanks, buddy.*

I pushed out of his arms. "Can we take tonight off?"

"Is everything okay?" He slid his fingers into my hair and turned me toward him.

"Fine. I'm just tired. Someone didn't let me sleep last night." *Please don't see my fake smile. Just let me get out of here.*

"I'd really like to not let you sleep again tonight." He tipped up my head and pressed a kiss on my lips.

I closed my eyes and almost let myself slide back into him. Back into the status quo we found without skipping a beat.

I cupped his face and ended the kiss, reluctantly opening my eyes. "Maybe tomorrow, okay?"

He sighed and pressed his forehead to mine. "All right. I have a ton of meetings this week anyway. I guess I should get ready for them. The birthday party kind of took over."

"See? Perfect." I swallowed down the lump in my throat and stepped back. "I'll text you later."

He frowned and twisted his fingers around mine. "All right."

Grabbing my purse, I strode out of the room and jogged downstairs. I didn't wait for him. I couldn't.

Not if I really wanted to leave.

I stopped in and said goodbye to Laurie, but she barely looked away from the screen. *The Care Bears* were far too enthralling.

He followed me to the door and dragged me back before I could go down the front porch steps. The kiss was hot and heavy and the lump in my throat grew even larger. So much that I thought I was actually going to choke.

I wouldn't cry. It wasn't his fault I didn't know how to keep up with how things were supposed to be.

I wasn't supposed to want more.

I pulled back and smiled. "I'll see ya."

His smile was soft and sweet and it took everything inside me not to let the tears brim over. "See ya tomorrow."

"Sure." I turned to leave and he snagged my hand.

"Hey. The munchkin's graduation?"

God, I'd almost forgotten. "Of course. I wouldn't miss it."

"Are you okay?" His eyebrows lowered.

"Yes. Just can't believe she's growing so fast." I sniffed. At least these tears made sense as far as Seth was concerned. Right now, I was more than willing to hide my face in his shoulder. "She's getting to be such a big girl."

He laughed. "I'm so glad I'm not the only one freaking out."

"Not just you." But if I didn't get out of there I was going to absolutely melt down and that wouldn't work. He'd never believe it was just Laurie growing up on us.

Him.

Me. Sort of.

God, what a damn mess. I stepped back again. "I've got to get to work."

"All right. But hey, wear something extra pretty. Not that you're ever anything else of course." He kissed my temple. "But I want to show off my girls."

"I'll do my best."

There was no way I was going to be able to hold off all the emotions running amok in my damn head.

I ran down the driveway to my car and turned to wave at him. As soon as he went back inside, the tears fell. I couldn't have stopped them if I wanted to.

16

ALLY

I sat in my car nibbling on oyster crackers from my stash from the diner. I'd been a complete wreck the whole night and anything I ate this morning made me nauseous.

Oliver and Seth stood together under the stately oak tree at the edge of the property. Main Street was alive with pedestrian traffic thanks to the shops, and the forty or so parents trying to wrangle children.

One of Laurie's boyfriends—the girl had a few—had escaped for the lake. Weston's dad, Dare Kramer, had him tucked under his arm as he hauled him back up to the white folding chairs.

He was a handful, but Dare was patient if a little frazzled most of the time. Another single dad who stepped up when needed. There were far too few of them in this world.

All the little perfect pieces of the town I loved so much.

The perfect place to raise a kid.

I'd been doing it informally with Laurie for years, and now Seth was dangling the possibility in front of my face.

I focused on the little girl twirling between the twin brothers. So different, and so much the same. Even here, when they were both dressed for work, somehow they were still on the opposite ends of the spectrum.

Seth with his laid-back summer-weight jacket in a perfectly acceptable wheat color over dark jeans and a white dress shirt sans tie. And then there was Oliver, who looked like he was about to head into the city for a meeting with people on Wall Street. His navy Savile Row suit was crisp and perfect even with the sun beating down on them.

The only thing that matched on the two men were the indulgent smiles for Seth's daughter. She was full of happiness from the colorful purple and pink dress with butterflies dotting the hem, to her slightly crooked blond braids. Somehow Laurie had turned into a little girl instead of staying the baby I'd helped to raise. Even when I'd drifted away from them for a few months, she was so much mine in more ways than I ever wanted to face.

Why the hell couldn't I just calm down about all of this? Let things happen as they happened.

Because you love him madly.

I slumped down in my seat and cursed when Laurie spotted me and came running. No turning back now.

I took a swig from my water to swallow the paste the crackers had become in my dry mouth. Then I swung the door open and rose, catching Laurie against my leg before she could knock me down. "Hiya, munchkin."

"Yay, you came."

"Of course I did. I wouldn't miss it." I crouched down in front of her and smoothed a flyaway blond curl around her ear. "I love your dress."

"Daddy got it for me."

"Did you guys go shopping together?"

"Yes." She buried her face in my neck and looped her arms around me. "Do I have to go up there?"

I laughed and wobbled on my heels thanks to the gravel path. "No. You don't have to. But don't you want to go up there and show your dad what a big girl you are?"

She shook her head against my shoulder.

I swung her up into my arms. "Yes, you do. You'll be up there with all your friends. And you want to show off your pretty dress, right?"

"Yeah." Her voice was small, but less scared.

"See? Oh, and you get a diploma. Just like the big girl you are."

"Diploma?"

I shifted her onto my hip. "Yep. A paper that says you are a very important little girl." I moved toward the brothers, still carting my precious cargo. "Even though we already know you are, right, Dad?"

Seth's eyebrows shot up behind his aviators. "Of course." He gave his little girl a huge smile. "What are we doing?" he asked out of the side of his mouth.

"She's a big girl now. She's definitely going up on stage to get her diploma."

"Oh, right. Definitely. I can't wait to take a million pictures of you, munchkin." He poked his finger into her side and she wiggled in my arms.

"No, Daddy."

"Okay, maybe one hundred pictures?"

She giggled. "No. Ten is good."

Seth laughed. "Ten, huh?"

"Yes. One for you, one for me, one for Grandpa, one for Unca Ollie…" She put her hand against my cheek. "One for Ally. She's just like a mama, right?"

I nearly dropped her.

Seth moved in close to me and slid his hand down my back. "Would you like that, baby girl?"

"Big girl," Laurie said quickly.

"Sorry. My big girl." Seth brought his hand up to my ponytail and stroked it absently. "Our big girl."

Laurie leaned into me and tangled her fingers in the chain of my arrow necklace at the nape of my neck. "I would." Then she reached up to her dad. "A lot, a lot."

I swallowed down a lump threatening to strangle me.

Seth hugged us closer to him. "I'd like it a lot, a lot too."

I looked up at him, but couldn't see exactly what was going on behind his mirrored glasses. His familiar cologne and the smell of coffee mixed with the watermelon scent of Laurie and they made my head spin.

Did he have any idea what he was saying?

Was he really saying it?

I opened my mouth, but screeching feedback from the podium cut me off.

Laurie winced and slapped her hands over her ears. "Loud."

A woman in a bright yellow dress leaned toward the microphone. "Parents, we're just about ready to begin."

"How about that? It's time to begin. Ally and Uncle Ollie will be sitting with me right there." Seth pointed to the left side of the folding chairs. "Let's bring you up there, okay?" He swung her out of my arms and up high in the air. "My pretty girl is graduating today."

She laughed and clutched at his arms. "Carry me, Daddy?"

"You got it." He turned back to me. "I'll meet you up there?"

I nodded and blinked back the sudden wash of tears threatening again. God, hadn't I cried enough last night?

I met Oliver at the chairs and noted that only three of them were reserved. None for me?

Oliver looked up from his phone. He took the program off the chair to his left. "I saved you a seat."

"Where's your father?" I sat down and crossed my legs under my long summer dress.

Oliver's jaw flexed. "Not here."

"Right." I swallowed and turned my attention to Seth and Laurie. How many times had the elder Hamilton bailed on these things? And yet there was Seth, bent down talking to Laurie as the teacher lined them up. He never missed a single event for her. Somehow I knew he was giving her a pep talk. A single father completely devoted to his little girl.

Even if his father and mother had been less than ideal in that arena, Seth excelled at parenting. So much so that I was afraid I'd never be as much of a natural as he was.

He headed back with a sweet backwards wave to his daughter before he took the seat beside me. His knee bounced as he cracked his knuckles. He scrubbed his palm down his thigh with a laugh. "I'm nervous. Crazy, right?"

"First of many graduations." I smiled up at him.

He flipped his hand, palm up and spread his fingers. "I guess you'll just have to hold my hand through all of them."

My throat clogged again, but I couldn't resist the gesture. I laced my fingers with his and turned to watch our little girl.

For the first time, I felt as if we could truly be a unit and it scared the crap out of me.

17

SETH

WHAT WAS THAT OLD SAYING? YOU CAN NEVER GO HOME AGAIN? I was learning that applied even when you'd never left your hometown.

The old homestead wasn't all you couldn't return to. You also couldn't go back to high school and pretend you were still eighteen when all you cared about were the three Ps—partying, Pabst, and pussy.

I still loved pussy. Ally's in particular. I sat back in my chair and rubbed my forehead. Actually, I didn't want any other.

Ever.

Christ, lightning bolts hurt. This one had jabbed me before, causing sizzling little bursts of revelation—usually quickly ignored—but now reality speared me between the eyes.

We weren't just making a baby. We were making a life.

"I think we need to go out the night before the reunion and get fucking trashed," JT said on the phone, and I grunted.

Not in agreement. Not in approval. Nope. Wasn't gonna happen.

"I have a kid, you know. I can't just spend the night getting lit."

"So what? I might have a kid out there too, somewhere. You don't see it slowing me down, man." JT laughed heartily and I swallowed a sigh.

I'd called JT to rehash old times while I ate half a turkey sandwich at my desk in between meeting with clients. Afterward, I intended to bike ride down to the bank before my slate of appointments later in the afternoon. It was a nice day out. Maybe I'd even stop at the bakery and see if they had any of those half-moon cookies Ally liked. If I brought a couple to the diner, maybe she'd soften up enough to talk to me.

It had been several days since the graduation. Surely by now she had to be over the whole wanting space thing she'd mentioned the day we'd made breakfast.

Her weirdness had started right around when she'd found that reunion invitation. But that didn't make sense. She'd had a good time in high school too. Or so I'd thought.

All I knew was that right now, JT wasn't funny, and I wasn't feeling the old times gig as much as I'd expected. Maybe because the best part of my past was also part of my present—and hopefully my future.

"Yeah, well, mine lives with me, and I'm not going out to get wasted. She's already spent the night with her uncle once this month."

"Come on, the kid needs some freedom."

"Freedom like I had? My dad never gave a shit if I was home, but I better not do anything to tarnish the precious family name."

Even as I said the words, I regretted them. My dad could be thoughtless, and he definitely wouldn't win the father of the year award, but he hadn't been a bad parent.

At least he'd stuck around, unlike my mother.

Unlike Laurie's.

Fuck, were we doomed to repeat every pattern in our lives? Just like I'd pulled a page out of my father's playbook by paying off Marjorie, I'd tried it again with that stupid contract.

I yanked open my top desk drawer where the contract still resided. I was going to set that stupid thing on fire.

Ally and I didn't need signatures between us. We weren't about that. We made our own damn rules.

"Look, dude, I'm just saying it'd be fun if we cut loose and partied like we did in the old days. But if you're not cool with that, then me and Brad will just see you at the reunion."

"That's probably a better idea. Maybe we can get a beer afterward," I added, though I already knew that probably wouldn't be happening. Ally would be with me, and she'd been clearly uncomfortable when the subject of high school had come up. I wasn't entirely sure why, but it didn't matter.

If she didn't want to do the whole reunion thing, we'd make our appearances, talk to a few people, and split. I preferred spending the night with her and my little girl anyway.

"Sure, man, whatever you want. I'm just glad to be seeing you and Brad again. I've been missing those old days something fierce. Nothing's been like them, you know? We had the life back then."

His words were still echoing in my head after I'd hung up. I'd had fun going down memory lane for a few minutes the other day, but perhaps I didn't need that blast from the past as much as I'd thought.

My present was pretty damn awesome.

I pushed aside the remnants of my turkey sandwich and flipped open the folder. I would tear up the contract. And in case Ally didn't get how serious I was about her—about us—I'd bring the damn thing back to her in pieces. Maybe then she'd relax a little and let things happen.

If that was even what she wanted.

My gaze scanned the page on top automatically. She'd faxed over the house paperwork separately, so the only thing that should be in this folder was the contract I'd given her. And it was, all signed, sealed, and delivered.

Just not with her name.

Your Ally Cat was written in her tight little scrawl, and fuck if it didn't make me smile.

She *was* mine, and she had been since high school. And if we went to that reunion together, there wasn't a person there who wouldn't know it.

Especially her.

I shoved the folder across the desk and rose. Actually, nope, I wasn't going to tear up the contract. Not where I had it in writing that she was mine. I'd take proof in whatever way I could get it.

She wasn't going to shut me out forever.

I'd made it halfway to the door when Oliver swung into the room, his briefcase in one hand and his eyebrow already climbing for greatness. "So you drove her away, hmm?"

Frowning, I stopped dead. "Drove who away?"

"Why, Alison, of course. She's the only woman in your life, isn't she? Perhaps not." Oliver moved forward to sit on the corner of my desk. "That would explain the secrecy. You have to know friends with benefits never works out well long-term. Or maybe you don't. Consider it free advice. Just another of Oliver's—"

"You don't have any friends, so what would you know about it?" I muttered, not caring if the jab hurt. My brother certainly never worried overmuch about his pointed remarks in my direction. "Oliver's Life Lessons", he called them.

I usually offered a lifted middle finger as thanks.

"I know Alison has called out sick all week to work and Sage grew desperate enough to ask me if I'd seen her. I indicated I had not. Clearly, she's not warming your bed either."

As if he'd dropped a giant weight onto my shoulders, I returned to my desk and sank into my chair. "She's called in? She never does that. Maybe she really isn't feeling well." Hope bloomed inside me as I did some quick calculations. It was early, but possible. She could definitely be feeling some twinges if something had taken root.

But she hadn't called me.

I reached for my desk phone just as Oliver snatched up the folder. And started to read while I stared almost unseeingly at him.

My slowness to react had to do with the possibility Ally could be pregnant. That was the only reason I had for not leaping to my feet and yanking the folder out of my snoop of a brother's hands.

"Well, now, isn't this interesting? A baby contract. Is Ally feeling the need to procreate? She is nearing thirty. I can see why she'd want to move on that sooner rather than later."

"Give me that, you jackass. And no, Ally wasn't feeling anything. I was the one who wanted the baby."

Oliver's brows snapped down as he peered at me over the folder I wasn't getting back unless I wrestled him to the ground—and that might end up happening. "I think you better cut back on those vitamins you've been taking. That ginseng-biloba-whatever mix must be messing with your wiring."

"My wiring is just fine."

"You have a baby. Why would you want another?"

"Laurie is four. Hardly a baby. And I'm not justifying my decisions to you." I narrowed my eyes. "Why is it so shocking that I'd want another kid? The first one came out pretty damn good."

"She did, but one is plenty. What do you think you're going to do? Quit your job and play house husband?" He glanced at the contract. "Seems like you just want her eggs and want her gone. Paying for her school, huh? Guess that explains why Sage mentioned her applying for classes in New York City. Free ride."

Oliver probably kept talking, but I wasn't listening anymore. All I could hear in my head on a constant loop was that she'd applied for school in New York City.

Miles and miles away.

I had no right to feel hurt. That was what I'd suggested all along. We'd make a baby, then she could go to school wherever she wanted. In the back of my mind, I'd always known it was a real possibility whether I gave her the funding or not. Ally mentioned splitting town much less frequently these days than she had right after her mother passed, but every now and then, it still came up.

She wanted a fresh start. Hell, she *deserved* one. My money could give her that.

Equal exchange. And hey, she could always come see our kid on weekends and breaks and holidays. The city was only a little over four hours away. Not that far at all.

"Fuck." I slammed my fist into the desk, barely registering the sting.

Oliver shut the folder. "Didn't know she was applying to schools in New York City?"

"No. I mean, I told her anywhere was fair game."

"You told her. As if she isn't an unencumbered adult capable of making her own choices."

I stayed silent for that one. The truth hurt as much as my now aching knuckles.

"Don't know if you know this, but Dad paid off mom."

My head snapped up. "What?"

"She didn't just take off. They made a deal. He'd finance her lifestyle elsewhere if she didn't try to take him for half in the divorce, thereby forcing him to expose her cheating and other misdeeds in court. Neither of them wanted messy, so she went for it. Last I knew, she was living in Cabo with her new family."

"Cabo?" I rubbed my thumb between my eyes. "Who the hell lives in Cabo?"

"Our mother does. From what I've heard, we have a younger half-sister too. Unsubstantiated, of course. Dad isn't exactly forthcoming on the subject, and the internet coughs up only so much."

I didn't say anything. My mind was so full of Ally that I couldn't focus on anything else.

If she missed work, she must've gone to New York to scope out schools. There was no other explanation. If she was truly sick, she would've been home with Sage. She didn't have any other friends in town she'd stay with. Nor did her budget extend to spur-of-the-moment vacations.

"I did drive her away. Somehow." I braced my elbow on the desk and raked a hand through my hair. "I don't know how to do this. Every time I think we're getting somewhere, we lose even more ground."

"Hamilton men are meant to walk single file."

Normally, I laughed off Oliver's certainty in that direction. For a long time, I'd been half convinced of the very same thing.

Not anymore.

"Meant to end up like Dad, you mean? Bitter and alone, with only his money to keep him company?"

Oliver adjusted his tie. "He has two rather strapping sons as well. One more so than the other."

"Keep trying with your workout routine. Persistence is key." I tipped back in my chair. "Fuck, Ol, how do I fix this?"

No sooner had the words left my mouth, I shook my head. "No. Never mind. I did not ask for your advice. There's desperate and then there's suicidal."

"Actually, maybe I should fix this."

"What? No. God, no."

His laughter was rich and throaty, like any good movie villain. "Seriously, man, pull yourself together. I thought you only wanted use of her eggs. And from the way you were making out the other day at Laurie's party," he cleared his throat, "I'm going to guess you already achieved liftoff there."

"We weren't making out. It was a kiss. We just kissed."

"Hmm, and here I thought you knew how babies were made already." Oliver whisked his fingers over the hairline-straight seam of his trousers. "That might actually explain a lot."

Despite everything, I laughed. "Why are you still here?"

"Because you need help, and I'm a giver."

"You don't even like Ally. I don't know why, but you don't."

"You are as dense as a two-by-four without all the uses." He gave a heavy sigh when I stared at him. "I was jealous. Possibly."

"Of Ally? Why?"

"Not of Ally, per se. Of your relationship with her. The two of you have always been a unit against the world. Before Ally, it was you and me, in case you've forgotten."

"It's different with Ally."

"No kidding. But you never fully realized just how much."

I shook my head. "No. Not until now. Even Marj—" I stopped. "You introduced me to Marj. Kept telling me she would be great for me."

Oliver shrugged and set aside the folder beside my sandwich wrapper on my messy desk. "I never thought you'd knock her up. Or marry her."

"One kind of led to the other," I said drily.

"Yes, well, some of us know how to bag it up. Then again, you're going bag-free intentionally now, so there's no understanding you, brother." Oliver rose and glanced down at me with all the paternalism being six minutes older brought to bear. "Let me try to fix this."

"No. Absolutely not. You don't even know what the issue is, and I'm supposed to let you sweep in and muck things up even further?"

"She's left you without a word. What further muck can I cause?"

I had no answer for that.

"As for not knowing the issue, it's fairly clear. You made up a nonsense reason to sleep with her that didn't require brutal honesty, and now you've finally realized you're in love with her."

"That's completely—" I exhaled. "Accurate."

"Now you'll be stuck with a kid too when all you had to do was admit you wanted to fuck her. As if she would've said no. That woman has looked at you with heart eyes since day one."

"So not true. I drive her crazy. If she had heart eyes—whatever the fuck that is—she wouldn't run away from me every time I get near her. It's like I have a fungus or something."

Oliver held up his hands, palms out. "Officially entering territory labeled 'do not need to know'."

I laughed again. "Oh, and the stuck with a kid part? Wrong. I want that kid with Ally more than anything. I want a family with her. Goddammit, we already are a family, and I want it to be official."

Oliver shook his head. "Oh no, you don't. I already reached my wedding quota with you, pal. One was awful enough. Another would be beyond the pale."

"I didn't say we were getting married. Yet." But now that the idea was rattling around in my head, I had to admit it wasn't displeasing.

She was having my baby, assuming all went to plan. Why not be my wife too?

"Why not?" I repeated under my breath while my brother gazed at me as if I'd grown horns, a tail, and sprouted red skin.

"Before you hear wedding bells, Romeo, you need a bride. Yours is currently MIA. I offered to help you, but if you're so certain you can continue to bungle this all on your own, then fine."

"Seth!"

We both glanced toward the doorway as Sage scuttled into the room. Actually, that was a misnomer. A few days ago, Sage might've scuttled. Her self-confidence appeared to waver with the tide, and she often seemed content to hug the wall.

Today was a different story. She walked into my office with her head held high and her assets swaying. *Visibly* swaying in her tight denim miniskirt and a top that barely covered her breasts. Not that I paid much attention. Sage was a cute girl—and I imagined she had gotten more than her share of catcalls on her way over here in that outfit—but my eyes were solely for Ally.

Now and forever.

"What are you wearing?" Oliver demanded, shocking me almost as much as Sage, who apparently had just noticed he also was in the room. She'd zeroed in on me at my desk like a laser pointer.

"Pretty sure they're called clothes." She sniffed at Oliver and returned her attention to me. "Ally hasn't been to work for three days. She hasn't been at your house so you can impregnate her, has she?"

My eyebrows lifted. So much for assuming Ally had employed discretion regarding our activities. Thanks to Ally sharing with the diner patrons her comical observations about my prowess the day after we'd first had sex, I'd understood it was known that we were lovers. But being lovers didn't mean babymaking necessarily.

"What has she told you?"

"Are the private details besties confide in each other really important?"

"I'm her best friend, and yes, they are."

"No, you're the best friend with a dick, which automatically slots you lower on account of the dick."

"She likes my dick, thank you very much."

Oliver stepped away. "Awkward moment."

"If she liked it so much, why did she run away? She never misses work. And she hasn't slept in her bed. So whose bed is she sleeping in?" Sage stepped forward and impaled my chest with a flame-red nail. "Huh?"

"Thanks for the vivid picture, but I can guarantee she's probably sleeping alone and is perfectly safe." I tried to ignore the icy jabs of panic pricking between my ribs. "She's extremely level-headed."

Sage made a noise in her throat. "Until she hooked up with you."

"Since when do you hate me?" I held out my arms. "I always thought we were good."

"You could hurt her, so I have you under a very watchful eye, buddy. If she's with child, she doesn't need additional stress from your inconsistency."

"With child?" Oliver snorted. "Welcome, Madonna. Oh, and I'll have you know, Seth said they only kissed. Virgin birth, is it now?"

"I did not say that. I said when you saw us—never mind."

As if I'd never spoken, Sage whirled on Oliver, swinging her hips in a way that made my brother's eyes flare wide. "Did I ask you? No. Why are you even here? Don't you have shameless hussies to lie with?"

"Shameless hussies? The fifties ended a long time ago. Oh, and newsflash." He dropped his gaze lewdly to her attire. "Depending on point of view, you might fit into one of those categories you're casting aspersions on."

I winced. Now he was going to get it. And he deserved it too.

Instead, Sage beamed. "Really? Do you honestly think so?" She fluffed her hair. "I'm going for a new look. Wholesome hasn't really been working for me."

"Why?"

"I'm hoping to encounter no-strings sex," she said matter-of-factly.

Oliver smirked. "*Encounter* it? Like sex is a living, breathing entity of its own?"

"In my world, it might as well be." She glanced back at me. "Anyway, that's irrelevant right now. I'm worried about Ally."

"I am too. But I'm sure she's fine. You've tried calling her?" I dug out my phone. I hadn't done anything but text her now and then, wanting to give her time and space.

"Yes. She worked on Sunday, then told me she was taking a few days personal time. But she didn't book it with the boss. She just keeps calling in sick. I don't know what's going on."

"You think she went to check out a school?"

Sage shrugged. "Maybe. She didn't say much about that either. Just that she had to start going after what she wanted. She mentioned before that she was interested in Baruch in the city." She tugged up her V-neck top. "Maybe we should drive down there, scope out the situation?"

"Scope out what situation? And I think we need a bit more to go on than to just pay a visit to some random school." Oliver glanced at me. "I'm going to play a hunch, and if it pans out, I'll get back to you."

"Oh, hell no," Sage said. "Any hunches get routed through me. She's my best friend." She pointed at me. "Quiet, you. You're the one who wouldn't know how to give a girl the fairytale if someone gave you a picture book with directions."

I stayed quiet. I was still tangled up thinking about my supposed inconsistency. And handing out fairytales—what the fuck was *that* about?

Perhaps I was the cause of Ally being so wary to take the next step. Hell, I'd never told her in so many words that I wanted to either. But she was my closest friend. Surely, she had to have some inkling about my inner workings. All of this had taken me by surprise. I was still feeling my way. It wasn't as if I was some expert.

I'd never fallen in love with my best friend before.

Never wanted to be with someone so much that everyone—and everything—else except my little girl paled in comparison.

So maybe I was screwing this up without even knowing it. By not coming clean. By not being clear and saying the words.

By not giving her the goddamn fairytale.

"I'm handling this on my own," Oliver told Sage. "I may be completely off-base. In any case, I have private business with Alison myself."

I pushed my phone back in my pocket and crossed my arms. I was still working out the proper method of handling this, but obviously the phone was not it. No fairytales granted there. "What private business?" I demanded.

"Private," Oliver repeated, already moving toward the door. "If I find out anything, I'll be in contact."

Sage chased after him. "I'll tail you in my car if you don't tell me where you're going."

His laughter drifted down the hall. "Honey, you couldn't keep up with me if you had a Ferrari. Stay here, pet."

"Pet?" Sage spun around and propped her hands on her hips. "He's a complete jerk. How can you even stand him?"

I jerked a shoulder. "Probably comes from sharing a womb. It creates a bond."

"Ugh." Sage flopped in the chair opposite my desk. "He's going to find her and make everything worse. She needs the womanly touch, not an interfering male."

"Ally knows her own mind. She can handle Oliver." I gazed at the folder on my desk. My fingers were itching with the need to trace the words she'd written.

Your Ally Cat.

If she wasn't mine yet, she would be.

A knock sounded at my door and it opened. "Seth, the Parsons are on their way in to sign the papers for the—" My father broke off, his gaze alighting on Sage. "Well, hello there, Sage. What a pleasure. I didn't expect to see you here." My father's smile could have burned a hole through glass.

"Hi, Mr. Hamilton. I'm sorry to interrupt business." Sage was already jumping to her feet.

"No, no, you're never an interruption. Stay, please." He glanced between us, a disturbing glint coming into his eyes. "I can talk to Seth later."

I frowned. What the hell was his deal? He was always sweet as could be to Sage. In fact, he was kind to most everyone in town except Ally, which royally pissed me off. Of course, Sage's parents had just landed one hell of a nice deal when they recently sold their B&B to a developer who had plans to make sleepy Crescent Cove "more cutting edge" and "more in line with the times." Whatever that meant.

As much as I hated thinking my father was that shallow, this certainly wasn't the first time I'd been confronted with evidence that money was all that mattered to him.

But it would be the first time I called him on it.

"No, we need to talk right now."

18

SETH

I ROSE AND WALKED TO THE DOOR. "SORRY ABOUT THE TIMING," I said to Sage as she sailed out. "It can't be helped."

"Par for the course from a Hamilton," she said under her breath before turning a sunny smile on my father. "Have a nice day, sir. It was good seeing you again."

"You too, Sage. Don't be a stranger. You're welcome here anytime."

With a bounce of her blond curls and a flounce of her non-flouncy skirt, she was off.

I closed the door and turned back to my father. He raised an eyebrow and gestured with the Hamilton Realty folder in his hand. "Why do I have a feeling this has nothing to do with the Parsons deal?"

"Because unlike you, work isn't the center of my world."

"Forget center. Sometimes it's barely even in your peripheral vision." Huffing out a breath, he sat in the chair Sage had vacated and crossed his legs. "What is it now, Seth?"

I didn't sit. I leaned against my desk and crossed my arms. "I'm starting a family with Ally."

Wow, those words didn't burn my throat nearly as much as I'd feared. Not because they weren't true, but because they were. Saying them to my father was acknowledging their truth. Their power.

And from the expression on my dad's face, I might as well have thrown down a gauntlet.

"Is this about that contract business?"

I didn't ask how he knew. In an office this small with paper-thin walls, he could've easily overheard us talking.

Which also meant Shelly had probably heard Ally and me having sex. That should probably embarrass me. And yet…

I wanted to tell the world she was mine, in every possible way. Even the graphic, inappropriate ones.

Or Oliver could have told him. I wouldn't have put it past my twin to hop on the phone to my dad the minute he had walked out of my office. The timeframe was insanely tight, but Oliver worked fast.

Still, he'd said he wanted to fix things with me and Ally. Telling my dad wouldn't fix anything.

Then again, there was my lawyer. My lawyer who golfed every Sunday with my father and had a shark emblem on his golf shirt rather than an alligator.

"Talked to Artie, hmm?"

My father glanced away, all the proof I needed. "Don't be ridiculous. That would violate client confidentiality."

Yep. I'd called that one right. At least it hadn't been Oliver who'd blabbed. I really didn't want to have to kick his ass since he was purportedly doing me a favor with Ally.

Though, God, I'd sunk low if I was accepting his help. Oliver's love life was even worse than mine. He went through women like ties. Actually, he probably used ties with women, since his tastes veered toward the dominant side. Yet another thing I had no desire to ponder.

"That contract was a mistake."

My father didn't reply for a long moment. "But she signed on the dotted line, didn't she? She agreed to take money for your child. Just like Marjorie did." He lifted his head and narrowed his flinty eyes on mine. "Women are all the same, Seth. You may think I was wrong for offering a payout to your mother."

"Considering I only learned about that today, can't say I've had much time to process. But wrong seems like a good place to start, yes."

My father went on as if I hadn't spoken. "The truth is, it was a test, and she failed."

"Ally didn't fail, and who tests someone you love?"

You did. You were probably playing Hamilton games without even realizing it.

"I wouldn't do something like that to someone I love. I won't do it again," I amended, though the situations were vastly different.

"You don't love Alison."

"How the hell do you know? Because you didn't love Mom? Because I didn't love Marjorie the way I should have?"

"I loved your mother. You will never understand."

"Then tell me. Explain it to me. I'm begging you." I spread my arms wide. "I'm standing right here, waiting. Listening."

"She wasn't faithful to me," he said in a nearly inaudible voice.

Laughter ripped from my chest. "So? You weren't faithful to her either. That's why we have that damn camp that you refuse to go near any longer. Which mistress lived there, Dad?"

He didn't look at me, just cracked his knuckles. "It doesn't matter. Your mother was unfaithful first. She bore another man's child." He forged ahead before I could finish processing what he'd said.

Did he mean the daughter she'd had with her new husband? Or...worse?

"Do you even know if Laurie is yours? Did you ever ask for proof?" he demanded.

Though I knew the question was just his version of lashing out, it hit me square in the gut just the same. I started to respond, but he cut me off, his low voice as brutal as a whip.

"Or did she use her as a bargaining chip as your mother used you and your brother?"

I gripped the back of my neck. "Laurie looks like me. She's mine. But you know what? Even if she wasn't, it wouldn't matter."

Deep down, it was true. I couldn't deny it would hurt like a bitch to find out she wasn't my child biologically. But I'd get over it. Because she was mine in every way that counted, and I didn't need a useless slip of paper to prove it.

Every time she called me Daddy, I knew the truth all over again. She was mine and I was hers. Against all odds, we'd made a family.

And now with Ally, hopefully our family would expand.

"Sure, it wouldn't." My father laughed mirthlessly. "How much of your savings did you use to buy her safety from her mother?"

"She wasn't in danger from Marj. Not physically. But neglect is just as hurtful. I would've emptied my bank account to ensure my baby didn't have to deal with a parent who didn't want her."

He lifted his head. "So would I."

I exhaled and moved around my desk, dropping into my chair. "She didn't sign it. Ally. She wouldn't. Even when she said she had, it wasn't legal. She didn't want a contract between us. If I'd been thinking straight—hell, if I'd been less of a coward—I never would have either."

When my father didn't speak, I leaned forward and braced my forearms on the desk. "I don't know why you don't like her, but I hope to God it's not for the reason I think. Because all these years, I've told myself there's some good in you, some decency. If you've let your feelings about her bank account color your attitude toward her all these years…" I trailed off before I said something I probably wouldn't regret.

Defending Ally came before everything else except protecting my daughter.

"You would see it that way," he said tiredly, and I jerked up my head, shocked to hear the fatigue in his tone.

My father was a bull of a man. Strong, healthy, larger than life in every way. Years had passed since I'd really looked at him and seen him as anything but a force of nature.

Until now. Now the lines on his face seemed like a roadmap, where most of the best days of his life were behind him.

I swallowed hard. "Then explain it to me. Please."

"She has the power to break you."

"You just insinuated I don't love her, and now you're saying she could break me?"

"I wanted to see if you truly knew your own mind yet, or if you were just playing games with a future you weren't ready for." His shoulders relaxed. "Maybe it's finally time."

Words left me. Just completely vanished from my head.

"I was you once." He leaned back in his chair. "I loved your mother more than was wise, and what did it get me?"

"Christ, did everyone see what I couldn't when it came to me and Ally?" I exhaled. "What I didn't have the balls to acknowledge?"

"You were smart enough to tread gently. Because you knew. You understood that once you committed to her, there was no going back."

I wasn't sure he was saying that as a positive thing, but I nodded. "You're right. There isn't. I love her and I want to spend the rest of my life with her."

Coming clean didn't scare me anymore. The truth just filled me with a sense of rightness. Like I'd been traveling down a road with my headlights off, and now I'd finally turned them on.

My future was right in front of me, and all I had to do was reach out and take it. And nurture it, and care for it, and protect it with everything I was.

My father nodded and steepled his hands over the folder in his lap. "Does she feel the same?"

"I don't know. I hope so. I think so maybe." I blew out a breath. "But if she doesn't, I'm a patient man. I'll just keep at her until she has no choice."

He surprised me by laughing. "Stubborn to a fault, you and your brother."

Questions sprung to my mind about what he'd said about my mother having a child with another man, questions I wasn't sure I was ready to hear the answers to. Not now. Today Ally and Laurie and our future family was where my head was at. As well as my heart.

"Yeah. Not too bright when it comes to pleasing a woman either," I added. My father coughed and I smiled. "Not like that. We're both good there. Well, I know I am. He's probably just all talk."

"He is about most things."

My smile grew. "I meant more about saying the words, giving out the romance. I kinda suck at that."

"Oprah," he said gravely.

I laughed. "What?"

"She told women not to settle. Now they all want a free car and a fairytale."

Back to that again. Obviously, the universe was trying to send me a message. I was listening.

"If any woman deserves one, it's Ally. She deserves the grand dream, all wrapped up in a big bow."

Maybe I did too.

I reached for my phone. I had some preparations to make before the reunion. Good thing I had money to burn, because I'd have to move fast.

It was fucking fairytale time.

19

ALLY

I snagged my keys on the way out the door. My phone was in my back pocket, but it was off. I wasn't stupid enough to go out without it, but I didn't want to talk to anyone. All the voices were too confusing.

Sage and her effervescent positivity.

Seth and his seductive laugh rolled in innuendo and faint promises.

Laurie and her wide smiles and happiness.

All of it was too much. I didn't know which to trust, especially when my own voice was so very silent. Tucked in like a turtle in front of a predator. The problem was, I didn't know where to turn, so the shell seemed prudent. Only my shell was Seth's house.

Again.

This one—one of the half dozen properties his family owned on the cove—wasn't often used. It was known as the Mistress House after one of the Hamilton men who kept his affairs away from the main house. Hell, Seth's dad may have done that too. Now it mostly lay empty and served as one of the few places I could be alone in this town. The small-town vibe of everyone in and out of each other's business was generally a comfort to me, but right now, every person I ran into wanted to know when Seth and I were going to get married and make babies.

How that little tidbit had gotten around, I had no clue. But I figured a certain blond might have something to do with it. The diner was the center of the town in more ways than one, and remarking on Seth's skills in the sack to several patrons certainly hadn't helped my cause.

Not that it mattered. No one could actually have a fling in this town.

Even if the mere idea of a fling and Seth in the same sentence made my chest tighten.

He'd never been that for me, even when I wanted him to be. When the idea of making a kid with him took hold, there'd been little hope for my heart to truly stay mine. It had always been his, but only I'd known it. That had been somehow easier than this.

All my dreams and happiness were wrapped up in his little girl and the man himself. I wasn't sure I could face all of that again. Loving him could be the one thing that would actually break me.

I hiked up the grassy hill into the trees and the path that rounded Crescent Cove. The house was beautiful, but not as pristine as the other Hamilton holdings. But that didn't much matter when it came to the view. The lake, the town, and the little gazebo looked picturesque from this vantage point. The sun glittered off the lake. No mirror sheen here. No, our cove was choppy and a bit wild. It suited me right to the ground.

The idea of moving out of Crescent Cove killed me. Because if things didn't work out between us, I'd have to leave. I wouldn't be able to face seeing him in town. My hand slid over my flat belly. Especially if there was a child growing inside me. Would he get what he wanted and be done with me? Or just keep me around in a mother capacity?

Would I be forever on the outside looking in?

I honestly wasn't sure how I was going to do that. Even though I wanted a family so very much, I wasn't sure I could take half-measures now.

I'd hiked these hills for days and still couldn't find an answer. So many fears churned inside me, and they were often the loudest voices of all.

Looking away from the town and the water, I caught sight of the little abandoned church on the far side of the cove. The only thing there now was the cemetery. The town had taken the church in the center square as their own many years ago, but the cemetery had always been up away from the lake.

I hadn't been there since we'd buried my mom that one sunny day. I'd been at peace about her leaving me. Mostly because the woman I'd loved had left long before. Even at the end when her body had turned on her so completely, she'd had a sweet smile until the very end.

She just hadn't been my mom.

I ducked through the trees and up the less used path to the little church. There was an old dirt road that the processionals used, but I didn't want to drive. The stretch of muscles and the sun helped the nausea that had been living inside me for the last week. Another thing I wasn't quite ready to face.

As evidenced by the plastic bag tucked away in my knapsack at the Hamilton camp. The one burning a hole in the worn canvas.

I'd traveled two towns over to buy it, visiting a nearby city where no one knew who I was. I'd wrapped the box in two bags and shoved it deep down. Fitting since all I ever did was shove things down so I didn't have to look at them.

It was getting really tiresome.

I lifted my face to the sun and uncapped the water bottle at my hip. Even if I didn't want an answer just quite yet, I wasn't stupid. A few signs might add up to nothing. Or a damn lot.

One of those signs was that a few hours in the summer sun could put me down like a puppy. So I guzzled down half the bottle and stuck it back in its little holster. I kept hiking, taking a shortcut up across the path instead of using the lazy walking trail.

Right then, it felt more important to get to the little hill under the Japanese maple at the far side of the cemetery. The headstones came into view and my chest ached. I ran my fingertips over the old stones at the front. The mausoleum to the left with Hamilton engraved across the top told the history of our town better than any story in the library.

Huge. Moneyed. Overwhelming.

I turned away from the testament to privilege and status and headed toward the edges of the cemetery where the plots were smaller, but no less taken care of. I aimed right for the ivory angel standing guard over my mom's grave. She was small and fairy-like beside the simple marker with her name and the dates. I brushed away the leaves and tugged out a few weeds before dropping cross-legged in front of her headstone.

"Hi, Mom."

I didn't even know what I really wanted to say, but it felt good to say hello. I cleared my throat. "I hope you can hear me. Even if you can't, I'll just pretend. I'm good at that." I dashed away a tear I hadn't realized was rolling down my cheek. "So I did a thing. I swore I wouldn't, but I did it anyway. I didn't mean to. Honestly. I look back now and wonder how I lasted as long as I did. Actually, that's probably one more lie I've told myself." I laughed before leaning forward to brush away dust on the base of her headstone. "I love him, Ma. So much that it scares the crap out of me. Like my chest feels overfull with it. And his little girl? God. She's the sweetest thing. She's gotten so big since you've seen her."

I dashed away another tear. "I think you'd remember her. Seth used to bring her to see you, but I know the stuff they gave you had you really out of it."

But I remembered the smiles. Whenever Laurie came over, there was always a smile on my mom's face. Of course, that little girl brought sunshine with her everywhere.

My little girl.

She was mine for all intents and purposes.

Just like Seth.

I bowed my head as the tears kept flowing. They didn't hurt though. Crying finally felt freeing. "I miss you so much. Sage is good to talk to for most of this mess I'm in, but I miss crawling up next to you on the couch and letting you play with my hair while you told me everything was going to work out. Because I'm so afraid it won't. I'm not sure I could bear it if he doesn't feel the same."

But it really felt like an empty fear. There was so much in my head. The touches, the laughter, the little moments with Laurie.

And then me running.

Always running away when things got too big, felt like too much.

Instead of staying to see how things went, I escaped before the answers could hurt me.

I tipped my head back to the sun and the breeze lifted my hair to whip my ponytail around. I laughed and brushed back the tears. "Okay, I got it."

If I didn't stick around, I wouldn't have to face reality.

The reality of asking for more. Of deserving more. I brushed my hand over my middle. For hoping for more.

"I think I'm finally creating a family of my own, Mom." I huffed out a laugh when the breeze whirled around me and leaves danced. "I *know* I am." I pressed my palm to the cool marble stone. "I know you always loved him. And you probably knew I did this whole time too."

I sniffed as the tears dried and the sun peeked from the clouds that were ever present thanks to the lake. I spun around and leaned against my mother's headstone and let the sun soak into my bones. It was peaceful here and that feeling had been a rare commodity in my life lately.

When a handful of people came to pay their respects to their own families, I stood and brushed off my pants. I kissed my fingertips and touched the angel then the marker. "Keep watch over her."

I went for the winding road this time. Then followed it down to the little picnic area to feed the bold ducks who swarmed the children. By the time I'd gotten to the little cabin I'd been hiding in, I was finally hungry.

I climbed the back steps to the kitchen and unearthed the peanut butter crackers I'd brought with me. It was the only thing that didn't seem to annoy my touchy stomach.

Cleaning up was definitely in order. I was dusty from the trails and sweaty from the sticky humidity clinging to the air. I grabbed my bag on my way down the hall to the small room with black and white tiles. My shower was infinitely more luxurious. The bathroom in the apartment I shared with Sage—sort of, considering I spent most of my time with Seth or working—had two shower heads and steamed up to a life-changing level. But the ancient claw-footed tub would do for today.

In fact…

I dug into one of the lower cabinets and found an old bath bomb I'd left there a few summers ago. The girls from the diner had given me a big spa kit to relax. Since I wasn't really great at relaxing, I'd left it here when I'd done an overnight with Laurie.

The only kind of camping I'd ever do was spending a night in this cabin.

I filled the tub and dropped the purple cake of soap into the water. It fuzzed and bubbled, releasing the sweet scent of lilacs and vanilla. I turned on my phone for music and flicked away the dozen messages that came through. I wasn't quite ready to face all my realities just yet.

I shrugged off my clothes and stepped into the scalding water with a hiss.

Nope, it was time for some Keith Urban and a bath to clear my head of the last of the cobwebs. I had to allow myself to really think through my options.

A glossy brochure stuck out of the top of my bag. Carefree students walking up pathways lined with lush green grass with stately buildings behind them. That could be my life.

My hand crept over my flat stomach. Or maybe I could embrace another life, while still achieving my hopes of getting my education. My mom had dreamed of me leaving and doing something grand. She'd worked her fingers raw to tuck a little away for me until she couldn't keep pushing on anymore.

The thing was, I didn't have to leave my home and start over in a new place to have a new beginning. It was hard to imagine a more perfect place for me than Crescent Cove. My home was here. My job, my friends. Sage.

Seth and Laurie—my family. My heart.

The pregnancy test hiding at the bottom of my bag.

It was probably too soon. My period was late. But that happened sometimes, so most likely it was nothing. I wasn't going to take the test here in any case.

When and if I took that step, I would do it with Seth.

My fingers drifted up to cup my sore breasts. My nipple tightened at the mere thought of his name. Seth, who'd shown me just what I'd been missing this entire time.

I slid up higher to the curls at the nape of my neck. Would our little one be dark like us? My rich brown hair, and his near black? Or would her hair be auburn like my mom's?

I lowered myself into the scented water that was rapidly cooling.

So much to deal with, so much to plan.

So much to discuss with Seth.

I stood up and rinsed with the little handle showerhead. It felt as if I was rinsing away the fear and excuses at the same time. I liked to think it was easier to hide behind them, but that wasn't really the truth either.

I tucked a towel around me and drained the tub, rinsing out the last of the bath bomb as I drip-dried enough to tug on my clothes. My worn jeans that I couldn't part with, the old lacrosse shirt I'd stolen from Seth.

Always Seth.

After grabbing my phone, I wandered back out to the main living space and my gaze drifted around the rustic, glass-walled room. We'd sprawled on the faded green rug on the first day of classes we skipped together junior year, passing back and forth a bottle of some foul-tasting stuff Seth stole from his dad's liquor cabinet. He'd stopped short of getting drunk, but I hadn't. I'd savored the freedom in laughing at nothing and lying on my back on the sun-warmed floor, staring up through the skylight at a sky full of marshmallow clouds. I was the girl with too many responsibilities, and he'd always been my ticket to fun and possibilities.

He still was.

I sat on the couch and dumped my phone in my bag, then reached for my iPad. I flipped the cover closed and tucked the tablet into my bag, setting it on the wicker chair beside me.

I couldn't even pretend to care about the class list on my iPad or the glossy school brochures anymore. Not right now, with so much else going on. As much as I wanted to make my mother proud, and to spread my wings, I had to admit the truth. Online classes might be something I investigated more someday, but right now, I was firmly invested in my life just as it was. Part of me always wanted to see what was out there, but my current reality was looking better and better.

If I didn't chicken out before I went for what I truly wanted.

The *thwack* of the screen door dragged me out of my musings. No one knew I was here. I reached for my purse and the can of pepper spray I kept in the zipper pocket. Sage insisted I carry it at all times, even when I had nothing on me but my wallet.

"Alison?"

I sagged back against the chair, still clutching the keys I'd pulled out and my safety spray. Not a burglar. A Hamilton. "Back here. What are you doing here, Oliver?"

He stepped into the sunroom, his back ramrod straight. His impeccable three-piece suit didn't dare look wilted. My T-shirt was already sticking to me. The little house by the water was usually cool, but there wasn't a single cool corner of Crescent Cove right now. Humidity and heat sat over the town like a shroud.

Not that you'd know it from Oliver.

"Finally. Do you have any idea how many people are looking for you?"

"I told Sage I needed a few days." I lifted my chin. "I wasn't feeling so hot."

"The whole town is buzzing about this stupid reunion and here you are, tucked away."

All the sureness I'd been feeling filtered right out of me. The reunion was tonight. Ignorance really was bliss. Why did he have to remind me?

He tilted his head. "May I?"

I shrugged. "It's your place." I sighed. "Actually, no. How the heck did you know I'd be here?"

He paused mid-step over the threshold. "Because I come here to think too."

I frowned. "You're the one who's been staying here?"

His eyebrow rose. "Just how often do you come here, Alison?"

"Not often. It's been months, actually, before the past few days. I didn't think anyone came here, but the sheets in the bedroom were far too fresh."

Oliver let out a frustrated sigh and tugged at his tie. "Yes, well sometimes one needs the simple and the quiet to think. May I come in?"

He owned the place, and he was asking *me* for permission. Unusually sweet for Oliver, but I needed some kindness right now. Desperately.

"Depends. Are you friend or foe?"

"I hope friend."

I couldn't remember the last time I had seen Oliver show an emotion other than disdain or disinterest or mild amusement, typically at someone else's expense. Especially toward me. "Since when?"

"Fair question. I believe we may have gotten off on the wrong foot."

"For thirteen years? I think that would be an understatement."

He dipped his hands into his pockets. "The Hamilton men aren't known for their grace with the fairer sex."

"Maybe you and your father, but I'm pretty sure Seth got the bulk of your share."

"Probably true."

Yet Oliver was the one who'd found me, not his brother. Did Seth even notice I'd been missing? And now I was just being melodramatic. Seth had been texting me a few times a day, every day.

I'd told him I needed a little thinking time.

I slid my hand over my belly self-consciously and sat forward, hunching my shoulders. I was already going into protective mode for a child who might not even exist. Along with heavily protecting myself.

Then again, perhaps Seth was waiting outside, planning a sneak attack.

"Is Seth with you?" I asked.

"No."

I breathed out a sigh of relief. "Good."

"Is there a reason you wouldn't want to see my brother?"

"No." I shoved my keys and pepper spray back into my bag. "Yes." I stood and crossed to the windows of the screened-in porch, hoping for a breeze off the water. It had helped earlier, but my mom wasn't talking now.

The vast, mirror-like lake shone and in the distance. Now I could see the white string lights around the gazebo, winding down the pier. Night was creeping over the town and the sun was sinking behind the trees with fantastic red and pink slashes across the sky. Music and laughter traveled with the occasional snatches of breeze on the heavy night. The pier and park was all tricked out already for the reunion. It was time to celebrate the ten years of our lives we'd put behind us.

Ten years I'd spent not moving forward.

I swallowed hard. "I don't know. That would be why I'm here. I don't know anything."

"Not surprising since my brother is the king of cowards."

"What?" I turned back to Oliver. "No, he's not. He—"

"No, that's exactly what he is. Both of you are. There's a reason no one ever fit either of you over the years. I may not want to tie myself to one woman, but Seth has been a family man since the moment that little girl was put into his arms. I just put the wrong woman in his path."

I flinched. "What does that mean?"

Oliver tugged at his tie again until it snapped out of his collar. He jammed it into his pocket before shrugging out of his suit coat. "It's too blasted hot."

I lifted a brow. "I thought you were impervious."

"Yeah, well, don't look at the line of sweat down the middle of my back. I'm not a fucking machine, no matter what you people think."

"I…" I didn't even know what to say to that, actually. Oliver had always been mostly cool and aloof around me. Had I started it? Or had he?

He blew out a breath. "This wasn't where I wanted to go with this. I'm here to save my meathead brother from making a mistake."

"Meathead?" I blinked. First, he was de-suiting and now he was plain-speaking.

I squinted at him to make sure he wasn't Seth playing a joke on me, but the edges of his tattoo demonstrated clearly which twin was which. They were both covered in ink, which was interesting considering Oliver's penchant for suits. But their ink was as opposite as their personalities. Seth's was more dark and heavy, while Oliver's contained more streaks of color.

Not that I would ever mistake the twin brothers for each other. The differences were staggering to me, if no one else. But there was a new glint in Oliver's eyes. Frustration and an openness I'd never seen before.

"Look, Ally." He swiped his hand over the back of his neck and my heart melted. Such a Seth gesture. For the first time, he really looked and acted like his brother. They'd always seemed like the opposite sides of a coin. "I may have had an idiotic moment when I pushed Marj into Seth's life. Intentionally."

I wrapped my arm around my middle, the quick flash of pain hitting me harder than I thought it would. A part of me had always known Oliver didn't want his brother with me. And it wasn't like the revelation was a total surprise. Oliver had mentioned introducing Seth to Marj at the diner. But a casual intro wasn't the same as an intentional one. I could tell from Oliver's expression he'd had a method to his madness far beyond Seth just meeting his friend.

"Why?"

"Because he didn't need me anymore, dammit."

My eyes burned and I blinked away the quick rush of tears. "What? Of course he did. Of course he *does*. You're his brother."

"The minute you came into his life, there was nothing else. We even went to different schools, for fuck's sake. He was supposed to try out public school for a year and then come back to prep school junior year if he didn't like it, but he met you. He didn't want to leave here after that, no matter what he thought of the school. He didn't say that, but that's the truth of it."

I frowned. "You think he chose me over you?"

"I know he did." Oliver's dark eyes were fierce. "And I hated you for it. Stupid, petty, and small, I know, but I did."

"We're just friends."

"You were never just friends. You both may have hidden in that role for the majority of your relationship, but deep down, you both knew it wasn't just platonic."

"I…" I had to swallow hard. I'd always loved him. Even when my mother's caregiving took over my life, I'd always put him in the back of mind as the end goal. The unattainable goal.

Maybe that was why I hadn't ever managed to choose a college away from Crescent Cove. The only thing I'd ever really wanted was here—Seth, and the family we could make. Simple maybe, but honestly, it was the only thing I'd ever really wanted.

"I love him so much," I whispered.

Just saying it was like dropping a burden. I'd held those words back for so long.

"I know you do." Oliver sighed. "And he loves you too."

"How can you—"

"Look, if you want to question it after all this? After he found every reason in the known universe to get you to stay in his life, then I don't know what to tell you. But I had to at least try to help out for once. Because that man is drowning. You're everything he ever wanted, he's just too stubborn to put the label on it because he's afraid you'll run." Oliver shook his head. "You're both so fucking afraid."

"Well, look at what we come from."

"Guess what, sweetheart? We aren't what we come from. We're exactly what we choose to be. You want that idiot I call a brother, then you go after him."

A loud pop and whistle startled me and I swung around. A huge spray of white fireworks fanned up into the night sky. In the center of it was a spray of red that shot out in dual arcs.

A heart.

My vision wavered when another one went up. Then another. A succession of them lit up the cove and kept on coming.

"Well, finally."

I tried to turn back to Oliver, but I couldn't pull myself from the display. "They're beautiful." And I should be enjoying them with Seth, not locking myself away in the little shame-shack his family owned.

We'd spent hours here as teenagers. We'd told each other secrets, we'd even confessed a few dreams, and shed some tears. But this was our past. Out there was our future.

Those hearts had to be a sign.

I stepped forward, then stilled, clutching my arms around my middle.

"Stop fighting it. Why the hell are you so afraid?"

I whipped around. "You're one to talk, Oliver Hamilton. I don't see you getting caught up with anyone."

"No one has ever mattered enough."

"No, you never *let* them matter enough." I was breathing heavy. But he was right. I'd let fear rule my life for long enough. "I'm sorry. That was uncalled for. I know how it is to hide."

Oliver's chin lifted. "There's a difference, Alison."

I tilted my head. So much Seth in him and yet, not nearly the same. Seth put Laurie first—put me first—in so many ways. Maybe Oliver would be the same someday.

But now I had to trust in Seth. And myself. "I'm going after him." I grabbed my bag off the chair.

"Hallelujah." Oliver lifted his arms then waved to the window. "He even gave you a map for once."

"Huh?" I hooked the knapsack over my shoulder and made sure I had my wallet, keys. My fingers brushed the early pregnancy test at the bottom of the bag.

"The fireworks. He said he was going for the fairytale."

My eyes flooded. "He did that? That's him?"

"God, you guys are so dense. Of course it's him. Even after he paid to put hearts in the sky, you still question it?"

I dashed away tears with my wrist. "Guess he should have taken out a skywriter."

"I'll tell him to do that next."

I laughed and jangled my keys. "Let's hope it doesn't come to that." I swallowed the nerves threatening to slow me down. "It's time to go get my man."

"Finally."

20

ALLY

I RAN THROUGH THE CABIN AND OUT THE FRONT DOOR. My fingers shook as I got in the car and tried to get my keys in the ignition. I saw more sparks through the trees and the fireworks floated higher into the sky with each explosion.

The white made the crinkly fuzzing sound that made my skin crackle in reaction.

Another heart speared the sky.

Then a succession of three.

For all of us?

The family we made?

The red and white shimmered as my eyes burned. I slammed my car into drive and hit the winding road with a scatter of dirt and gravel in my wake. The lake never felt so big as it did tonight. In my head, I knew it was a mere seven minutes into town. Thirteen years of traveling these roads had left an imprint. I could probably drive them blindfolded.

Good thing since my eyes kept filling when I glanced up at the sparkles and hearts dotting the sky.

"I'm coming." I didn't realize I'd said it aloud until my voice wavered. Sureness filled my chest and my heart pounded in my head, echoing in every nerve of my body.

I finally turned onto main street and slammed the heel of my hand on the steering wheel at the line of cars. Some were leaving the park, but others were simply sitting there in awe of the light show. The lake held fireworks for the Fourth and sometimes Labor Day, but it was pretty rare. They were expensive and the restrictions were a headache.

I only knew it because I'd stupidly signed up to help with one of the celebrations. Sage was a joiner and a pleaser. Watching her flounder during the Fourth of July preparations a few years ago had prompted me to help. Never again. Small towns were full of way too many helpful hands that never ended up doing anything but complain.

No thanks. I'd rather volunteer to babysit a dozen three-year-olds.

Right about now, I'd empty my bank account to get rid of every car on the road. I looked around for a place to park, but of course that wasn't going to happen either. My fingers ached from squeezing my steering wheel in frustration.

I rolled down my window and looked for a break in the line of cars to get to a side street. I slapped the side of my wheel when the hearts started slowing in the sky.

God, I didn't want him to think I wasn't paying attention.

I scanned the people on the sidewalks. I was about ready to scream for help from sixteen-year-old Madison Kohl when a familiar laugh floated my way.

Sage.

I twisted and turned looking for her familiar flyaway blond hair and my mouth dropped at the bouncing curls that swung down a woman's back. A woman with more curves than I'd ever seen in Crescent Cove.

Sage was talking to the new teacher, Mike London. And had she just tossed her hair over her shoulder?

"Sage?" I swerved over to the curb in a no-parking zone. This wouldn't work for long.

She twirled at my call then slapped her bare thighs. Sweet mercy, was she wearing Daisy Dukes?

"Finally! Where the hell have you been?" She turned back to Mike. "Um, sorry. I didn't mean to curse, Mr. London."

"Mike."

"Right, Mike." Sage's voice was unusually breathy. And loud. Her sunny smile lit up her face and Mike's eyes glazed over.

Of course, half of that was probably the miniscule strappy tank top Sage was wearing that showed off just how generous God had been when stacking her deck.

"Can you come over here, please, Sage? Like now?"

Sage carefully picked her way over the cobblestones of the sidewalk to the asphalt in her espadrilles. Navy ribbons climbed up her ankle to her calf. "Are you cock-blocking me?"

"I'd have to have a cock, Sage."

"Oh, right." She huffed out a breath. "You know what I mean."

I slammed my car into park. Now wasn't the time, and I knew I was going to regret asking, but I just had to know. "What the heck are you wearing?"

"Oh." She frowned. "Don't you like it?"

"You look hot as hell, girlfriend."

She smiled. "Well, thank you. Just something I found in my closet."

"You did not find that in your closet."

Sage gave a lengthy sigh. "All right, it was a store in Laurel. This isn't exactly the kind of thing you can buy in Kinleigh's"

That was for sure. But if Kinleigh got a look at that outfit, she might make some changes to her little shop. "Can you drive for me?"

"What?" Sage looked over her shoulder at Mike and wiggled her fingers. "Just a sec," she called out.

He waved and then slid his fingers into his thick black hair.

"Isn't he dreamy?"

I blinked and peered around her, then back at Sage. "For real?"

"I mean he's cute, right?"

"Um…" I honestly hadn't looked at anyone other than Seth in so long that it felt foreign to look at a man objectively. "I guess."

"You guess? Do you see how he fills out a pair of jeans? I mean, he's from Texas first of all, and then he wears honest to God cowboy boots. The kind that are actually broken in because he rides real horses. I mean just wow."

I nibbled on my bottom lip. "I'm sorry. Can I be the altruistic best friend tomorrow? I really need your help."

"Of course. I'm sorry. I'm just not even paying attention. All these blasted hormones are messing me up. That's why I'm on the hunt. I figure I gotta get this virgin thing done. How else am I going to breathe in this town? All the lovey stuff with you and Seth. He did those fireworks for you, you know?"

I resisted the urge to roll my eyes. "I know. I'm trying to go find him. But…" I waved at the traffic snaking down Main Street and around the park.

"Oh." She grabbed my door handle and hauled me out of the car. "Of course. Honestly, that man finally is listening and you went MIA. You two are going to be the death of me."

"You had something to do with this?"

"Well, not exactly. I just told him that he'd have to be knocked over the head before he did something really special to let you know how much he loves you. So I did a little knocking. A few well-placed insults never fail to get a man moving." She paused, her smile fading. "He does love you, Al. I saw it in his eyes."

My own eyes filled again and I blinked the tears away. I simply didn't have time for them. The sky was still smoky from the aftermath of the fireworks, but they were getting few and far between. "I really hope so."

"Oh, girl. He does. How can you even question it?"

"I'll remind you of this conversation when you've got real hearts in your eyes, not just the lusting kind."

Sage blushed and fussed with the strap of her tiny tank top. "He is dreamy. But we're not here to talk about Mike London. Go get that big hunk of real estate before he turtles again."

"You do have a way with words, Sage."

She bumped me out of the way and slid behind the wheel of my old car. "Go on."

I looked up at the sky, then to the pier. There was only one place that would allow for those kind of fireworks. "Can I have my bag?"

"Right." Sage leaned over and hauled my knapsack onto her lap. "Good Lord."

"My life is in there."

"It's heavy as hell." She handed the bag through the window. "Now go get him."

I grinned. "Thanks, Sage."

"I didn't do anything. I just told him to get with the program. Just like I've been telling you."

I resisted the urge to roll my eyes. Actually, as of late, she'd been lamenting how stupid Seth was, but it was just easier to nod.

At the moment, I had bigger fish to land.

I took off across the street and over the grassy hill that led to the path around the lake to the park.

My heart raced inside my chest as a single heart speared the darkness. My legs pumped and I was eternally grateful for my sneakers right then. They squeaked as I rounded the bend and the gazebo and lights came into view.

So close.

Don't lose patience with me now.

A stitch lanced my side and I slowed to a fast walk. I was not a runner by any means. I could hike for days, but speed was definitely not my thing.

I stared up at the star-strewn sky as sulfur and smoke burned my nostrils.

Please, just one more.

The pop and whistle of a single flame speared upward. A huge purple heart shined in the sky over the lake. A lonely boat was tethered to one of the fishing docks off the shore. Two men stood on the little steel deck.

But only one mattered.

Seth's broad shoulders nearly blocked the short, burly man at his side. They were arguing. Only snatches of conversation came across on the wind as it kicked up. Seth was shoving his hands into his hair and pacing the tiny space.

I dropped my bag as I got to the end of the pier.

Relief bubbled up inside me and out on a sobbing laugh.

247

"Seth!"

The wind was rising and the boats along the pier were slamming around. There was no recognition. Just more of Seth stalking around with his phone to his ear.

I dug into my bag, but I couldn't find my phone among all the clothes and books.

I stood up again and climbed onto the lower rungs of the rail enclosing the lookout at the end of the pier. I cupped my hands around my mouth and yelled his name again, but the wind was too strong and kept snatching my voice.

I turned around and saw people at the other end of the pier. Some I knew, some I wanted to forget. But there were so many of them—and they were all voices I needed right now.

I jumped and waved. When Brad, one of Seth's high school best friends, broke off from the group, I quickly motioned him closer. "Can you help him hear me?"

Nodding, Brad waved people up from the gazebo to the wide pier that jutted out of the park. Our entire class—or what was left of it at this late hour—came tromping toward me.

My eyes burned as everyone came to help. People I'd barely spoken to in my classes started jumping, shouting, and waving. Girls I recognized and others I didn't were jumping up and down like manic puppies.

Brad slung an arm around my shoulders and hauled me in close. He was a bit rounder than I remembered from school, but he had always been a sweet guy.

Jessica, the head of the cheer squad, clutched my hand. "I can't believe how romantic this is. Is this man for real?"

"Yeah, he really is."

She sighed. "You're so lucky. I don't think my husband has ever done anything like this for me. Like ever."

One last firework whistled into the night sky and the white sparks illuminated Seth's body.

I yelled his name and the assembled crowd parroted it behind me.

Seth finally turned around on the small dock and held out his arms. He tipped his head back and did a fist-punch into the air like Bender from *The Breakfast Club* and I laughed.

Jessica squealed in my ear and then started hopping around with the other cheerleaders. Brad slapped me on the back as Seth jumped into his boat and headed my way.

My heart raced as I picked up my bag and made my way through the dozens of people. The guys from his lacrosse team started chanting Seth's name and laughter thundered over the lake.

I took a shaky step onto one of the docks lining the right side and waited for him to come to me.

21

SETH

I PUSHED THE LITTLE SPEEDBOAT FARTHER THAN I SHOULD, BUT Crescent Lake had never felt so big in my goddamn life. Fireworks had brought her to me. I'd hoped, but I knew it was a big gamble.

If my girl wanted to stay lost, she would stay gone.

I blinked away the grittiness from the wind and spray off the water. The only thing that mattered was getting to the pier. Lenny let off one more spray of white cracklers and a waterfall from his waning arsenal. I'd been worried we were going to run out of them before she showed up.

But there she was, standing in front of a crowd of our classmates. All the people who had rallied around me in my days of lacrosse. While not as big as some of the other sports, we enjoyed a status of our own. Sometimes lacrosse was even more rough and tumble than the town's beloved football.

Ally hadn't really been in that scene. She'd always been on the fringes, thanks to her mother's health.

And if I wasn't such an asshole I would have realized that before I got so excited about the reunion. But there they all were behind her, hooting and hollering as if we were at a championship game.

She moved to the side ramp where the docks were.

I rode the waves I was making with the motor on my speedboat. I rarely took it off my dock, preferring to drive most of the time. Not to mention the small nightmares that my little girl would go flying off the back and be lost in the lake. So yeah—not so much of a boat guy these days. But right now? Right now, all I wanted was to get her alone.

I wanted to tell her everything that was bursting out of my chest.

It started with the silly hearts I'd shot off into the sky. I'd needed to get her attention. She couldn't deny that I was making a statement now. She also couldn't deny the truth that I was about to lay all over her. Even if it cost me more than a little to be that honest and vulnerable.

For her, I would.

I fishtailed on a wave and bumped over the wake I made in my haste to get to her.

I finally made myself throttle down the engine so I didn't come in too hot. I didn't want to hurt the one person on this earth who had been created for me. The person I'd been desperate to lock down, only to do the exact opposite in every way.

The last sparks of the waterfall fireworks lit her beautiful, smiling face. She dropped her trusty knapsack by her feet and folded her arms as I slowly puttered to the dock. Brad and JT hooted behind her, and a few catcalls from other members of my team rang out as well.

The front of my boat bumped into the mooring as I tossed up a rope to tie me off before I drifted back out to the cove. She rested her sneakered foot against the sloping bow and tipped her head. "Had to make a spectacle, huh?"

I widened my stance against the wild rocking from the waves. "Yep."

"Don't you do anything small, Hamilton?"

"Nope." I leaned forward and lifted my voice. "I've got a secret."

"Is that right?" Her lips twitched as she tried not to smile.

"Yeah. It's kinda a big one. Though maybe not such a big secret now." My stomach pitched in time with the waves banging my little boat against the moorings.

She pushed her dark hair out of her eyes as it whipped around her shoulders. "I'm listening."

I looked behind her for a second. No one was dispersing. At all. Everyone was leaning in to hear what I had to say.

God, please help me not to fuck this up more.

I took a deep breath. I valued my privacy, but this was important. "I love you, Alison. In a big, stupid, crazy way. So much that I can't even put it into words."

Her dark eyes widened and her hands fell to her side. "What?"

"Don't 'what' me. Deep down, you had to know."

Her hand flew up to her mouth and a smile broke between her fingers.

I glanced behind her and growled when I spotted JT with his hands over his heart.

She waved her hand toward the idiots catcalling behind her. "Never mind them. I'm not sure I heard that."

I pulled out of the slip that was too far away from her and moved closer. I didn't want her to have to strain to hear a word of this. "I love you. I wanna marry you."

"Marry me?"

I gripped the throttle and spun the boat around until it was sideways at the end of the slip. I held out my hand to her. "Yeah, you. This is the marrying kind of love. Being the mother of my kid kind of love. The one I already have," I quickly corrected at her crestfallen face. The last thing I wanted her to think about right now was that ridiculous contract. "I want to build a life with you. A family. I want forever, Ally Cat."

She blinked madly and looked down at me, her hands fisted at her sides.

"Please take a chance on me, Al."

She lifted her bag and tossed it into my boat then jumped in and I caught her. There was nothing else I could possibly do.

I wrapped my arms around her waist and dragged her into me. "You're killing me, Alison."

"I love you so much." Her voice was ragged and her eyelashes starred with tears. "Besides, if I didn't I would have after you gave me fireworks, for God's sake."

"Go big or go home, baby."

She lifted her arms around my shoulders and went up on her tiptoes. "I really like the idea of going home."

Jessica let out a "Whoop, whoop!" and everyone clapped on the pier.

Fairytale achieved? Maybe. At least the start of one. I had a lot of work to do yet.

I settled Ally in the seat beside me and waved as I throttled back away from the dock.

JT curved his hands around his mouth and shouted, "Lucky bastard!"

"You're damn right I am," I called back.

I sat down and dragged her close as I opened up the motor again and raced across the cove to my house—*our* house. We couldn't talk above the wind and waves, but I didn't need words right now.

I just needed her by my side.

It only took a few minutes to get to my dock and to moor the little speedboat. I tied off and jumped out to help her up on the dock.

She wouldn't look at me as I handed her the oversized knapsack she forever carried.

There was no way I was going to stand for that. Not now.

I dragged her close and lowered my head to catch her mouth in a swift, hot, heavy kiss. I poured everything I couldn't say into it, taking my time. She moaned and gripped the front of my shirt.

Reluctantly, I eased back a fraction. "You're all I've ever wanted. I was just too stupid to face the truth—never mind say it out loud. All I could think about was fucking things up between us and losing you forever. I'm still going to have nightmares about it," I said with a harsh laugh against her mouth. "But it's better than not having you be mine. And most of all, being yours." I touched my forehead to hers. "It's scary as hell to know you could break me into pieces."

"I'd never." Her voice was a sandpaper whisper.

"I know. That's what I figured out. I trust you." I sucked in a breath. "I know it didn't always seem like that. My dad has a way of looking at the world, and I think some of that seeped into me despite my best intentions. Sometime I'll tell you more about what I learned today."

She frowned, but she didn't push me. She just gave me the space to finish my thoughts.

"I don't want to live that way, mistrusting everybody. Assuming the worst. I believe in you. I want to believe in me too, that I can do this. We can make this work."

Eyes wet, she nodded. "We can. We will," she said fiercely.

"And I want to support your dreams. Whether that's going to school, or maybe traveling to see other places—whatever, I don't care. Your dreams are mine and we can make them happen together."

"Maybe school someday. Maybe traveling. But you know what I want most?"

Swallowing deeply, I shook my head.

Her fingers twisted tighter into my dress shirt. "You're all I've ever wanted. Just you."

Finally hearing those words was a goddamn miracle.

"Well, you've got me," I said hoarsely. "And you're never getting rid of me, baby or not."

Ally would always be enough, even if I couldn't help wanting to expand our family. Now and possibly even again in the future.

We'd take everything one day at a time.

She smiled, increasing her hold on me even more. "Is that so?"

"Oh, it's so. We can certainly practice all night long though," I teased, stroking her cheek. "Laurie's at my dad's place."

A little hiccup sneaked out along with a bubble of laughter. "Yeah, about that." She dug her hand into the endless contents of her knapsack and came out with a little white bag.

There was just enough illumination coming from the solar lights that lit up the dock and the path to my house for me to see a telltale logo through the plastic.

My chest tightened. My shoulders locked. Hell, my life flashed before my eyes. Not the one I'd already lived, but the one we would create together. "Are you?"

"I wanted to wait for you to do it with me."

I lifted her into my arms, and her canvas bag and the one with the test folded between us. "Can we do it now? Is it too early?"

She laughed. "It's a little early, but this test is made for that."

I blinked away the quick prick of tears. I didn't want to ask, but I knew I had to. "Is this okay? It's okay if you're not. We can wait until we get married. You know, make it all official. And if you want to do the school thing…" I swallowed down the nerves. I didn't want to wait, but I would for her.

I'd do anything for her.

"I don't remember saying yes. Or you really asking."

My breath stalled. "I mean, you're going to say yes, right?"

She tried to keep a straight face, but her lips kept twitching into a smile. Her fingers slid up my chest and around to the nape of my neck, then finally to the longer part of my hair where she could grip me tight. "I just might."

I looped her legs around my waist and kept on walking. "Well, then I'm just going to have to convince you."

She giggled. "Put me down, you idiot."

"And let you run again? I think not, lady."

"I'm never running again."

I lowered her to her feet. Mostly because I was afraid I'd do something stupid in the dark and drop her. No way was I ever going to let anything happen to her.

Taking her knapsack from her, I stuffed the test back in and put the bag over my shoulder before turning her around and slapping her ass. "Get going. We've got a test to take."

She dashed forward and we both ran up the stone steps to our home, then across the short distance to the back porch. When we reached the top of the stairs, I couldn't wait any longer. I scooped her up and fumbled through opening the door. Somehow I managed not to drop her, which was a feat because we were laughing like idiots.

Still carrying her, I rushed through the house, finally depositing her in front of the bathroom door. "Okay. Go, you know. Do whatever it is you do."

"What if I don't have—"

I pushed her into the bathroom and turned on the taps full strength. "Need a glass of water?"

She slapped at me and took back her knapsack before shoving me out the door. "Neanderthal."

I paced outside the door and was sort of glad that she left the water running. Not that her peeing on a stick was weird—much. I mean, I did have a kid. Bodily functions were just part and parcel of my day.

But this was a really important stick.

She opened the door and I spun around. "Well?"

"Five minutes, buddy."

My shoulders slumped as she dried her hands. "That's forever." I looked down at my watch and set the timer.

She grinned and walked into my space. "Then maybe we should make out for a few minutes."

"Well, I can certainly do that." I lowered my mouth to hers and slowly drew out the kiss. I tried to concentrate on the little things I knew she liked, but I kept sneaking glances at my watch.

She plowed her fist into my belly. "You're incorrigible."

I rubbed my ribs. "Ow. I can't help it." She tried to hide behind her curtain of hair, but I saw the nervous smile peeking through. "You want to know just as bad as I do."

"No, I don't. Well, maybe. What time is it?" She grabbed my wrist. "It has to be time."

"It's only been three minutes."

She dropped my wrist. "Ugh."

I tried to loop my arm around her waist but she wiggled free. "Seth, don't try to distract me now. You had your chance." She couldn't stop laughing as I grabbed for her again and again. "What time is it now?"

"Twenty seconds later." I banded my arms under her butt and lifted her until our mouths lined up. I stared at her as our lips met. "It doesn't matter what it says."

She looped her arms around my shoulders. "No?"

I shook my head, but then my timer started beeping and she scrambled down and we both raced to the bathroom. She elbowed me out of the way and grabbed the little plastic wand.

"What does it say?" I asked over her shoulder.

Her hand flew up to her mouth.

I banded my arms around her waist as we stood in front of the stick. "It's okay, Al, we've got—"

"Positive."

I swear I went blind and dumb for a full ten seconds. "What?"

"Positive." She twisted in my arms. "I think we're having a baby."

I crushed her to me.

"Seth, the stick."

"Who cares? I'm getting that sucker framed. My girl said yes, and the test said yes. Best day ever!"

"I didn't say yes yet."

I scooped her up into my arms again and strode out of the bathroom. "Oh, you will."

She grabbed my shoulder. "You're so certain?"

I locked my gaze with hers. "More certain than I've ever been about anything."

Her eyes were shiny, but the biggest, brightest smile lit her face.

Finally, I got the words right.

EPILOGUE

ALLY

THE AIR WAS CRISP, AND THE WIND FLUTTERED THE CURLS cascading down my back. The lace of my veil lifted and settled around my shoulders to brush my arms. Fingertip length. All the things I'd learned about weddings had gone in one ear and out the other, other than a little of the background on my veil. The piece offered a touch of the traditional. As did the empire cut of the gown that hid some of the swell of my belly.

I slid my hand over the bump growing larger every day. February was coming like a freight train and so here I was…getting married on the first of October.

I peeked around the gazebo to the long pier I had to walk down.

Alone.

"I'm here, I'm here." A little voice carried on the wind.

I glanced behind me to see Laurie coming around the corner in her pink tulle and ribbons. "What are you doing down here? You're supposed to be next to your dad."

"Nuh-uh. I walking you down the aisle, silly."

My eyes burned. "Oh, sweetie."

She held out her hand to me. Such a big girl these days. Four going on forty sometimes. Her nightmares had faded away with family reading time every night. We'd all settled into a crazy sort of normal. "It's okay, Mommy. I'm a big girl, I can do it."

"Oh, I know that you can. I just thought you had to be brave for Daddy."

She shrugged and stepped next to me. "Nah. He has Unca Ollie."

"Are you ready?" Sage rushed down the hill to fuss with my train. "What did you do? I told you to stay still."

I looked over my shoulder at my maid of honor decked out in a navy off-the-shoulder dress. "Wind."

Sage sighed and set down her tight bouquet of Gerbera daisies in burgundy, orange, and gold. "You're going to take off like a sailboat today with this wind." She fluffed my little train and shifted one of the buttons of my bustle. Why had I let her talk me into this thing? It was too formal for an outdoor wedding. I should have just gotten the little tea-length dress.

Sage tucked the daisy crown behind Laurie's ear. "Hey little mama, what are you doing down here?"

"I'm gonna walk Mommy down the aisle." Laurie clutched my hand.

"Oh, I swore I wasn't going to cry until the actual ceremony." Sage tipped back her head and blinked rapidly. "You're just the best little girl."

Laurie smiled brightly. "I know."

Sage and I laughed.

My maid of honor slapped her thigh. "Well, I think it's time to get this show on the road. I know there's a very nervy groom waiting at the end of that pier."

I slid my hand over my bump and the little boy kicking around like crazy. "I think both of us..." I looked down at Laurie and swung our clasped hands. "All three of us are ready to go down."

Laurie patted my belly. "He's gotta stay in there cooking."

I laughed. "Yes, we still have a few months to go."

"Okay. I'm heading down." Sage picked up her bouquet, stood, and looped her arm around my waist. "I'm so happy for you."

"Thanks." My eyes misted. "Now go, before I start bawling. You know all it takes is a stiff breeze these days."

Sage fanned her face. "Right. No tears. At least not for a few minutes." She blew out a breath. "Was the pier always that long?"

I laughed. "Yes."

"At least we've got two hotties to look forward to at the end."

"Yes. Well, at least one."

Laurie wrinkled her nose. "Ew."

Sage shook back her blond hair and checked her earrings. "Here we go."

My mouth went dry as she walked over the uneven ground in her stilts. I had no idea why Sage was suddenly interested in fashion and things like heels, but she pulled off the look.

As for me, me and my ballerina flats were going to do this long walk.

I tightened my hold on Laurie's hand. "You sure about this?"

She nodded. "I can't wait for Daddy to see your pretty dress."

"Then let's do this thing, huh?" I bent down, wrinkles in my dress be damned. I kissed her cheek. "I'm so excited to be marrying your dad."

"Me, too!" Laurie moved forward, tugging me after her. "Let's go."

There was no slow processional down the pier. White and red daisies dotted the railing with lace snapping in the breeze. I didn't really get to take it all in. In fact, I didn't even get to catch my breath before Seth came into view.

He took a step forward, and his brother yanked him back.

Seth lifted his fisted hand to his mouth and the shock and happiness on his face tumbled every nerve out of my body. Laurie and I nearly jogged down the pier to get to him.

To get to my very happily ever after.

I glanced down to the daughter of my heart and then to the man who'd owned it since I was fifteen years old.

Sage took the bouquet I forgot I was holding and then it was Seth's hand in mine.

The preacher behind Seth cleared his throat as he looked down at Laurie. "Would you be giving this beautiful bride away?"

Laurie squeezed my hand and looked down at her feet, then up at her father. She nodded. "I would."

Seth crouched down and held his arm open. "Thank you, Munchkin." She launched herself into his chest and he gathered her up against his hip, and never let go of my hand. He turned to me. "You're so beautiful."

"I love you so much." I leaned in to rub my nose with Laurie's. "Both of you."

His eyes were red-rimmed as he brought our joined hands to rest on the little life between us. I sniffled and laughed then all three of us turned to the preacher.

"We're ready."

ARE DIRTY HOT ROCKSTARS MORE YOUR SPEED?
ESPECIALLY THE BABYMAKING KIND?

ROCKSTAR DADDY

Never trust a cold condom.

Wait, let me back up. I'm Kellan McGuire, and I'm a rockstar in hiding, at least for the weekend. Enter Maggie Kelly, the famed Kelly virgin - AKA my small hometown's favorite good girl.

Did I mention she's really good? And I'm so...not.

Except Maggie isn't a virgin any longer. She actually just went through a rough breakup due to her ex's penchant for strippers.

And I don't want to be a rockstar this weekend. Not with her.

I just want to be Kellan, the wolf to her Little Red Riding Hood. The guy who shows her all the dark, dirty things she never dared to dream.

In return, she gave *me* something I never dared to dream about either - a baby.

A family.

Our family, if I can convince her I'm worth the risk.

Author's note: *this book may be called Rockstar Daddy, but the emphasis is on lots of babymaking practice, laughter, a few tears, and a serious case of insta-love.*

READ ON FOR AN EXCERPT...

CHAPTER 1

KELLAN

Fucking blizzard.

Again.

Why was I even surprised?

I was the jackass who had grown up on the outskirts of Turnbull, New York, snow capital of the northeast, and had escaped to sunny LA only to return.

Voluntarily.

No one had held a gun to my head or shackled my wrists. Nope, I'd strapped my surfboard to the roof of my SUV and made the trek home to buy property on the very edge of town. Outside of town, truth be told. Because the icy tundra in the city proper—ha ha— wasn't enough for me. Might as well build a damn shack with my own two hands and surround it with pine trees and solitude.

So much freaking solitude.

True, it was just my vacation home. Cue more laughter. My place to escape from the rigors of being a famous rockstar.

At least the rockstar part was right. In my head if nowhere else. The famous? Working on that. Wilder Mind's first single was due to drop just after the holidays, and our manager, Lila Crandall, was prepping us for the big time. A lot of that was smoke and mirrors designed to build us up into being the showmen we weren't quite yet, but under her bluster, there was a kernel of truth.

Wilder Mind was poised to take on the world.

Me? I was poised to chop some wood so I could hole up in my cabin and spend New Year's Eve soaking up the silence.

No other company. No other voices. Especially no incessant interview questions or even the shrill scream of fans. Not that we'd dealt with much of that yet. Only a taste. A hint of things to come if we were lucky enough to make it big.

In the meantime, it would be just me and my old Taylor acoustic, a roaring fire, and a case of Coors.

Hey, I never said I had highbrow tastes. So sue me.

Blowing out a breath, I heaved the ax through the chilly air, savoring the pleasant burn in my muscles. I was chopping way more wood than I'd need for a weekend at the cabin. If I was lucky, I'd make it back to Turnbull a few times over the winter. With the single dropping, we'd be branching out. Spreading out to do shows some distance from LA, which meant all the press that went with that. I'd be talking myself hoarse before I was expected to go up and bleed out onstage for the price of a ticket.

That was my role. My *new* role. The one I'd craved since I was a kid with a cheap thrift store guitar, a joint in my back pocket, and the requisite amount of teenage angst that made me think I could be a great songwriter.

Now I was getting my shot, and the battered composition notebook I'd been lugging around for years—first in backpacks, then in briefcases during my brief stint working at Ripper Records—was definitely getting a workout.

Just like my arms. I slammed the axe into the snowpack and threw back my head. Shit. The chill seared my lungs, yanking out my breath in icy puffs. And I still wasn't smart enough to go inside.

Nope, I kept splitting logs, continuing on until the overcast afternoon turned into dusk. The foggy dark hung in ribbons of mist around my forest, and I didn't stop until the distant cry of a lonely coyote made me think maybe it was time for that fire.

We didn't get a lot of coyotes out this way, but we had some. In this much dense forestation, you got quite the range of creatures. Even the occasional black bear. My mom had told stories about one coming up to the back door and rattling the knob of her folks' old ramshackle place, but I had to think that was bullshit.

Maybe I just hoped it. If a frigging bear couldn't just break down a door, fuck the rest of us who rued being so goddamn polite all the time.

Still, much as I lobbied for the rights of bears and coyotes, I wasn't stupid enough to be whaling on logs after dark. Not when I had a twelve-pack and a hot shower waiting for my sore ass.

"Getting soft," I muttered after stowing the axe and piling up the wood to haul inside.

I grunted as I made my way around the side of the cabin in the knee-deep snow, part of a cord of wood in my arms. Obviously, I needed to hit the gym harder before Wilder Mind went out on tour. My body freaking hurt. I was covered in sweat. Probably looked like a frigging maniac with snow sticking to my beardy face.

I jumped around night after night onstage in closet-sized clubs and bars, but I wasn't as hardy as when I'd lived in good old Turnbull full-time. Back when I'd worked on cars and picked up odd construction jobs to get by.

It had been blind luck and a dose of small town friendliness that had even gotten my ass out to LA. Lila's mom and pop ran the local orchard, and my mom had gotten to talking to Lila's mother one day about how I didn't want to be stuck working construction for the rest of my life. One thing led to another and under six months later, I'd been on a place out to LA to meet with Donovan Lewis, the head of the record label Lila worked for. We hit it off and though I didn't know shit about selling anything that didn't come in a bucket or wrapped in cellophane, I'd ended up as an account rep.

Representing artists. Me. The guy who'd barely graduated high school but could schmooze a quart a milk out of a cow. Or so my mom had claimed to Lila's mother.

Because a way with cows surely meant a way with egotistical, often drugged out musicians. Right.

Somehow it had worked though. Lila said I had a knack. Donovan had given me raises. A bunch of them, in short succession. The mogul some jokingly referred to as Lord Lewis didn't shortchange his talent, and he'd seen something in me. I owed him and Lila a shit-ton of gratitude. First, for hiring me to represent some of their musical acts, and then for trusting me to front a band.

The band part I had more familiarity with. I'd been stroking an acoustic long before I'd stroked my first girl. Let's just say I'd done my share of touching both, and leave it at that.

One more thing about Turnbull? They had some damn fine women, but it was hard to see them clearly under all the layers of outerwear when it snowed for what felt like half the freaking year. I preferred California women anyway. They seemed more good-natured as a rule. Maybe all the sunshine and hot temperatures put them in a better mood.

And goddammit, I loved me a woman in a bikini.

When I reached the front of my property and heard the squeal of tires, I didn't react fast enough. Put the image of a half-naked, tanned woman in the mind of a man who'd nearly frozen his nuts off and who wouldn't miss a car fishtailing off the road?

Right into my ditch.

Tires spun, spewing up snow and dirt and tiny rocks, and a horn went off about sixteen times. And I stared, my wood in my arms. Shocked as hell that anyone had even come down this practically deserted road in the first place, never mind took the curve way too fast and gone ass up in the ditch.

The chick was now attempting to shimmy her way out of the driver's side window. Painfully. With no shortage of groans and screeches and noises no adult female should ever make.

Since she was moving—and frantically at that—I had to figure she couldn't be too badly injured. Still, she could have done harm to herself she'd yet to realize.

With more than a small sigh, I set down the wood on the short set of steps to the cabin, brushed off my hands on the thighs of my jeans, and trudged down the snowy hill to where the squealing damsel's car was lodged.

She turned her neck and gave me the biggest, brightest smile I'd ever seen. I was a little taken aback, since she was half in and half out of a window and her car was fucked up, if not totaled. It appeared to be an older model under the snow and grime, and an accident like hers could screw up the frame. If that happened, the vehicle was shot.

Not that she seemed worried overmuch.

"Hi!" she called over the rushing wind, her voice as cheerful as her expression. "Thank God for you."

I didn't know how to respond to that, so I came around the ditch and eyed her lopsided car. "Yep, well and truly stuck."

She blinked at me from under the pink fringe of a stocking cap. "It's just a little fender bender."

"Oh yeah? Then why are you climbing out of the window?"

She wiggled. "Because the door won't open."

"Seems a bit worse than a fender bender to me." I came around the driver's side, hooked my hands under her armpits in her heavy down coat, and simply plucked her out of the car.

Only afterward did I think of possible internal injuries. Though what possible injury could've allowed her to jump and dance around now that she'd been freed, I did not know.

The other thing I noticed about her right away? She was dressed as if she was in competition with the Michelin man, except her bulk was made out of layers. Many layers. She had earmuffs under her hat to go with her bulky scarf, huge coat, ski pants—likely layered over thermals —and some serious freaking boots with enough snaps and ties to secure a horse.

And yet she was still jumping around, blowing on her gloved fingers, and laughing like a crazy person.

"Whoa, that was nuts. I seriously feared for my life. I saw Jesus and heard angels and all that stuff." She frowned at her car with its likely bent axel. "I paid extra for the best snow tires. I still skidded. That seems like a warranty violation. Don't you think?"

What I thought was this chick was going to talk my head off.

"The forecast predicted two feet today. Typical lake effect. Are you not from around here?" Though it was hard to believe someone from a warmer climate would've been that well-prepared, but maybe. They did tend to have thinner blood than us hardy northern types.

Though what the hell was I saying? I was a California boy now too. Happily.

I'd never actually heard someone roll their eyes at me before, but her disgust was palpable. "Hello, look at me. Do I seem unprepared for this weather? If anything, I *over*prepared. In my trunk, I have a spare battery kit, a First-Aid kit, a tire repair kit—"

"Lady, I got it. You're prepared. You just spun out. It happens."

She propped her hands on her hips. Or at least where I figured her hips would be. Hard to tell with her coat.

"Very pragmatic of you, buddy, but now what? I'm stuck and I need to get to Mrs. Pringles' before she goes to New Year's Eve mass. This is her first year without her husband, and she puts on a brave face, but she and Joe were so in love. It was sweet to see, really. And if I can't get there before mass, then I'll have to wait until she gets back, or worse yet, go join her in the church, which would be okay except I kind of got ex-communicated last year."

I wiped away the flakes collecting on my face. I would've hoped my expression coupled with how I looked might've intimidated her— big, burly, bearded—but if anything fazed this one, it wasn't me glaring at her during her endless monologue.

"I'm sure I'll regret asking this, but why, exactly, do you need to go to grandmother's house?"

She brushed snow off the arms of her coat. It was coming down faster than she could efficiently whisk it away. "Oh, she's not my grandmother—"

"That was a joke, Red." I gestured toward her attire. Red and pink everything, which didn't go together but somehow seemed to suit her. "You also have a car instead of a basket, but let me mix a metaphor or two."

"Ah. Big bad wolf, is it then? Sorry, you don't seem to fit." She marched toward me and grasped the side of my pants. "Wile E. Coyote sweats aren't exactly scary, tough guy."

"Don't touch," I growled and that made her step back and cock her head, much like a puppy. Instead of a floppy ear, she had the bouncy pouf on top of her hat. "I can't just touch you."

She seemed to think about that. It was getting darker, and the snowflakes falling between us were coming faster and harder. But if I wasn't mistaken, she was pondering that comment as if I'd just said the most important thing she'd ever heard.

"No," she said after a moment. "I guess you can't. You shouldn't. Just because Derek ran off with Trini isn't a reason for me to let strange men touch me. Especially ones wearing sweatpants."

"What's wrong with sweatpants?"

The most ridiculous thing about this whole conversation? I didn't *want* to touch her. I was almost sure. So what if it had been a while for me? That was by choice. God knows I had women throwing themselves at me front, back and center, and it only promised to get worse as things took off with the single. I'd backed off the fuck-and-duck game simply because I'd gotten bored.

I was tired of fake women cloaked in pretenses who just wanted me for my fame. As much as I exploited my growing fame to get any damn thing I wanted.

Never said I wasn't a fucked-up bastard, now did I?

"There's nothing wrong with them, per se. They're just not fashionable."

In spite of the fact that my face felt like it was freezing into place, I cocked a brow. "Oh, and that eye-searing combo you have on is? You practically have on a snowsuit. Like a child."

Her cheeks reddened. I don't know how I could tell the difference considering she'd been awful damn pink from the wind to start with, but somehow I knew I'd gotten to her. "I'm not a child. I'm a grown woman who likes to be prepared."

"Huh." I crossed my arms and jutted my chin toward her car. "So how's that working out for you?"

She stepped forward, kicking up snow with her gigantic boots. Then she let her gaze wander down the front of me and let out a little *harrumph*. "And you know what else? Statistics say that eighty-eight-point-six of grown men who wear sweatpants are either still living in their mother's basements or they're serial killers."

Deliberately, I moved into her space, dwarfing her with my size. And yet again, she did not back down. "Those are some odds, Red. Are you feeling lucky?"

~

CHAPTER 2

MAGGIE

I was supposed to be afraid of this guy. That was what he wanted me to be anyway. Why else would he be looming over me as if he wanted to do me bodily harm?

But I wasn't buying it. Let's go over the evidence.

Wile E. Coyote sweats.

Enough concern to pluck me out of my car like a wilted vegetable.

Back to the Wile E. Coyote sweats.

Also, possibly the kindest, softest, most intriguing brown eyes I'd ever seen. Surrounded by a frame of inky lashes. Such a heavy fringe that snow kept gathering on them until he grew impatient and blinked it away.

But that was neither here nor there.

"First of all, there are most likely no serial killers in Turnbull or the surrounding towns. That's extremely improbable, given the size of the population."

"So are your dumbass statistics, but I didn't call you on them, did I?"

I wasn't pouting at being called a dumbass. Lord knows I'd been called much worse. As the youngest of six, I'd gotten used to verbal abuse at a young age. I almost enjoyed it.

Just because I looked small and defenseless didn't mean I was. I tended to sneak up on people like a bunny.

Aww, she's so cute and fluffy—CHOMP.

"Then again, you're not making any effort to assist a stranded traveler, so maybe you are planning to Ted Bundy me. Where's your fake cast, huh?" I gave his arms in the sleeves of his surprisingly thin coat a glance before pretending to search the snowbanks around us. "Where's your VW Bug with the passenger seat taken out?"

"What the hell are you talking about?"

"Ted Bundy. One of the most famous serial killers of all time. Don't you people respect the titans in your field?"

"What people is that, exactly?"

His bored tone was making me feel stupid. So much for going toe-to-toe with this giant behemoth. He didn't find me amusing and he obviously had no intention of helping to free my vehicle.

So time for plan B.

"I'll just get my bread." There was no helping my clipped tone as I stomped back toward the ditch. Not that I could even be sure he'd heard me. With the howling wind and the crunch of my boots on the snowy, uneven ground at the side of the road, maybe he hadn't heard a word I'd spoken.

Then his big hands clamped around my upper arms and he hauled me back as if I'd been on the verge of falling into a fire pit. "Hold it. What bread?"

"Kindly unhand me."

He made a low noise in his throat and without looking back at him, I knew he'd done that cocked brow thing again. Pretty hot. I couldn't move one eyebrow independent of the other, so I tended to appreciate skills in others that I did not possess.

"You have no reason to try to get back in that car."

"Yes, I do. I need my bread before it gets cold." I sighed. "Well, any colder than it already is. My hot bag can only do so much."

"Your hot bag? Woman, you make no sense."

"Stop calling me woman, and it's an insulated bag to seal in warmth. I used it to protect Mrs. Pringles' bread. It's her favorite, pumpkin chocolate chip." I craned my neck to look up at him, intending to shove his big paws off me, but his head was tilted and his lips were parted, revealing just a hint of bright white teeth.

And those dark assessing eyes were searing right through every damn layer of my clothing.

"Kindly unhand me," I repeated, not missing the slight chatter of my teeth. I wished I could blame the cold. It was so much worse than that.

I was by the side of the road with a disabled car and a possible Ted Bundy wannabe with soulful eyes, and I didn't even really care that he was keeping me from my bread.

Mrs. Pringles' bread. Same difference.

"You might injure yourself further if you attempt reentry. Let the professionals handle it."

"Further?" I frowned. "I'm not injured."

Was I? Quickly, I took stock. Everything still worked. Arms, legs, mouth. Definitely mouth. Sure, my heart was beating a bit too fast and my thoughts were skidding out of control, but that was normal for me. My dad called me "fanciful," which he partially blamed on my obsession with the macabre. My mama said I spent too much time with my head stuck in a book. My brothers—all three of them—called me some variation of Magpie, my childhood nickname that had stuck like a damn flytrap. Maeve and Regan, my perfect older sisters, just sighed at my supposed antics and went on with their lives.

So yeah, mental babbling was typical for me. And often, actual babbling, though the dude hulking over me was not inspiring to foam at the mouth as I usually might.

I didn't know men like him. The guys I attracted were safe, nice boys. The kind who went to church on Sundays and pulled their elderly neighbor's newspaper out of the bushes and always referred to my parents as "Sir and Ma'am." They didn't have edges. They didn't skimp on their manners. They definitely didn't miss their morning shave.

As far as assisting someone with car trouble, they would've been sweet and helpful and fixed the problem before I could ask. Not brusque and dismissive and now rough as the brute hauled me around and set me a few feet away from my vehicle.

"Stay there." He pointed at me. "I'm going to take care of your problem so you can get on your way."

"About time. Do you have a truck hoist?"

He was already moving toward my car. He studied the door for a moment, then yanked on the handle. It opened for him with only the slightest effort.

Traitorous car.

Fumbling inside, he realized my window was the crank-up kind and shut it so the front seat didn't fill with snow. "Guess the door wasn't so stuck after all," he shouted over the wind.

I rolled my eyes. Sure, if I had the strength of an ox, no problem. "I asked if you had a truck hoist?"

"A truck hoist?" he echoed, clearly not paying attention as he studied my car.

"Yes, to pull me out of the ditch."

"No, I don't have a truck hoist. What I do have should do the trick though." He shut the door without grabbing my bread or any of my belongings, then climbed out of the ditch, pulled a cell phone from his pocket, and hit a button. Smugly, I might add.

This man did not have an air of friendly cooperation, that was for sure. As for neighborly concern? Nope. Nada.

After a minute, his smug expression flattened. His mouth thinned out and he gazed at his phone as if he'd misdialed. He hit a button again, waited, then yanked the phone from his ear. "What the fuck?"

I tried not to blanch. Of course, I'd heard swearing before. I was a college student, wasn't I? But in my family home, we had a tip jar. Anyone who swore put in a five-dollar bill. Forget a one-dollar bill. My parents had wanted us to learn appropriate words swiftly, and parting with five dollars of our allowance had worked fast.

Pretty sure this dude didn't have a jar. If he did, he'd probably smash it with one of his hamhock fists.

"Is there a problem?"

"No. Definitely not. The tow truck place isn't answering. No big."

"It's New Year's Eve."

"You don't say?"

I ignored his sarcasm and lifted my voice to speak over the growing wind. The darker it got, the more frigid it was growing outside. But I'd be damned if I shivered. If he could seem impervious to the weather, so could I. "If you're not using a national company and instead supporting a local business, it's not surprising. This is a holiday. Therefore, holiday hours."

"Thank you, Miss Know-It-All, but I'm well aware of this particular company's hours. It's a family business."

"Your family? Yet you don't own a truck hoist?" I cocked my head. "Seems fishy."

"I said family business, not my business."

"Ah, like your dad? Or your brother?"

"Look, they aren't answering, so we'll have to just wait." He glanced around at the gathering snow as if he planned for us to wait at the edge of the road.

If that was the case, I was definitely going to try to get back into my car. As much as I loved Mrs. Pringle, I knew my stomach was on the verge of roaring. That bread was going to be mine. I'd skipped lunch, and boy oh boy, I knew better than to take shortcuts. They never paid off.

"Okay. Well, thanks." Even if he couldn't be polite, I could. "I appreciate your…" But I wasn't a liar. "Conversation."

I couldn't be certain in the near darkness, but I was almost sure his lips twitched. "Conversation, is it?"

I shrugged.

"Come on," he said, indicating with his chin for me to head up the short incline to a dark, forbidding, *tiny* house.

Immediately, my back went up. And my spidey senses started to tingle.

Or that might have been my extremities due to frostbite setting in.

"No, thank you. I don't think that's a good idea. I'll just stay here and call AAA."

"You have AAA?"

"Of course I do." I bit my lip, vividly picturing the expired notice on my desk at home. I'd paid that, right? It had been at the top of my To Do list, but with the holidays…

Okay, maybe not.

"You seem uncertain."

"Not really."

He gusted out a sigh. "It's freezing out here. Let's go inside and get warm. I'll call the towing company again later."

"If they're not answering now," I shouted over the wind, moving closer when my voice seemed to get sucked away, "what makes you think they will later? It's a holiday. People are out celebrating."

"Are you?" He pointed at himself. "Am I? No. Not everyone is in a fucking party mood. Now come on."

When I didn't budge, he gave me a stern look that made me half expect him to haul me over his shoulder like a sack of Maggie. Then he let out another of those windy breaths. "Please?"

My frozen face cracked into a smile. "Did that hurt?"

"A little. Not as much as my nuts shriveling up into my spine though."

I swallowed. Along with not hearing a ton of swear words on a daily basis, I also wasn't privy to men referring to their nuts as if that counted as ordinary conversation.

Hi, my nuts hurt. Pass the crackers.

"You, um, should definitely go inside then. That sounds painful."

"It is. Come on. I won't bite."

"Are you sure?"

Now he did more than almost smile. He barked out a laugh. "Not unless you want me to, honey, and even then, I'm pretty sure you aren't my type." He tilted his head and lifted his voice above the howling wind. "I'm not into church girls. Even the ex-communicated kind, which does sound interesting."

"It is. No, I'm not telling you." I rubbed my mittened hand over my stinging cheeks. "What happens between a girl and her priest is private."

"Wow. Some *Thorn Birds* shit? Kinky little thing, aren't you?"

Was that actually approval I saw in his midnight eyes? They'd definitely warmed. Speaking of kinky…

"Hardly." I sniffed, and not out of haughtiness.

I had to sneeze, and I had to pee. I was also freezing and starving and desperately in need of a long, hot shower.

Then again, did I dare get naked within the same four walls as this guy? Even if I wasn't his type?

Serial killers had types too. They also didn't kill everyone they met. I couldn't be sure this guy was safe, but if I wasn't in his target victim group, he could be a homicidal lunatic and I wouldn't necessarily be in danger. Plus, I knew some judo.

Oh, the rationalizations a girl who urgently needs a bathroom will make.

"Okay. I'll go inside with you. Briefly. Until we can reach the towing company. Otherwise, I will have many people out looking for me, and they will descend on your place like a swarm of locusts if I'm not home in a matter of hours."

Much to my consternation most of the time. I was well and truly sick of being so overprotected by my family, though I loved them for their concern. It was just hard to have much of a life when you were watched like a rabid animal expected at any moment to go on a rampage through town.

In truth, I just mostly studied and worked, along with spending time with my bestie and my boyf—

Yep, not going there.

"Not if I tie you up and make you call them to say you're okay and not to look for you. Then I might throw your chair in the basement and leave you without food and water."

His voice was entirely too serious, which was how I guessed he was lying. It was a gamble, but I was going to bet that the usual serial killer didn't advertise his intentions so brazenly. "You forgot to add that you'd have your way with me first."

"Hoping, Red?" Before I could stammer out a response, he grabbed my arm and towed me behind him. "Not my type, remember?"

"I didn't say yes," I called.

He promptly ignored me.

After dragging me up a short snowy hill, we made our way up a scarcely shoveled path to a short set of rickety steps. He stopped to pick up some wood, then stomped up the steps and pressed his shoulder into the door. "Come on," he shouted in my general direction before barreling into the dark house.

Hell, I didn't even know if it was truly his. He could be an illegal squatter there for all I knew.

The fact of the matter was that I knew most of the people in Turnbull. This was on the outskirts, true, and the occasional person came or went without stirring my notice, but we lived in a small, self-contained area. We might be surrounded by trees and hills and blocked in by mountains of snow for almost half the year, due to our proximity to Lake Ontario, but we kept track of our own.

Also, it was hard to make quick getaways when a snowpocalypse wasn't a disaster so much as a way of life.

Biting my lip, I cast a quick glance back toward the road. In the time it had taken us to walk up to the house—though calling it that seemed to be an overstatement—my poor car had become even more buried. The snow wasn't coming down in flakes now. More like pellets.

"Red," he growled. "Forget the damn bread."

Something about his irritation made me laugh. I clapped a hand over my mouth, then bent at the waist when more laughter rolled out. I couldn't catch my breath and what breaths I could take were laced with ice. Crappy time to be on the verge of hysteria.

Guess my accident had shook me up more than I'd thought. Or else it was due to the man himself.

So I stood up straight, threw back my shoulders, and strutted inside in my giant boots to my beheading.

At least he'd turned on the lights. As I shut the door behind me and shifted to survey my surroundings, from down the hall came a string of curse words shot off in succession like gunfire.

My eyes widened. If he was trying to ease me into feeling comfortable before he struck, he wasn't too good at it.

"Are you okay?" I asked carefully, darting glances right and left as I crept up the hallway to where his voice was coming from.

And stopped dead at the mouth of the sparse, rustic kitchen.

He was standing at the stove in nothing but a pair of silky black boxers with a spatula in his hand, poking at whatever congealed mess was in his dented pan. It was one like you'd see in a camping kit, meant to be used on nights under the stars and no other time, ever. But that was his home cookware.

Fit him somehow, as did the intricate swirls and lines of dark ink that wrapped around his muscular shoulders and biceps. More ink covered his back and sides. He was a human canvas, tattooed and rippling with muscle.

I didn't find that arousing. That he was the exact opposite of my lanky, inkless ex was merely something I noted.

"Fucking burner is fucking out." He stabbed at the red mass in his pan. Without sparing me a glance, he continued. "Why are you still dressed like a damn polar bear? Get out of those wet clothes. You were standing in a snowbank for a good fifteen minutes or more."

"Polar bears don't need clothing, as they have fur."

That he only growled made me laugh. And cautiously unwind my scarf.

While he continued to fiddle with the non-working stove, I cleared my throat. "You have a microwave. Just heat up the soup." Cautiously, I stepped closer and peered at the gross stuff he kept trying to stir. "That is soup, right?"

"Yes. Tomato. I was going to make grilled cheese to go with it. Can't now, because fucking burner is—"

"Fucking out," I finished, surprised by how liberating it felt to curse. There weren't any tip jars here.

No furnace either apparently, as it was nearly as cold inside as it had been out. Or else I'd caught a serious freaking chill.

"Look at you. Your teeth are chattering." He turned to me and yanked off my fuzzy hat, causing the long hair I'd tucked underneath to come tumbling out. He gazed at it as if he was surprised I had hair at all, then managed to shake off his shock and tugged off my earmuffs too.

Sound rushed into my ears, including the uneven hiss of his breaths through his tightly clenched teeth.

I raised my gaze to his. He was staring at me in a way I wasn't used to from men. When a girl grew up in a small town with three strapping, overprotective brothers, you got used to guys being too afraid to take their shot. As such, I'd grown accustomed to dating the safe, parental-friendly boys. I liked them. They were predictable. No serial killers in the bunch.

None of them made my blood heat the way this one was with merely a heavy-lidded look.

He gripped my hat and earmuffs in his hands, crumpling them. This close to him, without even the buffer of his clothes, he seemed even more huge. Tall, muscled, dangerous.

I didn't know that kind of male. Had never wanted to.

Until now.

"Keep going," I said softly, challenging myself as much as I was him. I gestured to the rest of my outerwear. "Lots more clothes to strip off me, Wolf."

For more information on this title see tarynquinn.com.

ALSO BY TARYN QUINN

Unwrapped

Afternoon Delight

Dirty Distraction #1

Drawn Deep #2

Wilder Rock

Rockstar Daddy #1

Coming Soon

Rockstar 3 #2

Sinful in Seattle

Thrill Seeker #1

Coming Soon

Thrill Chaser #2

Dirty DILFs

Have My Baby #1

Coming Soon

Claim My Baby #2

Filthy Series

Filthy Scrooge

USA Today Bestselling author, **TARYN QUINN,** is the redheaded stepchild of bestselling authors Taryn Elliott & Cari Quinn. We have been writing together for a lifetime–wait, no it's really been only a handful of years, but we have a lot of fun. Sometimes we write stories that don't quite fit into our regular catalog.

Do you like shorter and dirtier reads?

Anything goes with this penname.

• Sexy—check.
• Erotic—check.
• Sweet—usually mixed in with the sexy…so, yeah—check.
• RomCom—check.
• Dark—oh, yeah…check.
• Paranormal—check.

Did we mention that we like all the genres?

So, c'mon in. Light some candles, pour a glass of wine…maybe even put on some sexy music.

For more information about us…

tarynquinn.com
tq@tarynquinn.com

Made in the USA
Monee, IL
25 August 2020